at
Midnight

JAMES PATTERSON PRESENTS...

Kisses
at
Midnight

Jen McLaughlin
Samantha Towle
Tabitha Ross

BOOK**SHOTS**

GRAND CENTRAL
PUBLISHING
NEW YORK LONDON

Copyright © 2017 by James Patterson
Excerpt from *A Wedding in Maine* copyright © 2017 by James Patterson

Grand Central Publishing
Hachette Book Group
1290 Avenue of the Americas, New York, NY 10104
grandcentralpublishing.com
twitter.com/grandcentralpub

The McCullagh Inn in Maine was first published in July 2016.

Sacking the Quarterback was first published in September 2016.

First Mass Market Edition: January 2017

Grand Central Publishing is a division of Hachette Book Group, Inc. The Grand Central Publishing name and logo are trademarks of Hachette Book Group, Inc. The BookShots name and logo are trademarks of JBP Business, LLC.

The publisher is not responsible for websites (or their content) that are not owned by the publisher.

The Hachette Speakers Bureau provides a wide range of authors for speaking events. To find out more, go to www.hachettespeakersbureau.com or call (866) 376-6591.

ISBN 978-0-316-32007-8

Printed in the United States of America

OPM

10 9 8 7 6 5 4 3 2 1

FOREWORD

When I first had the idea for BookShots, I knew that I wanted to include romantic stories. The whole point of BookShots is to give people lightning-fast reads that completely capture them for a couple of hours in their day—so publishing romance felt right.

I have a lot of respect for romance authors. I took a stab at the genre when I wrote *Suzanne's Diary for Nicholas*. While I was happy with the result, I learned that the process of writing a romance novel required hard work and dedication.

That's why I wanted to pair up with the best romance authors for BookShots. I work with writers who know how to draw emotions out of their characters, all while catapulting their plots forward at breakneck speeds.

All three of the BookShots in this omnibus—by Jen McLaughlin, Samantha Towle, and Tabitha Ross—have those same fast plots and heartwarming characters. In *The McCullagh Inn in Maine*, you'll read about two people who fall back in love as they repair an old home. Next, you'll encounter another set of characters who try to deny their attraction in *Sucking the Quarterback*. Finally, in a brand-new BookShot called *Seducing Shakespeare*, one woman will sacrifice everything for her heart. You've got a book of three romantic BookShots in your hands. I dare you to try to read just one.

James Patterson

CONTENTS

The
McCullagh Inn
in
Maine

Jen McLaughlin

Chapter 1

THE SICKLY SWEET scent of dying roses drifted over me as I backed down the driveway, moving too quickly to check for traffic first. My heart raced faster than the engine of the stolen Volvo XC90 as I stepped on the gas. All good plans allow for improvisation, right?

My fingernails were digging into the wheel. I forced myself to relax. There was no room for weakness, for panic, in my life. Not anymore. Whatever lay ahead was guaranteed to be better than what I was leaving behind, and it certainly couldn't be worse than what I'd already survived.

I took a deep breath and held it as I ran a red light, feeling more alive, more like myself, than I had in years. A horn blasted, and I gripped the wheel hard. It was a miracle I didn't break my swollen knuckles off at the joints. I was temporarily blinded by the oncoming headlights and I instinctively stepped on the gas, tensing as a truck headed directly for my door. The lights veered left and the pickup skidded off the road and into someone's yard. Not my fault, not my problem.

I never wanted it to turn out this way. Sure, I saw the writing on the wall, kept a bag packed, and made contingency plans, but I was supposed to just disappear. Vanish into the night, be an unsolved mystery. Instead, I was going to have to spend the next couple of days fleeing for my life, hoping no one put two and two together. If I could just make it to the inn…

I screeched onto the ramp for I-95 with the scent of burning rubber filling the car, but I didn't slow, not hesitating as I headed toward safety. *North.* I wouldn't stop until I reached the one place where I knew I could escape. The same place I fled from years ago, with dreams of being something—some*one*—else. I was older now, and wiser, and I'd learned people never change. My current circumstances proved that point. All you could do was play the cards you were dealt.

No one would think to look for me in the sleepy Maine town I'd once called home, the one I'd erased from my record.

I'd sworn never to go back.

Sirens wailed at a distance, and I eased up on the gas pedal, forcing myself to obey speed limits. The last thing I needed was to get pulled over right now.

Once I put a little more distance between me and Miami, I'd find a rest stop, change my clothes, and wash up. Dyeing my brown hair could wait until I found some hole-in-the-wall to stop at for the night. I'd go blond. No one would expect me to go for that color. I hated blondes.

They led charmed lives the rest of us could only dream about.

My phone lit up, the screen showing a picture from my former life. I cursed. Keeping my eyes on the road, on that horizon, I fumbled around on the seat until I found the phone. Grabbing it, I chucked it out the window. A glance in the rearview mirror showed it disappearing under the wheels of a semi.

I gave a quick look at the object still remaining on the seat. My fingers flexed on the steering wheel. If I could only get rid of the gun the same way....

This hadn't been the plan, but then again, neither was murder.

Chapter 2

IT'D TAKEN TWO days of back-roads driving before I reached North Carolina. Ditching the car, I hopped on a bus for twelve hours. I looked like a preppy sorority sister going home for the weekend, my society persona left behind with the car. Once I hit the Maine border, I hitchhiked to the nearest used car dealer and bought a rusted old Chevy with some of the cash I'd stolen.

My destination was Hudson, Maine, which was only listed on the most thorough maps, a tiny pinprick of ink among shades of green. If you've ever heard people tell jokes about towns where the wild animals outnumber the humans, it's possible they were talking about Hudson.

This late in the season, most of the autumn leaves had dropped, and the nearly bald tires of my junker car crunched over pine cones as I navigated roads I hadn't seen in years. Finally, I arrived at the only home I'd ever known, the McCullagh Inn. My aunt, who'd owned it, had died six months ago, leaving me the business. I hadn't been able to go to the funeral, but I knew a heaven-sent opportunity when it arrived, and so I'd made discreet arrangements to keep the lights on and get a cleaning service to come through once a week.

I'd never told anyone down in Miami about the inn or my life before I arrived there, so if I had any luck left in my bones, no one would search for me here. Sure, it might seem like someone could track me down easily enough, but I came from a long line of less-than-law-abiding folks. There were ways to muddy the water.

My father had taught me to prepare for all outcomes. I knew how to fade off the face of the planet so no one ever found you again. I'd done it once before, when I ran away from home. But now I was back....

And I couldn't shake the feeling that this was where I was supposed to be all along.

I flipped the TV on, muting it as I dialed my brother on the burner phone I'd bought at a Virginia convenience store. I may have tried to go straight, but Paul had stayed in the family business.

I turned away from the morning news and caught a glimpse of myself in the tarnished, ornate mirror over the fireplace. The pale green walls of the foyer and the wood paneling of the living room weren't doing a damn thing for my complexion, and I could see the faintest shadow of a bruise beneath the makeup I'd slathered on. As I listened to the phone ring, I looked into my own blue eyes, wondering if I knew the person looking back at me. Then I turned back to the news, watching to see if what had happened in Miami had gone national. My newly blond hair swung in its pony-tail. I really should've cut it, but, hey, even a girl like me is entitled to some vanities.

"Hello?" My brother's raspy voice cut through the cheap phone.

I closed my eyes for a second, nostalgia making my throat ache. Or it could've been the abuse my vocal cords had recently taken. Nothing had a greater hold on you than family. "Paul?"

"Yeah?" Silence. A lot of silence. And then: "Chelsea? Is that you?"

I licked my lips. "Yes."

"You're alive," he said flatly.

"Yes," I said again, staring at the old tree outside the front window, next to the driveway.

"I'm going to kill—"

"Paul." I swallowed again, eyeing the whiskey I'd brought out from the kitchen. It would hurt in the morning, but it might be worth the pain. "I need help, and I need you not to tell anyone I called, or where I am."

There was no hesitation. "What do you need?"

Relief hit me in the chest. It was true what they said about family. "A new ID. A completely new identity, actually."

"You're on the run. Again." At my silence, he sucked in a breath. I'd learned at a young age that people would say anything to fill a silence. "Did you dye your hair yet?"

"Yeah."

"Nice." He sighed. "What happened, Chels?"

A phantom gunshot filled the empty inn, and for a second, I was back in that moment. I eyed the table by the front door, where I'd shoved the gun in case I needed it again. It would've been smarter to ditch it, but it was the best protection I had right now.

When the silence continued to stretch, Paul cleared his throat. "Where are you?"

I thought of the bruises I was trying to hide, the secrets I carried, and I knew my older brother would see right through me. I had no choice. I needed that ID. It was the only way I'd get my fresh start. "I'm at Aunt May McCullagh's inn, *my* inn."

There was a brief pause.

"The lawyers found you," he said.

Ignoring the accusation in his tone, I focused on the cloudy skies above the Atlantic Ocean. I'd left all the shades drawn except for one on the bay window overlooking the cliff, where a trail led down to the beach. On either side of the trail was an overgrown garden, filled with lobelia. I'd spent half my life sitting in that window, reading and looking at the storms raging over the ocean while dreaming of a future away from this tiny town. "Yeah, I know. I suck."

"No argument here," he grumbled. I could picture him sitting behind the wheel of his car, glowering at nothing in particular. Paul was happiest unhappy. "She left the inn to you, wanting you to fix it up and breathe new life into the place. She never gave up hope that someday, you'd come walking through those doors alive."

I remained silent again, because, really, what was there to say? The past was done. I couldn't go back and fix it, even if I wanted to. And those mistakes, those choices I'd made, had turned me into the woman I was. I couldn't regret that. Now I was here, ready and willing to make a new life for myself. And I'd make this the best damn inn in all of Maine.

Like a phoenix, I'd be reborn once Chelsea O'Kane was dead.

He sighed, dragging the sound out longer than a wave crashing on the shore. "Look. I'll get you what you're asking for. Meet me at Joe's to discuss it." There was a beat of silence. "It's the coffee shop on Main Street, in case you forgot."

How could I forget?

Main Street was the only street in town with any shops. There was a coffee shop, a church, a liquor store, a grocery store, a bar, and a Rite Aid. They were all on one block, with enchanting brick facades and quaint dark-gray clapboard on the old buildings. "When?"

"An hour from now. Don't be late."

Exactly an hour later, I walked down Main Street. The second I saw its Victorian architecture, I was comforted by its familiarity. But I tugged my baseball hat down to shadow my face and looked at the cracked sidewalks to avoid the usual small-town curiosity that would inevitably be thrown my way. I was always good at blending in, and I congratulated myself for not losing my touch…until I bounced off a brick wall.

Or, rather, a man.

His muscular arms closed around me, saving me from hitting the ground. The second his skin touched mine, a bolt of desire mixed with the panic that shot through my veins. I jerked back sharply, stumbling backward, and glanced up. The tall man who caught me was handsome, his wavy brown hair swept back off his face, and it was like the ground opened beneath me when I recognized him. Suddenly, that bolt of longing made perfect sense.

Oh, for God's sake. I couldn't catch a break. I'd had more than enough drama to fill ten seasons of a soap opera, and all I wanted was to lie low and nurse my injuries, but *nooo.*

It was Jeremy fricking Holland.

Damn it, he wasn't supposed to *be* here.

Chapter 3

JEREMY HOLLAND HAD been an object of infatuation since childhood—from the time I understood the difference between boys and girls up until college. He'd been a major part of my "wish on a star" phase. We'd been best friends, the kind who were supposed to be secretly in love with each other, so when he got together with the preppy blond cheerleader Mary Walker, I was pissed. When he went and proposed to her like the idiot he was, I skipped town the night before their wedding. I hadn't planned to return.

And I hadn't spoken to him since.

I may have googled him from time to time, though. Last I'd heard, he was living in Bangor, dribbling his life away at some desk job.

His gaze met mine, and the casual look in his familiar green eyes brightened to recognition. I quickly turned away—like I should have done the second I realized it was him. My heart raced, and the old undeniable attraction between us jerked back to life like a tangible thing, all because our bodies had bumped against each other on the street.

Damn his muscular arms.

And damn his outdated online profile.

"Sorry," I mumbled, sidestepping his large frame and tugging the baseball hat even lower so he wouldn't stop me. I didn't need this. Not now.

I didn't want him to focus on me.

He easily stepped the same way as me, blocking my escape effortlessly. "Are you okay?"

"Yeah." I cleared my throat, forcing my voice to drop a few octaves. Between that and my altered appearance, maybe he wouldn't recognize me. He'd married Mary, after all. How smart could he be? "I'm fine."

I walked past him, making sure not to brush against him. The last thing I needed was to feel a pull toward him. I was more panicked than I had been during my entire journey from Miami.

"Chelsea?" he asked, his voice dipping sexily. "Is that you?"

I stiffened, a few choice curse words flitting through my brain. But I bit them back, because nothing indicated guilt more than freaking out—and my father had trained me better than that. "Who?" I asked without turning around.

"Chelsea. Chelsea O'Kane."

I shook my head, balling my fists at my sides, ignoring the way his voice made me feel. All shivery, broken, and empty. "Never heard of her, but I hope she's pretty if you've got us confused."

As I attempted to saunter away, forcing myself to unclench my fists and keep my body language relaxed, he called out, "No matter how hard your daddy tried to teach you, you always were a lousy liar, Chels. Drop the act, and turn around."

I took a deep breath and considered my options. If I kept walking, Jeremy would come after me, and the ensuing argument would draw more attention than I wanted. If I faced him, I risked getting sucked back into his "help your fellow man" world, and right now, I could only help one person—myself.

Luckily for me, I saw Paul's truck turn the corner of Main and Birch. "Whoever you thought I was, trust me, that girl is long gone."

There was an intake of breath from behind me and I paused, for the briefest of moments, at the sound. I wanted so badly to turn around, to run into his arms and tell him everything that was bothering me, like I'd done when we were kids, but then my self-preservation instincts kicked in. I crossed the street, not bothering to look both ways—in this town, I'd hear a car well before it ever reached me.

Paul's truck pulled up to the curb of the coffee shop, and I yanked the door open at the same time as he opened his, one foot out the door. He glanced at me in surprise. "I thought we were—"

"Change of plans," I growled. "Drive. Fast."

He frowned, closing his door without hesitation. "Is that—?"

"Yep," I gritted out. "And he recognized me."

"Shit," Paul said, jerking the truck into drive. "He won't let it go at one conversation."

"I know." I scanned our surroundings through the passenger window, sucking in a breath. "Son of a bitch."

Damn it, why did I have such lousy taste in men? The recognition in Jeremy's eyes scared me more than Richard's fists ever had. If I wasn't careful, Jeremy would ruin everything....

And then I'd be the one facing down the barrel of a gun.

Chapter 4

PAUL TURNED DOWN the road that led to the inn, a ramshackle gem framed by old forest. His grip on the wheel was unyielding. He stared out the windshield, flexing his jaw, ignoring me. More than likely he was about to spout the perfect reprimand for this situation—one he'd probably been rehearsing since I'd left. "You look like shit."

"Thanks," I said dryly.

"Where did the bruises come from?"

Of course he saw them. "A problem that no longer exists."

He pressed his mouth into a tight line. "What did Jeremy say?"

"He asked if I was Chelsea O'Kane. I told him I wasn't."

"That was stupid," Paul snapped. "Now he'll be focused on you and why you lied. You need to shake him off."

I dropped my head back on the seat. Damn it, he was right. And I didn't need that kind of attention right now—especially not from *him*. "I'll find him. Tell him I want nothing to do with him and ask him to leave me alone. He will."

Paul snorted. "Yeah. Sure he will."

"He will," I said, knowing it was true. Jeremy had picked Mary, after all.

There were new wrinkles around Paul's eyes, signs of a

life filled with laughter and worry earned while I'd been away, which made me feel a little emptier inside. Otherwise, he had the same brown hair and blue eyes that were, as always, tinged with something between a touch of mischief and anger at the world.

"What the hell did you get yourself into this time?" he asked.

I shook my head, staring out the window at the trees blurring together as we sped by, my mind still on Jeremy and the threat he posed. I hoped he dropped the idea of reconnecting and disappeared out of my life again. "You don't need to know the details."

"The hell I don't," he growled. "You're blond, Chels. *Blond.* Obviously, shit got real."

Wincing, I touched my hair self-consciously. I looked ridiculous in this color and we both knew it. "The less you know, the better. Just trust me on this."

"But—" He sighed. "Whatever."

I swallowed and glanced in the rearview to make sure we didn't have a tail.

"You have to admit it's pretty shitty that you disappeared from my life, only to show up when you need me to get you a new ID, so you can…what? Run again?" he snapped.

"I don't just need a new ID," I said softly. "I need Chelsea O'Kane to be legally pronounced dead. And after that, I'm not going anywhere."

He braked, the tires squealing softly at the sudden movement, and slowly turned to me. *"Dead?"*

I nodded once, knowing I was asking for a lot, but it was the only way I stood a chance at coming out of this mess alive. "Can you do that?"

He stepped on the gas, pulling into the inn's circular gravel driveway without answering, but I didn't make the mistake of assuming his silence was a good thing. I knew better than that. The second he put the truck into park, he turned to me, scowling. "I understood why you ran. You wanted to get away from this life, from Dad's legacy. You wanted to be clean. Normal. *Legit.* Right?"

That had been the plan, yeah. But apparently, I wasn't the type of girl who got clean. Gripping my knees, I nodded, still not speaking.

Paul needed to say his piece, and I intended to let him.

"So you ran, and you never called or told me where you were. I didn't even know if you were still alive."

I stared at the faded gray clapboard and peeling blue shutters on the front of the house. The gardens were choked with weeds, but renovating the inside was my first priority. "I'm sorry. I was living in Miami, working as a lawyer, when things went…" I trailed off and made the *kaboom* motion with my hands.

"A lawyer, huh?" He stared at me, his gaze filled with pain and accusation. "You can't get any more legit than a lawyer. Can't remove yourself from this family any further than that, right, Chels? The only thing worse would've been becoming a cop."

"I'd never—" I stared down at my legs. That's exactly what I'd been thinking when I chose my major. I'd been so desperate to be a better person. That had been all Jeremy's fault. Him and his do-good attitude that never faltered. "I mean, right."

"And now you're here, asking for a favor…." The crisp wind, carrying the taste of salt water, buffeted the overhanging branches, casting shadows on his face. Paul continued, "Asking for *my* help."

I nodded, grabbing hold of my knees.

While I'd done what needed to be done, I was older now,

and I never should have cut ties with my brother, no matter what he did for a living. No matter how similar he was to our father.

Coming home to Maine meant safety, but it also meant a chance to start over, to rebuild my relationship with my brother. I needed him and this inn.

"Tell me, Chels. Was it worth it? Did you find what you were looking for?"

"No. Is that what you want to hear? I thought I could be someone who made a difference in the world, who changed things for the better, but all I did was make things worse. So that's why I came home to the inn, to you. To start over. Again."

Paul rubbed his forehead, letting out a sardonic laugh. "How far up shit creek are you? You going to end up in jail like Dad?"

"This isn't some penny-ante con man scam." I pressed my lips together and shrugged. "If I get caught? Well, let's put it this way. You'll never find the pieces."

Stiffening, he dropped his hand. "Jesus."

"Can you do it or not?"

He tapped his fingers on his thigh. "It's not going to be easy. Declaring someone dead takes a shitload of paper-work." He let out a long breath, drawing it out. "But I have some connections in Bangor who can pull it off, as well as the name change."

I collapsed against the headrest. "Thank you."

"After you're 'dead,' what then? You got a plan?"

"I do what I should have done all along." I gestured at the inn, eyeing the mildewing posts on the wrap-around porch. "Fix this place up. Open for business. Make Aunt May proud. *Stay*."

He cocked a brow. "And when people ask why your last name is different?"

"Divorce." I twisted my lips. "Or maybe I'm widowed. Whichever draws less curiosity."

"Divorced, I think," he said hesitantly. "You're really staying?"

"Yes. I'm done running. Whatever happens, happens. This is where I make my stand."

"All right." He nodded, placed his hands on the wheel, gripping it tightly. "How do you want to die?"

Chapter 5

THAT NIGHT, I turned on the big-screen TV. Settling into the corner of the couch with my glass of whiskey, I tucked myself in with an afghan Aunt May had crocheted. My notebook of lists and plans for the inn's renovation slid between me and the couch. I smiled at the roaring fire I'd managed to get going before focusing on CNN, which was covering a bombing in Kuwait.

Not a shooting in Miami.

I hadn't eaten all day, but that was okay because I wasn't really hungry. I didn't need food, just some whiskey to help me survive the night ahead. Anything to help me sleep, without knocking me out so deeply I couldn't hear danger approaching.

Even an hour of shut-eye would be nice.

Rubbing my face, I yawned and set my drink down. I froze when someone knocked. The only person who knew I was here was Paul, and he was in Bangor taking care of my identity crisis.

Heart pounding, I stood on the scratched hardwood floors, slowly creeping forward. A floorboard squeaked under my foot and I half expected to hear gunshots, but only silence followed. I opened the drawer I'd slid my gun into, resting my fingers on the cool barrel of the Glock.

Pulling the curtains back hesitantly, I peeked outside. And damned if I didn't want to use that gun even more than before. Gritting my teeth, I let the doorknob go, glowering out the tiny slit of the curtain opening. *Fricking* Jeremy Holland. He stood underneath the flickering light on the porch, holding food and a bottle of wine, the soft amber glow making him look too hot for my liking.

There was no way in hell I was letting him in.

He rocked back on his heels and knocked again. When I didn't move, he grinned and leaned in close to the door. "I can hear you breathing."

I winced, covering my mouth, which was stupid, because unless he'd become a superhero over the years, he was lying.

"I know you're in there, Chelsea O'Kane. Open up."

Announce my identity to the whole world, why don't ya?

I hesitated, pressing my hand against the door. What were the chances of him giving up and going away? Slim to none. Jeremy would never give up on anything so long as the slightest shred of hope remained.

"I have your favorite Chinese food. General Tso's chicken, rice, egg rolls, and red wine." He waited, and when I didn't unlock the door, he sighed. "If you don't let me in, I'm going to have to assume it's not you in there. And if it's not you, it's a trespasser, so I'll call the police."

I closed my eyes, counting to three. Such a damn idiot. The best way to get yourself shot was to *inform* a possible criminal that you were going to report him. How had he survived all these years without me around to beat some sense into him?

Oh. Right. With his pretty *blond* wife.

Mary Walker—no, Mary *Holland.*

"All right." He looked the door up and down before stepping back. I hoped he wasn't about to kick it down. The damn thing wouldn't stand a chance. "Suit yourself." I saw him fish his phone out of his pocket.

Fricking Jeremy Holland. Pressing my forehead against the metal, I called out, "Call the cops and I'll shoot you myself, asshole."

He laughed, his finger hovering over the screen. "There's the Chelsea I knew and loved."

"You didn't love me," I replied coolly, resting my hand on the knob. "How's Mary?"

He didn't say anything to that. "Let me in."

"No." I shook my head, even though he couldn't see me. My heart raced and my blood rushed. Knowing he was just inches away, on the other side of this door, made me feel more alive than I'd felt in…years. "Go home. Forget all about me."

"Not happening. Why did you lie about who you were?"

"I didn't," I said quickly. "I'm not Chelsea O'Kane anymore." I took a deep breath and focused on my story. It was imperative I convince him. "I was married, but he's gone now. I kept his last name, though. Wanted to leave my ties to the O'Kanes in the past. You know the family motto, keep looking forward."

"You got *married?* To who?" he asked, his voice hard.

"No one you knew."

"Try me." He jiggled the knob. I sucked in a breath. "Don't make me break down the pretty pink door your aunt special-ordered all those years ago because it reminded you of a fairy palace. I just want to talk."

I tightened my grip on the knob. "I'm talking to you now."

"Doesn't count." He sighed. "Open up. Prove it's you."

Rolling my eyes, I turned the lock, because there was no way he was going to leave unless I told him to, and I'd promised Paul I'd contain Jeremy. Yanking it open, I glowered at him, breathing heavily because, God, he looked good. He'd changed into a flannel shirt, which was unbuttoned and hanging loosely over a tight gray T-shirt. And those jeans—God, those *jeans*—left nothing to the imagination. "Happy now?"

His gaze raked over me, and I swore he somehow closed the distance between us without moving, because I could *feel* it. When he finally met my eyes again, there was a heat that set me on fire. "No."

"Too bad. Go home to your wife," I said, stepping back, wrapping my arms around myself, holding on tightly. Being this close to him shook me off my axis. "I'm sure she wouldn't be happy if she knew you were hanging around over here."

He entered the house, shutting himself in with me. I could feel the power radiating off him, and damned if he didn't smell exactly the same as he used to—like male, cologne, and fresh aftershave. I wanted to bury my face in his neck and breathe him in until his lips met mine like I'd fantasized about for years. Everything else faded away, but I didn't move. *That* had been a onetime deal.

After sliding the lock home, he set the food and wine down on the table—the same one that held my gun. I quickly glanced at the slightly opened drawer but focused on the real threat.

Him.

He crossed the room and grabbed my chin, clearly ignoring the *back the hell off* vibes I was throwing his way. The second his fingers touched my skin, sparks of desire laced through my blood like heroin, as he stared at me like he had every intention of picking up where we left off all those years ago. "You're blond."

"Yeah," I breathed. "So is your wife."

His grip on me tightened. "You *honestly* think I would still marry Mary after you and I slept together the night before my wedding?"

Chapter 6

JEREMY HELD HIS breath, waiting for her reply. She stared at him with wide blue eyes—eyes he'd never truly forgotten, despite how much time had passed since he'd last seen them. He scanned her face, not missing the bruising on her pale throat and underneath her eye, no matter how much makeup she'd used.

Her blond hair was...out of character.

She was beautiful, of course. Nothing would ever change that. But Chelsea as a blonde was like seeing the White House painted purple. Her lips were as plump and tempting as he remembered, and the attraction between them was as strong as ever. He'd missed her more than he'd thought possible. It felt like it was just yesterday that they had gotten drunk, kissed for the first time, and ended up naked in bed together...the night before his wedding to another woman.

That had been the shittiest thing he'd ever done.

And somehow the best, too.

"You didn't marry her?" she asked softly, swallowing hard. She winced, like it hurt to do so. It took all his control not to pull her into his arms, hug her close, and demand she let him help her with what she was going through. "I thought we both moved on."

"How could I, after what we did?" he asked angrily. Even if it hadn't been morally wrong, he'd realized the truth that night. It had always been Chelsea.

She gripped her arms tighter, letting out a little laugh. "You loved her. What happened that night was…" She faded off and he stiffened. If she said it was a mistake, he'd show her just how much of a mistake it *wasn't*.

She sighed. "It was wonderful. But it was just a night. We both knew where your heart really belonged."

Yeah, he had thought he'd known, too. Until he kissed Chelsea and saw just how very wrong he'd been. He ran his thumb over her jawline softly. "A man who truly loves a woman isn't going to sleep with someone else the night before their wedding. My relationship with Mary was over the second you and I kissed."

"Lots of things were," she muttered, pulling free from his touch and backing up a few steps. "You shouldn't be here, Jeremy."

"Because your name change magically erased our connection?" he asked dryly.

"No." She shook her head. "Because I don't want you here. You're part of my past—a past I have no inclination to revisit. I'm moving on. Starting fresh."

"Funny, because right now, I can't think of anyone else I'd rather be with, revisiting memories." After years of searching, he'd be damned if he wanted to waste any more time playing games now that he'd finally found her again. He wasn't that same stupid kid he'd been before—the one who had been too blind to see what he wanted until it was too late.

She shook her head, biting down on her lower lip. "Well, that sucks for you, because I'm not interested. You broke my heart before. I won't let you do it again."

"You broke mine, too," he said softly—honestly—trying

his best to act as unthreatening as possible. If he pushed too hard, she'd take off again. If you looked up *flight risk* in the dictionary, her picture would be next to the definition. "Why are you here? What are you running from?"

"Nothing," she said quickly.

Too quickly.

"We both know that's not true," he said, stepping closer to her. She stiffened but stood her ground as he reached out and tugged on the lock of hair that always fell into her face. He missed her normal chestnut color. "What trouble did you get into after you left?"

"The kind that's none of your business," she spat back, yanking her hair out of his grasp. "It stopped being your business when you asked Mary to marry you."

"I left her at the altar. For you."

"Not for me," Chelsea argued, shaking her head. "I was *gone.*"

"Yeah." He stopped once their toes touched. "Guess I didn't know just how *gone* you were."

"Poor you. Go home, Jeremy."

"I brought you some dinner. Something tells me you haven't eaten all day, and even if you don't want me here, you need to at least take the food."

She shook her head, biting down on her lower lip. "Stop it."

"Stop what?" he asked, cocking a brow.

"Taking care of me. This isn't just like old times. Take your food, and yourself, out of here. I'm not the same girl I was back then."

He reached out and brushed her hair out of her face. "I'm not the same boy, either. This time around, I know what I want—and I plan on getting it."

She sucked in a breath, her cheeks flushing. "Good for you. Should I clap?"

"Why are you so angry with me?"

"I'm not angry," she shot back. "I'm *busy.*"

He cast a quick glance around the inn, which was in shambles and empty except for the two of them. "Clearly."

She pointed to the door.

"All right, all right. I'm going." Laughing, he turned around, opening the door and stepping outside, leaving the food on the table. The second he was on her porch, she started to swing the door shut, but his deep voice made her stop what she was doing. "I'll be seeing you soon, Chelsea."

"Don't count on it," she shot back, her voice clipped. "I'll be too busy here."

"Curious," he said, his tone soft.

She scoffed at him. "Haven't you heard what happened to the cat?"

He cocked a brow. "No."

"Curiosity killed it."

And with that, she slammed the door in his face, locking it immediately.

But underneath the anger in her voice, he heard it. The fear that caused the slight tremor in her words. Chelsea wasn't the type to be frightened, so if she was scared of something, or someone? He was going to get to the bottom of this.

Even if it did kill him.

Which it very well might.

Chapter 7

THE NEXT DAY, I slept late in an attempt to ward off the hangover pounding inside my temples, but it didn't get the memo and lingered like a bitch. Should've stuck with whiskey instead of moving to the wine Jeremy had brought over. Now I trudged up the cracked cement walkway that led to the front porch, juggling supplies from the hardware store. Pamela Mayberry ran the place now, since her father retired down to Boca Raton. Pamela peppered me with questions, trailing me around the store as I made my selections. It was only through the grace of God that I managed to carry on a polite conversation without snapping. You can take the girl out of a small town, but that small town will never forget her.

It was time to start ripping the inn apart, room by room. I'd begin with the ugly wood paneling in the living room, which would be used by guests as a common space. There would be coffee, croissants, and tea, and soft music playing as the fire roared cheerfully…

That was about as far as I'd gotten.

But it painted a pretty picture.

Smiling, I unlocked the door, almost dropping the bags in my left hand. After heaving them inside, I turned around, breathing heavily, and headed to my car for the next batch.

By the time that was inside, my back ached and my palms were abraded. I started to shut the door and froze, fear shooting through my chest. There was something else on my porch, obscured by the dead potted plant to the left of the door.

Roses.

Not just any roses.

Red roses.

I glanced around the yard, looking for signs of anyone watching—*waiting.* Nothing moved except a few birds in the nearby apple tree. They chirped happily, flapping their wings, completely unaware that I was about to lose my shit. When no one jumped out to attack, I took a deep breath and bent down, grabbing the brass vase before going inside.

Slamming the door shut, I leaned against it, heart racing. I longed to throw them out without reading the note tucked among the petals, but that would be a foolish move. If there was a threat, I needed to face it head-on, not cower behind false ignorance like a scared child. That wasn't my style. I preferred using my fists for cover instead.

I glanced down at the card—and fear immediately turned to anger when I realized it was a different ghost from the past haunting me. I'd recognize that cursive *J* anywhere. That son of a bitch didn't know when to quit. Without thinking my anger through, or identifying the true cause of it, I was in my car heading for town. For *him.*

Even though I knew rationally that I shouldn't be doing this, and that I was playing right into his hands by seeking him out, it didn't stop me. When it came to Jeremy, I wasn't rational.

Which was why he was such a danger to me.

I couldn't afford to mess up right now.

Angrily, I aimed for the run-down motel off Main Street,

which was the only lodging in town. I saw Jeremy's late model truck parked in front of the motel and I screeched into the parking lot. It was like it was meant to be—I'd found him so easily—but I refused to look too deeply into that. I wanted to give him the damn flowers back, and make sure he understood that I meant it when I said to stay away, since he seemed to think this was some kind of game.

He should know better.

I'd never been the playful type.

Pulling up next to his truck, I picked up the flowers and marched up to his door. Lifting my fist, I knocked hard enough to wake the dead. The door swung open, and there he was, wearing nothing but a pair of black sweats, which clung to certain parts of his body I tried very hard to forget about, thank you very much. The lack of a shirt only highlighted how good he looked, because good God, those abs had to have been chiseled by Michelangelo himself. There was no way those were *real*.

He'd always been fit, but now…

He was a freaking Adonis.

Damn him.

At my obvious appraisal of his body, he grinned and gripped the opposite side of the doorjamb, leaning closer. "You look good, too, Chels."

That annoying childhood nickname snapped me out of my haze of abs and pecs. Gnashing my teeth together, I ducked under his arm, barging in his room without invitation.

After all, he'd done the same thing to me.

"Please," he said dryly, closing the door behind me. "Come in."

The room was tiny, and being shut inside with *him* wearing practically *nothing* was too much. I needed that door open again…better yet, I needed to get the hell out of here. Away from him. "I'm not staying. Keep your stupid flowers and stop showing up at my place. I don't need you coming by, scaring the shit out of me—"

"Scaring you?" He raised a brow, crossing his arms. "Why the hell would flowers on your porch *scare* you?"

I lifted my chin, knowing I'd said too much and cursing myself because of it. When would I learn that less was more, especially when it came to Jeremy Holland? "When will you realize all I want is for you to stay away—"

"—from you." He walked across the room, not stopping until he was directly in front of me, in my personal space, doing the very *opposite* of staying away from me. "I know. I heard you. When will *you* realize I don't give a damn what you want, because I know that you're hiding something, and I'll keep asking questions until I get some answers?"

I sucked in a deep breath, watching him closely, my chest rising and falling way too rapidly. He always could read me like an open book, and clearly he hadn't lost that skill during our years apart. I needed to do something to throw him off balance.

So I did the most unpredictable thing I could think of.

I kissed him.

Chapter 8

THE SECOND OUR lips touched, I knew I'd made a big mistake. *Huge.* It came second only to running away to Miami to chase after a new life. And look where *that* had gotten me.

He gripped my shirt at the small of my back, taking over the kiss without any hesitation. His lips moved over mine, claiming me, and he moved my body so I was trapped between him and the dirty wall. There was no escape, which is the first thing I should have been focused on, but instead...

All I could think was *more.*

More tongue. More hands. More heat. More *everything.*

He lifted me up as if I weighed nothing and edged between my legs, pressing his hardness against me. I'd only felt him like this against me once before, and yet it was like my body had never forgotten just how right he felt.

Growling, he slipped his tongue between my lips. The second his touched mine, I gasped into his mouth, curling my fingers over his impossibly hard biceps. For the first time since leaving Miami, I felt like I wasn't lost. For the first time...

I felt safe.

And it was all Jeremy's fault.

I pushed at his shoulders, inhaling deeply, and turned my head to the side so he couldn't claim my lips with his own again. He was stealing the air right out of my lungs. The room was spinning, and his muscles were pressed against me, and I wanted more of him. *Oh, my God,* I couldn't breathe when he was touching me.

Sliding his hand under my butt, he thrust against me, his sweatpants and my leggings creating only a thin barrier between the two of us. Part of me wished they were gone, and the other part knew if they were, nothing would stop us from having sex right here, in his drab motel room.

"You taste so damn good," he mumbled, nibbling my ear.

I shivered, digging my nails into him. Warning bells went off in my head. I knew I had to put a stop to this before things went too far. The whole reason for this ill-advised kiss was to throw *him* off balance.

But, God help me, he didn't seem to be falling victim to my master plan.

Not even a little.

Instead, he was acting like he'd been waiting ten years for this to happen…just like I had. I skimmed my fingers down his arms, exploring his muscles as I went. Relearning the way he felt, pressed up against me. He still felt like Jeremy, but at the same time, it was like he was an entirely different man. I wasn't sure if I could handle the emotions coursing through me, but I knew one thing.

If we kept doing this…

I'd regret it.

Shaking my head, I pushed at his shoulders again, a moan escaping me as he brushed the sides of his thumbs across my nipples roughly. "We can't—oh *God.*"

"Yes. We can," he rasped in reply. "We really can."

He claimed my mouth again, his hand dipping in between

our bodies. The second he ran his fingers over me, I knew my defenses were gone. His tongue brushed against mine, and I clung to him, some small part of me never wanting to let go. The feeling was so familiar that it was like putting on a sweatshirt you hadn't worn in years.

It just *fit*.

Pleasure built in my stomach, spreading slowly over my body, and I rolled my hips against his fingers, and his erection. He put me down and ran a hand across my nipples, squeezing them as his other hand moved over me, and with an embarrassing quickness…

I came.

Hard.

His mouth tore free, and he dropped his forehead to rest against mine with a ragged moan. "Jesus, Chels. That was the hottest orgasm." He slipped his hand under my butt again, palming it, and lifted me. "I want more."

He sought my mouth, but I turned away at the last second, panting. "No."

"No?" He asked in surprise. "Seriously?" I pushed at his shoulders and he immediately set me down, nostrils flaring as he stepped back. "All right. I get it."

"This never should have happened. We had one night and that's it. It's done," I said, still trembling. "Finished."

"I don't know about you," he said slowly, dragging a hand through his hair, which made it stand up in a sexy, *GQ* model way. "But when I'm done with someone, I don't kiss them like I'm going to die if I don't fuck them in the next five minutes."

My cheeks heated, and I backpedaled—which was stupid, because we both knew exactly what had happened here. Panicked, I said, "I only kissed you because I thought it would scare you off."

"Why the hell would you think that?"

"Because it scares *me*." I wrapped my arms around myself. "I've spent the last few years forging a new path, doing what I want to do, and playing by *my* rules, not my father's. But after two days back here, I'm kissing you like nothing's changed at all."

He reached out hesitantly, brushing my hair behind my ear. "And that's a bad thing?"

"Yes. I'm no good for you and never have been."

Shaking his head, he pressed his mouth into a thin, hard line. "I disagree."

"That's because you always look for the good in people. Sooner or later, you'll realize there's none in me." I slid away from him, avoiding his eyes. If I looked at them, I'd get lost in their green depths, and I'd end up right back in his arms— endangering him. "Don't bring me flowers again. I don't like them."

"Why not?" he asked softly.

"My ex used to give them to me, as an apology, after he…" I broke off, refusing to say any more. It was enough. It was more than enough. "They just—they hold a different meaning for me now. Don't give them to me again."

Something crossed his eyes—rage, maybe—and he stepped closer. "I'm sorry."

I opened the door, grabbed my purse off the floor, and swallowed hard. "Stay away from me, Jeremy."

Far, far away.

Chapter 9

LATER THAT NIGHT, I was on a ladder, shoving a pry bar between the last of the wood paneling in the living room, when headlights hit my window. I sighed and shoved harder, successfully knocking down a portion of the dated wood, sending a puff of dust flying through the air in the process. I let out an exasperated breath, because I had no doubt who had just pulled into my driveway.

It had to be Jeremy.

Clearly, my warning to stay away hadn't taken.

I hopped off the ladder and removed my dust mask, heading for the door. I grabbed the bottle of whiskey off the upside-down bucket and uncapped it, swallowing a mouthful before setting it back down. My body still hummed from the orgasm he'd given me. Even though I wanted him to stay away from me and the danger surrounding me, my traitorous heart sped up at the thought of seeing him.

No matter how logically I looked at the situation, one thing wouldn't change: My body remembered Jeremy Holland, and it wanted more of his touch.

Much more.

A girl could only save a guy from herself so many times before she stopped trying.

Being a good person didn't come naturally to me, and re-
sisting temptation wasn't my strong suit. Eventually, I'd stop
pushing him away.

And then he'd be in as much danger as I was.

Footsteps sounded on the porch as I swung the door open.
"You just can't take no for an—" I broke off, the words choking me, because it wasn't Jeremy on my doorstep this time.

It was a cop.

Oh, shit. They *knew*. They found me.

"Chelsea Adams?"

"Wh—?" I blinked. Chelsea Adams…? *Paul.* He'd come
through. "Y-yes?"

"I'm Officer North. I'm afraid your brother has been attacked." He removed his hat. "He told an officer you're his
sister, and his emergency contact."

Paul. Oh God.

Paul was the only family I had left who wasn't behind bars,
and I couldn't lose him. "What happened? Where is he?"

"He was jumped outside his office, on his way to come see
you." The officer fiddled with his hat, as if unsure where to
look or how to act around me. "He's in pretty bad shape, but
he should recover. I can take you to him, miss, and the doc-
tors can tell you more."

"I'll drive myself," I said quickly, reaching for my keys.

"Ma'am?" He leaned in, locking eyes with me. I stiffened,
because I didn't need him all up in my face. "I can smell the
whiskey from here. I think it's best I drive."

My cheeks flushed and I nodded, ducking my head down.
In my worry, I'd completely forgotten about that. That wasn't
like me. Then again, I'd done a lot of uncharacteristic things
these past few days…my behavior with Jeremy was just the
most recent example. "Right. Thank you."

The ride in the cop car was filled with awkward silence.

For a moment I reveled in the novelty of riding in the front for a change. Then I started quietly panicking. Paul had just been attacked, and the timing was a coincidence, right? My brother had his fair share of enemies. I shouldn't jump to the conclusion that this was the work of the people after me.

But when I walked in the room and saw Paul lying in the hospital bed, I knew. His eyes were nearly swollen shut, and parts of his head were shaved, with thick bandages covering wounds. A thin white blanket concealed most of his body, but I could see that both of Paul's thumbs were splinted. I knew what that meant.

They were here.

Chapter 10

JEREMY PUSHED THROUGH the doors of the hospital, his heart racing as he dodged an old guy in a wheelchair. Nurses in colorful scrubs walked the halls, some clearly at the beginning of their shift, others obviously at the end. One of them, someone he vaguely recognized from high school, smiled at him as she passed, so he nodded back politely. People sat in those horrible plastic chairs in cramped waiting rooms, waiting to find out if they were losing someone they loved today.

He hated hospitals.

They reeked of desperation and death.

When he'd heard of the attack on Paul, his stomach had sunk. This wasn't supposed to be *happening*, damn it. He pushed the elevator button harder than necessary, tapping his fingers on his thigh impatiently. *"Come on,"* he growled.

He needed to see her in one piece.

With his own eyes.

The second the doors started to open, he slipped through the crack, hitting the button for the third floor before anyone could join him. Paul had already been admitted, and word was that he'd be in the hospital for a good couple of weeks.

Paul had been beaten and tortured.

It was a miracle he was still alive.

The only reason Paul was still breathing: He was a message. A warning. One intended for his sister, and one *Jeremy* intended to take very seriously.

The doors to the elevator opened and he took a left, heading toward Paul's room. They hadn't spoken much over the years, but Jeremy had kept tabs on him. As he approached the room he slowed, walking lightly when he heard the sound of Chelsea's voice. He stopped just short of the door, where he could see them without being seen.

She spoke again and her voice washed over him like the first warm spring rain after a long, cold winter. Creeping closer, he stole a quick peek. She sat beside Paul, resting her hand on his arm gently, talking so quietly he had to struggle to hear her words. He was taken back to a time when he'd gotten his appendix out and she hadn't left his side as he recovered. Why hadn't he understood what she meant to him back then? How could he have been such a fool to lose her?

History wouldn't repeat itself this time.

"…and that's why you were attacked tonight. They're trying to flush me out."

"Shit, Chels," Paul growled.

Jeremy couldn't see her face, but her shoulders were drooped, and her head was as low as her voice. "I'm sorry. I never intended for this to happen, for you to get dragged into my fight. If I'd known they would do this…"

"I know." Paul stared at her, his bruised face looking like a sick artistic interpretation of a face rather than the real thing. "How are we going to get out of this mess?"

"There's no we, just me—" She stopped midsentence, stiffening. He held his breath. Something told him she'd discovered his presence. Or rather, sensed *someone* standing there, listening. Now she would clam up. "How did they get the drop on you?"

"What? Why—". Paul stared at her, then nodded once, glancing toward the door. I stepped back quickly, heart racing. Damn them and their silent communication. "I was leaving the DMV—" He broke off, wincing. "They came out of nowhere."

She nodded, smoothing his hair out of his face tenderly. "Criminals are good at that."

Footsteps approached, so Jeremy slid into the empty room next to Paul's, holding his breath. After a moment, the door to Paul's room shut, and he heard Chelsea say, "They're gone."

Jeremy pressed his ear to the thin wall.

"Assholes," Paul said. "How did you get mixed up with those guys anyway?"

"It's not like I meant to," she practically whispered.

"They were trying to find out if I knew where you were. I told them the truth, that we hadn't talked in years. That last I heard, you were some kind of hotshot lawyer down in Miami. I think they bought it, but you should leave, Chels. They might have someone watching the hospital."

"Shit," Chelsea said after a long pause. Jeremy could picture her sitting there, covering her face, looking exhausted as hell.

"Yeah. 'Shit' is right. The cartels don't mess around. And with what you did, they might never stop looking."

She sighed loud enough for Jeremy to hear it through the wall. "I did what I had to do, Paul. But you know what, it doesn't matter. You're right, I need to leave. Find someplace else to hide out."

Anger rushed through Jeremy's veins and he balled his hands at his sides. No. *Hell, no.* He didn't come back from Bangor for her only to watch her skip town.

She was right where he needed her to be.

Chapter 11

AFTER PAUL·DRIFTED off into a morphine-induced sleep, I sat by the bed in the white room with fluorescent lights overhead, watching over him with dry, weary eyes. This was on *me*. I had assumed they would be too busy dealing with the mess I'd left behind to chase after me already. Paul had paid the price for my mistake. It was my duty to make sure it didn't happen again.

At least three people had stopped by to check on him, so news was traveling fast. After the third drop-in, I requested that no one else be allowed in, so Paul could rest.

"Chels?" Jeremy said from behind me.

I stiffened, closed my eyes, and prayed for the patience the good Lord had never given me. "How many times do I have to tell you to *leave me alone* before you finally listen?"

"Is he okay?" he asked me, coming into the room and completely ignoring my words…as usual. Sometimes I wondered if he even heard them. "What happened?"

"Some punks jumped him outside his office," I said quickly, sticking close enough to the truth. While I thought I was an excellent liar, Jeremy did always have an uncanny knack for knowing when I was stretching the truth. "It wasn't enough to just mug him, they had to beat him, too. Assholes."

Jeremy came up beside me, staring at Paul with a furrowed brow. His hands were in his pockets, and his jaw was hard. "Some street kids took the time to break his thumbs?"

"Yeah." I gripped my knees, staring at my brother's hands. Bile rose in my throat, but I swallowed it back. Now wasn't the time or the place to lose it. "Sick, right?"

His mouth pressed into a thin, tight line. "Unbelievable." After a few moments, he let out a long breath and put his hand on my shoulder. "Let me take you home."

"I can manage on my own."

"That wasn't a question. You're exhausted, and sitting here worrying isn't going to help Paul. You need to rest."

"No." I pulled free, my heart racing and my skin burning where Jeremy had touched me. His hand stayed open, palm up and empty between us. "I need to make sure they don't come back."

"Why would a bunch of 'punks' go to all the trouble of sneaking into a hospital to attack Paul again?" he asked, his perfect brown brow arching. I hated when he did that. "I feel there's something you're not telling me. Am I right?"

"Of course you'd think that," I muttered, knowing I was skating on the edge of giving him information he didn't need to know. "No. I'm just being paranoid. I'm worried about my brother."

"He has a police guard." He pointed out the door and I looked. Sure enough, there was a uniform outside his door. Weird. Wouldn't Paul love to know that law enforcement was lurking? The officer waved at me and I blinked at him before I recognized him. His name was…uh…Harry? No, *Larry*. He'd asked me to prom. I'd gone with Jeremy. I should've gone with Larry instead. "Paul will be fine on his own tonight. I want to make sure you're okay."

I crossed my arms, forcing my attention off the officer and

back to Jeremy. Paul would have to deal with it, because having a police presence around was actually calming me. For once. "I love how you continue to think that I give a damn what you want these days."

With that, I moved closer to Paul's side, intent on ignoring Jeremy. He'd get bored watching me watch Paul sleep soon enough.

"Fine. You want to stay?" He walked over to the other chair in the room. It had been in the corner, but he dragged it right next to mine and sat. "Then we'll stay."

"Seriously?"

"Dead serious." He crossed an ankle over his knee, his heel brushing my thigh because he was so close, and leaned back as if he didn't have a worry in the whole world. "It's been ten years since we had a sleepover. And that last one was…*eye-opening*, to say the least."

I still couldn't wrap my head around the chain of events that had led us here, or what it all meant. Jeremy had chosen me over Mary. He was still choosing me. I guess, in a way, he always had. His mother had hated me because of my father, but Jeremy had never cared, always keeping his bedroom window unlocked for me whenever I needed to get away from my family. He had loved me. Of course, he apparently didn't realize he was *in* love with me until I decided enough was enough and left. Jeremy was the love of my life.

But, man, he could be such a *guy*.

"Yeah, that night was definitely eye-opening." I looked back at Paul for any signs of distress. He didn't so much as twitch. The beeping of his heart monitor remained slow and steady. "Despite, y'know, earlier, I have no interest in repeating history."

"Yeah. Me neither."

I lifted a shoulder. "Glad we're on the same page."

He leaned forward, resting a hand on my thigh. His brown hair fell on his forehead, and his piercing green eyes called for me to give him what he wanted—me. He wore a flannel shirt and a pair of ripped jeans, and his huge arms strained against the fabric of the shirt. He was so strong, so steady, and I ached to borrow some of that strength. To let him take care of me…

Again.

"You misunderstand me." Hesitantly, he reached out, cupping my cheek. "I plan on kissing you again, but I have no intention of losing you this time, Chels."

I stiffened, holding my breath, because having him here, touching me, made it oh-so-tempting to lean on him for support. Just like he wanted. Just like I *couldn't*. I wasn't that naïve girl who believed in love anymore. I lurched to my feet, shaking off his touch. If only it was as easy to lose the emotional hold he had on me. "What's it going to take to get rid of you?"

He smirked. "Easy. Let me take you home."

"Done." I grabbed my purse, checking to make sure the officer was still there. He was, and he looked a hell of a lot more alert than I felt. "And then you leave me the hell alone. Look forward, and leave the past where it belongs."

Every moment I spent with him was another moment he crept closer to my heart and threatened the new beginning I was fighting so hard for. Every moment brought danger and risk to things I wasn't willing to lose.

Like his *life*.

Chapter 12

THE SECOND JEREMY parked behind my car, I was opening the door, hopping down, and heading for the inn. I'd been too close to him for too long, and I needed space to breathe. I inserted the key into the lock with steady hands and slipped inside my sanctuary. I pushed the door shut behind me with my hip but collided with something hard. I bounced off it with a soft *oof.* This was a lovely sense of déjà vu. "What the—?"

"I want to look the place over," Jeremy said quickly, sliding inside uninvited... *again.* "After all, your brother was just attacked."

"And what will you do if you find someone?" I asked incredulously, unable to believe how incredibly hard it was for him to get the damn message. It was exhausting trying to constantly push him away—and I was all out of energy. "You're an accountant. You gonna throw a calculator at him?"

"No." He shot me a look out of the corner of his eye. "How did you know I was a CPA?"

Well, shit. I'd as good as admitted to looking him up online. I hadn't meant to be so transparent, but after Paul's attack, I was a little off my game. "Paul mentioned it once, I think. Or maybe it was Dad."

He lifted a brow. "You visited him in jail?"

Nope. Dad got locked up with a six-year sentence for breaking and entering. If he was lucky, he'd be out next year. But given his history, his freedom wouldn't last long. "What exactly are you going to do if you find someone?"

"Just because I'm an accountant doesn't mean I'm weak." He shot me a hard look. "Don't make the mistake of thinking I am."

I held my hands up defensively. "I'd never *dare.*"

Brushing past me, he glanced in the living room. "Damn. Did someone break in here and steal your walls?"

"Yes. They absolutely did," I said dryly, following him. "There's a real market for old wood paneling on eBay these days."

He snorted and moved into the kitchen, stepping over fallen paneling and nails. I'd have to clean it up at some point, but I wouldn't tonight. I was too tired. "Wow. I didn't know brown vinyl floors were back in."

I clenched my teeth. "Spare me your sarcastic comments. I know the inn needs a lot of work. Like I said yesterday, *I'm busy.* I wasn't making that up."

He glanced over his shoulder, saying nothing at all—and yet somehow saying everything at the same time. As he moved into the pantry, glancing at the bare shelves, he flicked the light on in the kitchen. It flickered, then turned fully on with a pop. "Electrical issues. Probably old knob-and-tube wiring. It'll all have to be updated to pass inspection."

I wrapped my arms around myself. "Thanks, Captain Obvious."

He grabbed a pillow off the couch on the way, holding it in front of himself like a shield and shooting me a charming grin. "I'll bring this in case anyone attacks. You know how to do wiring?" he asked, heading to the stairs.

I rolled my eyes. "Nope."

"I do," he called over his shoulder.

"Congrats?" I followed him up the stairs, trying not to stare at his butt. I failed, with a capital *F.* "Want a cookie?"

"Sure. I love cookies." He rounded the corner. "I did the wiring at Dad's place, you know. I learned a few tricks fixing up his old place before he sold it."

"How is he?"

"Dead." He flicked on the hallway light, glancing at me briefly. Shadows covered his eyes—or was it the pain from his loss? "Died two years ago. Mom shortly after."

Well, damn. I hadn't seen that on his Facebook page. Despite his parents' feelings about me, they'd been good people. They never knew about my private entrance—Jeremy's window—but they'd invited me to dinner more often than not. Jeremy wasn't allowed near my place, but I preferred his house anyway. His mother always had fresh-baked goodies on the counter, like Betty Crocker. If Betty could also shoot a deer with a rifle at a hundred yards. Mrs. Holland had been a woman of many talents. "I'm sorry. I didn't know."

"I miss them every day," he said simply. He opened the next door, glancing into the Blue Room. Or the room that would be blue, anyway, once I was done with it. Right now, it was covered in faded, peeling floral wallpaper. "You need to paint in here. Maybe something pale. Like…light blue, since it faces the ocean. That would remind your guests of the nearby beach."

I stiffened, my heart picking up speed. We used to joke that we shared a brain, because we always came up with the same ideas at the same time. Years apart and yet it was like no time had passed at all. I gestured to the cans of blue paint in the corner of the room. "That's the plan."

We studied each other. Our connection hadn't died, no

matter the distance between us. It would be so easy to fall back into "us," to resume our relationship as if nothing had changed, but I couldn't. I needed to focus on the inn, on making it the warm and welcoming place I knew it would be—not on Jeremy.

He went through all the rooms, stopping when he reached mine. Slowly, he pushed the door open, turning the light on. He strode in, glancing under the bed for hidden monsters, the way he had in all the other rooms. My monsters didn't hide under beds. I leaned on the wall, watching him check my closet. Having him here was...nice. All the more reason to make him go.

As he walked away from my closet, he tossed the pillow on my bed. "I could stay here. Help you fix the place up. I'm handy."

"No, thanks," I said, shutting that idea down immediately, mostly because it made my heart soar and my legs go a little weak. The idea of having Jeremy under the same roof as me, helping me transform this place...it wasn't exactly a *bad* one. "I don't take charity."

He flexed his jaw. "It's not charity. I'm paying an arm and a leg to stay at that cheap-ass motel because it's the only lodging in town. Fixing up the inn gives people like me options. This place is much nicer, and you can play the whole 'short walk to the beach' angle that the motel could never claim. It's the perfect small-town getaway. You could host honeymooners—any couple, really, looking for a romantic weekend. Maybe even weddings."

"That's the plan," I repeated. "You think I didn't think of that?"

"I know you did. But the thing is, being here, looking at the rooms?" He smiled, locking eyes with me. "I can *feel* it. I can feel the things this place could be, what it could offer people. And, damn it, Chels, I want to be a part of it. I want to help you rebuild."

I didn't say anything. Mostly, because all I could think of saying was *yes*. But I couldn't. He'd suck me back into his world of goodness and I wasn't naïve enough to think that world existed anymore.

"Let me help you open this place up sooner. I'll be in town for a week, so let me lend you a hand while I still can." He gestured toward the hallway, walking across the room. My bedroom felt a million times smaller with him in it. I stared at him as he crept closer, one step at a time. When he was directly in front of me, I crossed my arms in front of me defensively. "I think it's really special what you're doing here, rebuilding the inn. Let me be a part of it. Of you." He blinked. "That came out wrong. I meant…screw it."

And then, without warning, he cupped my cheek. Before I could exhale, he was kissing me, and I was clinging to him, and his hands were everywhere. I couldn't think of any other place I'd want Jeremy to be than *here*. I wanted him with me, fixing up the inn, building a future that was so real that I could feel it, too. He slid his hand up my shirt, cupping my breast, and claimed my mouth with no mercy and no hint of hesitation.

He just…took.

And I gave. *Willingly.*

Arching my back, I dug my nails into his shoulders, letting out a soft moan. His phone rang, and he stiffened, his lips going hard against mine before he pulled back. "Shit."

I shoved at his shoulders. "If you didn't want to kiss me, then you shouldn't have—"

"It's not that. I just didn't want to push you when you were vulnerable," he said, pulling away from me and ignoring his ringing phone. "I meant what I said, though. Can I help you?"

Swallowing, I stared at him, knowing I was in over my head. There's only so much you can learn from construction how-to books and YouTube. Besides, no matter how much I pushed Jeremy away, he kept showing up, so I might as well save my energy for more important things…like staying *alive*. "If you're going to help, you can stay here for free as payment."

"Deal." His grin lit up the room better than any flickering light ever could. "You won't regret this."

That might be true, but one way or another…*he* would.

It was only a matter of time.

Chapter 13

THE NEXT MORNING, Jeremy was under the sink with dirty water dripping on his face and the edge of the cabinet digging into his back. The TV was on in the living room and he could just barely make out what the news anchor was saying. He'd heard the telltale dripping under the sink when he came down to the kitchen to make coffee, and he figured that there was no time like the present to start earning his keep. He intended to make sure Chelsea had no valid reason for kicking him out, since he was exactly where he wanted to be. Sooner or later, she would trust him again and tell him the truth she was trying so hard to hide. Footsteps approached, and he torqued the wrench harder. "Morning, Chels."

The footsteps stopped at his side. Though he couldn't see her, he could easily picture her frowning down at him, arms crossed. "What are you doing under there?"

"Admiring the old lead pipes."

"Ha-ha," she muttered. "So funny."

He pushed out from under the sink, swiping his forearm over his forehead as he eyed her. She wore a loose pink shirt and a pair of leggings that hugged her curves. "There was a leak in the pipes where they joined."

She frowned, and he glanced down at her soft lips. "Since when?"

"I don't know. I just got here, but judging from the damp wood under me, I'd say a long time. But it's fixed now." As Jeremy stood, Chelsea's eyes drifted down his shirtless torso. "Neighbors brought pie, casserole, and those."

She eyed the red roses he'd deliberately thrown away. "And questions about Paul?"

"Of course." He grabbed the mug off the counter, filled it with coffee, and handed it to her. "Still like it black?"

"Yeah." She took the mug and her fingers brushed his. It was just like old times, when he used to bring her coffee every day before class, since they had gone to the same college. She could've gone away to school, but when he got a baseball scholarship for the state university, she followed him there. As her fingers left his skin, he swallowed hard. Just that simple touch was enough to make him want to pull her in his arms and kiss away the worry he could see in her eyes. "Some things never change."

"Guess not."

She set the coffee down, leaned on the old maple cabinets, and stared at him. Chelsea had a way of staring at a guy that made it feel like she saw all the way to the bottom of his soul. It was enlightening and scary all at once. "Why didn't you marry Mary? After all those years together, telling me that she was the love of your life, you just…left her behind."

"I was wrong. I didn't love her," he said simply. "Why'd you marry that guy?" He was curious to see what she'd say, since they both knew she'd never been married. "I gather from what you've let slip that he was a dick."

"I don't know. I keep asking myself that question." She tapped her fingers on the counter. "Why did you take the boring desk job?"

"I was looking for something different. A change." He shrugged. "Why'd you run away?"

"Same reason. I didn't want to be the girl who was in love with a boy who didn't love her back. And I definitely didn't want to be known only as Johnny O'Kane's daughter anymore."

Her words touched him. He'd always told her that she could be more than her family. He couldn't help but feel that even though she'd done her best to leave him in the past, there was still a small chance he'd be in her future. "I always loved you. I just didn't know the truth until it was too late. After I canceled the wedding, I went down a dark hole. Drank too much. Slept too little. Was angry at the world."

She turned away. "Yeah. I know the feeling all too well."

"Fixing up this place with you, I think it'll be good." He glanced around the kitchen, seeing it as it could be, not the cracked wood on the cabinets and the peeling wallpaper. "For both of us. What do you think of white cabinets?"

"*Love* them." She came alive at the mention of the renovations, no longer looking as if she'd rather be somewhere else. "I think they'll brighten this place up, especially if we do a blue-and-white backsplash, too. I'd like to have pastries and coffee in the living room, over there, for guests who don't want room service. Or they could eat in the formal dining room with the other guests, and I could have a buffet-style breakfast in here."

"That's a great idea." He rubbed his chin. "You seem pretty experienced at this stuff. Where have you been? I heard you were down in Florida."

"I was," she said hesitantly.

"Were you in hotel management down there?"

Just like that, the excitement died in her eyes. "No."

"So what did you do?"

Chelsea stiffened the second he pried into her past. It was infuriating. What would it take to get her to open up to him? "I was an assistant district attorney."

"And now you're back here…fixing up inns?" He worked his jaw. "It takes guts to walk away from that degree, if you ask me. Why leave all that?"

"I didn't." Leaving her coffee untouched on the counter, she bumped shoulders with him as she started to leave the room. *Escape* was more like it. "I'm going on a few errands. Won't be back till later tonight."

"We'll continue this conversation later," he called out.

She didn't reply. Just banged the front door shut behind her.

Jeremy trailed after her, watching her from the window as she got in her beater. He wanted to tag along to keep her safe, but he knew he'd be pushing his luck. He'd already wormed his way into her home. If he pushed any harder, she'd snap. If this was going to work, he needed to stay close to her.

"And in other news, a district attorney is the latest victim of increased gun violence in Miami. Dental records have confirmed that Richard Seville, who was a popular candidate for the mayoral office in Miami due to his generosity with the people of the city and his conservative political leanings, has been murdered. Authorities say someone broke into his home late Monday night, killing him. Police are looking for help to identify and locate the woman seen fleeing the scene, who is described as…"

He stopped listening, pulling out his phone and quickly dialing. "The story went national," he said, as soon as the other person picked up. "We need to move faster."

Chapter 14

I'D NEARLY DRIVEN into a tree when I got Paul's text. CNN's covering it. I still remembered what a comfort my brother had been to me as I'd spilled all my dirty secrets. It was bad enough that Paul had put two and two together with the little bit I'd told him, but what if Jeremy did, too? I guess I had let myself fall into a false sense of security as the days ticked by with no repercussions. Now I had a brother in the hospital and the media shining a spotlight on things.

I pulled over to check out the link Paul had texted. I scanned the article quickly and breathed a sigh of relief, dropping my phone back onto my lap. They didn't seem to have too many details. It said that Richard was shot in his home and that his death was further proof we were losing the War on Drugs. No duh.

The situation clearly called for junk food, so I swung by Ollie's Diner to pick some up for me and Paul. In his hospital room, we talked about the new development, but that only led to circular arguments. There was nowhere to go with this mess.

A day later, I sat in my car again, trying to muster the courage to head into the inn. Jeremy was painting in the living room and I had a bag of supplies on the passenger seat. I had to admit, once Jeremy had started pitching in, a lot more progress had been made on the renovations. I flitted from project to project, doing whatever caught my attention at that moment, but Jeremy always liked to finish what he started.

I couldn't help but compare him to Richard. Richard never let me "flit around." He was a massive control freak and needed to oversee everything from start to finish. That included people. We had met at the holiday party, back when I first started at the DA's office. He was already a rising star. I thought we'd been swept away—that our relationship was like something out of a romance novel—whereas he saw a puppet he could manipulate.

Little did he know that there ain't no strings on me.

My reverie was interrupted by a woodpecker doing its thing in the trees. I should run again. I knew I should, but...I didn't really want to. Maybe I needed to be more like that woodpecker and just keep banging away until I got what I wanted. Maybe it was time to stand my ground and fight. Turning my head, I looked at my inn, the place I wanted to make my sanctuary. Over the past few days, Jeremy and I had bonded over our plans to renovate, and for once, things felt *normal*. I was dreaming of a future like any other average person.

And then it got blown apart by CNN.

All the blinds were pulled up in the living room, and I could see Jeremy standing on a ladder, painting the walls that I'd taped the other night. He'd sanded them yesterday, and now the plaster was getting new life under his roller with the paint I'd carefully picked out. My dreams were coming to life, but at any moment, they'd die in front of me.

God, could I be any more melodramatic?

Shaking my head, I cut the moping, straightening my spine. I wouldn't be *that* girl. I would be the girl who fought. Look at what I'd done to get here. If the cartels wanted a fight? Well, then, I'd give them a fight on *my* turf. If they wanted to come at me, they'd have to do it in the broad light of day. No more shadows for me. That part of my life was over. It *had* to be. I was Chelsea…Adams.

And I wasn't going *anywhere*.

Besides, if they knew where I was, I'd be dead already. They were obviously using the cops to try to flush me out, so I had time to come up with a game plan. My aim was to win. I grabbed the supplies out of the backseat and trudged up to the front door. Rock music blared out the open windows, and Jeremy sang along loudly and out of tune. Smiling, I glanced up at the old inn and saw home.

And Jeremy was undeniably a part of that picture, whether I liked it or not. I wasn't sure if I did yet. But that was okay. For once, I was okay with being unsure. Waiting to see how things worked out between the two of us should have scared me, but with danger lurking…yeah, it didn't. It was freeing to not give a damn anymore. Opening the door, I set the bags down. Jeremy's biceps flexed and hardened as he stroked the roller up the wall, set on making my dreams a reality. I took a second to admire the view, then called out, "I'm home."

"Did you get everything?"

"Yup." I came into the room, studying his workmanship. It was flawless. Excitement built inside me and I smiled. "That light peach is even prettier on the walls than it was on the card."

"It really brightens up the place," he agreed, grinning. "Did you decide whether you want the fireplace painted?"

"Yep." I pointed to the cans of paint at my feet. "Antique white won."

He nodded. "Good choice."

"Yeah. Paul suggested it." I tucked my hair behind my ear. "He'll be coming to live here, with us, once he's out next week, by the way. Once he's healed, he can help us out with renovations."

"Do you think that's——?" He gave the wall one more stroke before turning around mid-sentence. As he did, his sleeve brushed the wet wall. "Well, shit."

I laughed, but cut it off quickly when he shot me a narrow-eyed look. Forcing a straight face, I asked, "Do I think it's what?"

"Funny?" he asked, ripping his shirt over his head and hopping off the ladder effortlessly. He landed on both feet, dropping the shirt as his feet touched. I gulped down air, because, God, those *abs*. He stalked toward me, his eyes narrow.

I forced myself to stand my ground, even though I wanted to flee for my life. The cartel didn't send me running, but give me a shirtless Jeremy and I was a goner. "Yes?"

That brow shot up, and he took another step toward me. "Is that a question?"

"No." I lifted my chin. "I think it's funny you got paint on you, without a doubt."

Reaching out, he rested a tender hand on my shoulder, skimming his hand over the bare skin of my shoulder by my tank top straps. "Good. I'd hate to make you uncertain about anything when it comes to me. I know what I want from you, and I want you to feel the same certainty I do."

He lowered his face to mine, his eyes seductive.

I closed my eyes, breath held, ready to be kissed, and then he…

Ran the paint roller down my face.

Fricking Jeremy Holland.

Chapter 15

I GASPED, STUMBLING back with wide eyes, my mouth parted in surprise, and trying my best to act as if he'd taken me off guard by painting me instead of kissing me. Well, I mean, he *had*. But I wasn't so off balance that I couldn't start plotting my revenge. Dad had taught me a few tricks, and Jeremy wouldn't see me coming till it was too late. "I can't believe you just did that," I shrieked, lurching backward until I bumped into something.

He started laughing hysterically, bending over, taking his attention off me. *Jackpot.* "You...should...see...your...*face.*"

"I can't," I answered, creeping closer and closing my fist around my target. His laughter washed over me like a million lights in a gloomy basement. "But I can see yours."

He glanced up just in time for me to swipe the paintbrush I'd grabbed from the can across his entire face—and into some of his hair. He jumped back, but not quickly enough. He blinked at me, his eyes standing out comically against the light-peach paint, and his lips bright pink in contrast. I burst into laughter, pointing at him. "Oh my God. If I look anything like that, then—*agh!*"

I hit the floor, his arms cradling me so I didn't get hurt. The second we settled, he caught my arms over my head, trapping my weapon, leaving me defenseless with Jeremy Holland between my thighs. As he struggled to hold both my wrists with one hand, he lifted the roller threateningly. "Oh, so you want to play dirty?"

"You started it," I accused, arching my back, trying to throw him off. It did nothing besides let him settle in between my legs more firmly. I gasped when he rolled his hips, teasing me with his hardness. "*Now* who's playing dirty?" I said.

"Baby, you have no idea how dirty I can get," he murmured, dropping the roller and cupping my cheek. Tilting my chin up, he stared down into my eyes, his grip tightening on me. "But I'm willing to show you, if you'd like."

"Yes," I breathed, anticipation making my nerves tingle. "God, yes."

The breath I'd been holding burst out at the exact moment his lips touched mine, making everything seem right in the world again. He was hesitant at first, probably giving me a chance to change my mind, but when I strained to get closer, he claimed me fully. It was as if I'd been walking a labyrinth for the last eight years, and the second he was holding me, *kissing* me, the maze went straight, and suddenly I knew exactly where I was going and why.

He didn't let go of my wrists, but ran his thumb over my pulse gently as his tongue swept inside my mouth. He tasted like beer and Jeremy, a combination I missed more than I cared to admit. I slid my hand over his lower back, pressing closer to him as I curled a leg around him, locking him in place. There was no doubt. No fear. Okay, that was a lie. The way he made me feel scared the hell out of me. But even so?

It just felt *right*.

Skimming his hand down my sides, he deepened the kiss, stealing the last bit of coherent thought from my mind until all I could focus on was getting him naked and buried inside me. I needed Jeremy with a passion that burned me, that changed me, and there was no stopping now that we'd begun again.

I tugged at his shirt, moaning and writhing beneath him impatiently. Tearing my mouth free of his, I sucked in a breath, the room spinning around us. "I need you. *Now.*"

He slid his hand under my butt, nodding, pressing his forehead to mine. "You have me. You always have." He caught my mouth again and rocked his erection against me, sending pleasure through my veins. I pushed closer, desperate for the release only he could give me, and dug my nails into my palms, tugging for him to free my wrists.

He let go immediately, like he'd just been reminded he had been holding them, and stopped kissing me. Instead of keeping his lips on mine, he brought them down my body, one torturous inch at a time. My jaw. My throat. Directly over my pulse. My collarbone. The top of my breast. The lower he went, the faster my heart raced, and it got so loud, I swore he heard it, too.

So loud, I could feel the glass of the window above shattering over us, slicing my skin with its jagged edges—wait, what?

Jeremy threw himself over my body, completely shielding me, and it was then—oh God, it was *then*—that I realized the pounding I'd heard wasn't my heartbeat. It had been bullets, breaking windows, and implanting themselves in the freshly painted plaster. And those bullets were still coming, showing no sign of stopping anytime soon. Jeremy cursed, covering my body even more, pressing me down into the floor so hard that I couldn't breathe.

We were going to die.

Chapter 16

JEREMY GRITTED HIS teeth, growling as the bullets whizzed over his head, somehow miraculously avoiding them. One second, he'd been in heaven in Chelsea's arms, and the next, the threat of danger became all too real. He'd let his guard down, forgotten for a split second that he was supposed to be keeping her *safe*, and look what had happened. She'd almost been killed.

The second the bullets stopped, he was on his feet. They might just be pausing to reload, but he didn't give a damn. With Chelsea in danger, he wouldn't stand here waiting to find out and not fight back. "Stay down. Got it?"

She nodded, eyes wide, opening her mouth. She had small cuts on her cheeks and arms from the glass but otherwise looked fine. He didn't wait for her to speak. Instead, he took off out the front, taking the gun that she'd stowed in the table by the door. He didn't bother to look back when she gasped. There wasn't time. He had to catch those assholes who dared to shoot at his girl, damaging what she was trying to fix. Hell, he had to save her life, so she could be *his* girl, and so this place could become an inn again.

He bolted onto the porch, leaping off and raising the gun at eye level.

A dented black Cadillac screeched around the corner, out of shooting range. His finger tightened on the trigger. He ached to put a few holes in those sons of bitches, but he didn't have the shot. *"Shit."* Lowering the gun, he pulled his phone out, sent off a quick text, and headed back inside the inn.

Chelsea stood shakily, pressing a hand to her stomach. Her face was pale and she looked seconds from falling over, so he shoved the gun back in the drawer and rushed to her side, running his hands over her in case he'd somehow missed an injury besides her superficial wounds. "What's wrong?"

Shaking her head, she pressed her lips into a thin line and gripped his bicep, holding on to it tightly. She choked on a laugh. *"Everything's* wrong. Someone just shot up my home and tried to kill us."

"Yeah. They did. But they failed." Jeremy took a deep breath and pulled her into his arms, curling his hand behind her head and cradling it protectively. She was so brave and so strong that sometimes he forgot she wasn't in this line of work. Or at least she wasn't supposed to be. "I've got you, Chels. I won't let anything happen to you."

"That's sweet." She buried her face in his chest, breathing deeply, and for the first time since she came back, she leaned on him. "But it's a foolish thing to say. You have no idea what's going on."

He held her close, preparing for the worst. "So tell me."

"There's nothing to tell." She pushed off his chest, but her hands lingered. "The decisions I made, the messes I created, they're mine. I don't need anyone trying to fix them for me. If you know what's good for you, you'll stop trying. You've seen what happens when people try to help me. From here on out, I go it alone."

He caught her hand, refusing to let her go. "Tell me what you're planning to do."

"What makes you think I'm planning anything at all?" Chelsea crossed her arms defensively.

It was on the tip of his tongue to tell her the truth, but he didn't say a damn word. Sirens sounded outside. "I—"

"Shit." She pushed her hair out of her face, going even paler than before. "Someone called the cops?"

"There was a bunch of gunfire. Of course someone called the cops. Do you have a reason to hide this from them?" he asked slowly, locking eyes with her. "Is there something you want to tell me before they get here?"

"I…" She opened her mouth, closed it, and then shook her head. Disappointment hit him in the chest like a lingering bullet. "Nope. Nothing."

"Okay." Clenching his jaw, he headed for the door. "Stay in here. I'll take care of this and send them on their way." As he walked out the door, he shut it behind him, heading for the closest car. The red-and-blue lights blinded him as Larry stepped out of the driver's seat. "What happened here, Jeremy?"

He sighed, pulling his wallet out of his pocket. Larry's gaze dipped down, then shot back up immediately. "I'll tell you everything you need to know, but then you need to get the hell out of here."

Chapter 17

WITH JEREMY OUTSIDE, handling the cops, I rubbed my hands up and down my arms as I surveyed the damage to the walls and windows. This would easily set us back a few days and a few hundred dollars. But that wasn't what really mattered. What mattered was that *they* were getting closer. Soon they'd discover the truth about Richard. It was a truth I couldn't accept, but I'd done what I needed to do to survive and get out of there alive.

If I wasn't careful, my past was going to destroy everything I loved. It was time to take care of business. Obviously, my plan to escape and fade into the sunset wasn't working out, so I needed a new one. One that wouldn't quite have a happy ending for me.

If I was going down, the least I could do was make sure no one else went down with me. I had to make sure Paul and Jeremy would be okay. There was one course of action left available to me. The door opened and I stiffened, waiting for the cops to come in and question me. Instead, Jeremy came in alone. The flashing lights outside turned off and headlights hit the windows as the cars pulled away. "What's going on?"

"They got a lead on the shooters, headed down on Main

Street." Jeremy locked the door but didn't come any closer. Just stood there. "After they investigate, they'll be back to ask questions. Probably in the morning."

I blinked. "They just…" I held my hands out, their palms facing up. "…*left?*"

"This isn't Florida," Jeremy said dryly, rubbing the back of his neck. "There are four cops in town, and there's never been a drive-by. When it happened, they sent the two on-duty cops here. When Mr. Brady, down by Route 22, called in to report some kids joyriding in a city-slicker car, they went to see if they could catch them. An off-duty officer was told to keep watch here, in case the shooters come back, but Larry—from high school, you remember—he thinks they'll catch the kids tonight."

"Good." I wrapped my arms around myself, shivering. "I thought this was supposed to be a safe town. It's why I came back."

"It is a safe town, relatively speaking." He crossed the room, pulling me into his arms. He ran his hands up and down my bare biceps, warming me the way only he could. "I don't know why this keeps happening to you guys."

"What do you mean?" I asked hesitantly, resting my cheek on his chest for a second. *Just one second.*

He shrugged, still running his hands over my arms. I melted into him more, even though I knew better than to lean on a guy like Jeremy. If I let him, he'd swoop in and try to fix all my problems, and I needed to do that all on my own. "Weird, huh? You and Paul having such a run of bad luck?"

"I guess." I swallowed. "Why did you come back?"

"To town?"

I nodded. "Yeah."

"I missed small-town life. I don't know what I was looking for when I left, but I didn't find it. The second I knocked on this door, though, and you opened it…" He pulled back, tipping my chin up gently with his hand so our eyes could meet. "I found what I've been looking for all this time. This inn, and you…it just feels right."

He stared at me silently, his eyes asking a million questions. Questions I couldn't answer. I glanced away, staring at the drawer he'd so fluidly opened earlier since it was easier than looking at him. It wasn't that I didn't trust or care about him. It was that I saw how all this was going to end, and it didn't include him and me together.

Stepping out of his reach, I felt the loss of his heat immediately. "How long have you known about the gun?"

"Since I moved in." He crossed his arms and leaned against the door. "Does the fact you're keeping that gun handy connect to your recent misfortunes?"

I lifted a shoulder. "Not really. Like you said, bad luck. Or maybe karma, coming to collect."

He laughed, but there was no warmth to it. "So you're not worried about this?"

"Aside from the fact that we now have to fix up all the damage they caused? No." I crossed the room, opening the drawer. His green eyes followed my every movement as I picked up the gun. "But I think I'll bring this up with me tonight, for safekeeping."

"I want to stay here to renovate longer than we originally talked about." He rubbed the back of his neck, ducking his head and watching me. "I spoke to my boss. He said I can work remotely for as long as I want. You clearly need more help here than you thought—"

I stiffened. "I do not."

"Chels. Your walls are literally shot up."

My cheeks heated, and I turned my face away. The idea of him sticking around wasn't unpleasant, but shouldn't he *want* to leave? We'd just been shot at, for God's sake. I had a feeling that wasn't something an accountant was accustomed to. "I'm fine on my own. You need to stop worrying about me. As a matter of fact, in light of these new events, if you're gone in the morning, I totally understand."

He flexed his jaw, staring at me through narrowed eyes. "*I'm* not the one who runs away."

"Then you're an even bigger fool than I thought."

I headed up the stairs without another word, and, miracle of all miracles, he let me. As I walked down the hallway to my empty room, I tightened my grip on the gun more with each step. By the time I closed the door behind me, I was breathing heavily. My knuckles hurt, my throat ached, and my chest burned...but I refused to give in to the urge to cry.

Big girls don't cry. Dad's voice echoed in my head, filled with reprimand and disgust. He'd hated shows of emotion, so at a young age, I'd learned to show none. My mother had taken off pretty much the second she finished pushing, and I hadn't heard from her since. All I'd had was Dad, and Paul...and Jeremy. Leaning against the door, I took a deep breath in, exhaling it slowly. *Repeat until you regain control.*

After a few times, the burn eased and I was able to breathe...until I looked at the bed. On my pillow, bright against the white pillowcase, were four red roses. Anger choked me, and I stalked to the bed, picking them up in one swipe. A small card read: *together again.* Clearly, Jeremy hadn't listened when I'd told him to stop with the flowers.

I tossed them in the trash and slid the gun under my pillow. Sinking onto the mattress, I opened my MacBook and clicked on the e-mail icon. I'd need all the help I could get. It wasn't every day a girl gave up everything she fought hard for to save someone else.

Especially not a girl like *me.*

Chapter 18

JEREMY WATCHED CHELSEA from across the living room as he held the white crown molding against the wall, lining it up to see what it looked like. It was going to match the fireplace perfectly. After the drive-by three days ago, they'd been on overdrive to get the living room put back together. They'd replaced the broken windows, plastered the bullet holes, and repainted. The room was coming back to life.

Chelsea hadn't been much of a talker these past few days.

Instead, she'd been single-mindedly focused on finishing everything as quickly as possible. Jeremy couldn't help but think it was because she was racing against some kind of inner clock. He was losing any grip he had on her. She had a certain air that screamed defeat, but if he had anything to say about it, she'd never lose. It would help if she would just trust him and tell him what he needed to know instead of leaving him to fill in the blanks himself. He knew he could fix this with minimum damage.

Aside from the inn.

Then they could continue reconnecting. There had been a few passionate kisses here and there, but for the most part, she was still holding him at arm's length. What she didn't know was that he was scared, too. But that's when you know it's real.

When it scares the shit outta you.

"Jeremy?"

He snapped himself back to the present. "Yeah?"

"You mentioned wanting to stick around here, while working remotely. Said you wanted to live in a small town again. Right?"

He swallowed. "Right."

She stroked the brush over the mantel, leaving it a shiny antique white. Paul had been right. It complemented the peach walls perfectly. "Well…if I had to leave again for, for reasons, would you keep working on this place, bringing it back to life even if I wasn't here?"

He froze, staring at her, his heart pounding. And there it was, the confirmation that she was planning something that would result in her leaving all this work undone. "Of course, I'll do whatever you need me to do. But where are you going?"

"Nowhere." She stroked the brush again, still not looking at him. "Just hypothetically thinking out loud."

Bullshit. She was up to something. While he was honored she trusted him enough to leave the inn in his hands, he'd rather she trusted him with the goddamn truth about why she was running away…*again*. "Did the cops come by yesterday?" he asked casually.

She nodded, staring at the mantel as she ran the paintbrush over a spot she'd missed. "Yep."

"I heard the investigation into those joyriding kids didn't pan out, and they still don't know who shot at us. Did they give you any new details? Something that sparked these hypothetical thoughts you're having?"

She stiffened at that last part. "Nope. I told them that I moved here to fix up the inn, and that my place got shot up."

She swiped the brush across the mantel harder. "That's all I know, so that's all I told them. End of story."

Jeremy gritted his teeth. Enough was enough already. Obviously, she trusted him enough to put him in charge of the inn. Now she needed to trust him with her secrets, too. "Really, Chels? After all this time, you still won't let me in, not even a little?"

"I don't know why you keep asking me about this. You were there! You saw everything I did. Maybe even more." She turned around, her cheeks slightly red and her lips parted. "You're turning out to be a lousy worker, more interested in gossip than actually helping. Are you going to nail those strips of molding to the wall, or are you hoping they magically attach themselves?"

He threw the wood down and held his hands out at his sides. "I don't know. You seem to believe in the impossible, as if I wouldn't remember that your voice goes up when you lie, so maybe you believe in magic, too. Or, better yet, maybe you could, I don't know, tell me the *truth*. Why do you need a caretaker for the inn? You running away again?"

For a second, just a brief fucking second, she opened her mouth, and he thought she was going to finally talk. But then she closed it, shrugged, and shot down his hopes with a single word. "Whatever."

When she turned back to the mantel, ignoring him again, something inside him snapped. He stalked across the room, rage consuming him, and spun her around by the shoulder. "Damn it! Stop *ignoring* me. I'm trying to save your ass, and you won't let me."

Her nostrils flared. "No one asked you to ride back into my life on some quest to save me. I don't need you, or any other man, trying to be my knight in shining armor. I can defeat my own dragons, thank you very much."

Suddenly she looked more alive than she had in days. So that was the way to get her talking. Piss her off. Luckily, he was good at that. He gestured to the formerly shot-up wall and said, "Looks like you suck at it."

Her cheeks flushed, and she pointed an angry finger at him. "Screw you. You think you can just come in here and the world will arrange itself to your will, that everything will be sunshine and rainbows just because you say so. Guess what? It doesn't matter if you're a good person or if you try to do the right thing, because evil will triumph over goodness every time. And I hate...I hate...." A frustrated sound escaped her, and she stomped her foot, just like she used to do when they were younger. Just like she had ten years ago, when she told him she loved him and that he was a fool for agreeing to marry someone else. "I hate *you*."

He did the same thing he had done all those years ago, when she said those same three words to him. Growling, he wrapped his arms around her, hauling her against his chest, burying his fingers in her hair and splaying the other hand across her back.

"Yeah, well, I love you. So tough shit." The second he said it, he knew he had made a huge mistake. Chelsea and feelings didn't mix, and he was going to scare her off before he had a chance to save her life. Her eyes widened and her lips parted, and he did the one thing guaranteed to shut her up.

He kissed her.

Chapter 19

I STRAINED AGAINST him, trying to get closer, knowing I should be pushing him away. He loved me, and I was only going to break his heart. When this whole thing was over and the dust had settled, he would be left alone, sad, missing me—and I didn't want that for him. He deserved more than memories. I broke the kiss off, trembling, every inch of my body begging for more. "Are you sure?"

He grabbed my hair and my shirt, nodding, not letting go. "You're the best thing that ever happened to me, and I'm not losing you again, Chels. Yes, I'm sure."

My heart twisted, and I opened my mouth to tell him he *had* to lose me again. I did trust him, but I'd already put plans in motion. The other night, after mourning the loss of the life I wouldn't get, I'd contacted the feds. I hated them even more than the cops—being an O'Kane and all, I couldn't help it. But in a few days, I'd disappear again with my brother at my side, and there would be no finding me this time.

It would be over between Jeremy and me, and he'd be better off because of it.

But the second his lips touched mine, I swallowed the words. He backed us out of the living room, his lips never leaving mine as we stumbled toward the stairs. By the time we made it to my bedroom, I was a mess of trembling need and untapped emotion—a dangerous combination. We fell back on the bed and it felt so right that it stole my breath. All the more painful that soon, I'd be losing him all over again.

Over the past few days, I'd pictured an actual life with Jeremy by my side as my accountant and jack-of-all-trades. And damn it, that life we could have shared had sounded good. Him. Me. Falling in love all over again. Turning this inn into a home for us and a sanctuary for others. It had been everything I ever wanted.

His hands roamed over my body. Down my hip, around the swells of my breasts, across my ribs. When he closed a hand over my breast, dragging the side of his thumb across my hard nipple, I gasped. Desire pooled in my belly, and I wrapped my legs around his waist. He took advantage of my open mouth, his tongue slipping inside to claim mine as he squeezed my nipple between his fingers.

We undressed each other with unsteady hands, clothes flying everywhere. By the time I was down to a thong, its matching red bra tossed on the floor, all rational thought fled my brain. I lay on the bed, breathing heavily, as he tugged his boxers down. When he stood there, naked, staring down at me as if I meant the whole world to him, I sucked in a breath.

And I didn't exhale. If I did, I'd say something stupid like how I loved him, too. I'd say he was the only man who had never lied to me.

He rolled a condom on and crawled up my body, leaving kisses in his wake. My calf. My knee. He placed a love bite on my inner thigh, then rolled my thong down my legs, his fingers burning on my skin as he went. A fire was hot within me, and there was only one way to put it out.

I spread my legs, letting my knees fall to the side. He slipped his hands under my ass, lifting me up to his mouth, and finally gave me what I wanted—his mouth on me. It was magical, and crazy, and so powerful that for a second I thought I might be dreaming this whole thing. But then his fingers dug into my skin, his teeth scraped me, and I was breathing heavily, panting, and writhing against his mouth as the pleasure rose higher and higher. I couldn't *breathe*.

After a few minutes of this perfect torture, he rolled his tongue over me, once, twice, and with mind-clearing clarity, I came hard, my whole body hardening impossibly before I collapsed, breathing heavily. He didn't stop there, like any other man would have.

Instead, he tapped my sensitive flesh, sending me soaring over the edge again, tears running down my face because it was so intense. Every nerve, every sensation, was heightened because this was Jeremy. He was the one. He'd always been the one. The only reason I'd been with Richard was because I didn't think I deserved this—I didn't deserve a guy like Jeremy. Especially after what we'd done the night before his wedding. In a way, I was punishing myself by ruining the only good thing I'd ever had in life.

I'd stayed with an abusive asshole because I let myself believe it was what I deserved. Once this was all over and I turned state's evidence, they would take me away to my new life in protective custody, where I'd keep lowballing myself.

I would lose Jeremy all over again.

And this time, I had no one but myself to blame.

Chapter 20

JEREMY HAD WAITED for this moment way too damn long, and now that he had Chelsea in his arms, clinging to him, limbs trembling from the pleasure he'd given her, he wasn't quite sure what to do with himself. Ever since she'd left him, sex had been just that—*sex*. Meaningless. Empty. A way to fulfill a basic need, but nothing more.

With Chelsea, it was everything.

This wasn't about lust or desire.

It was a promise from him to her, a way to show her she could trust him to stick around no matter what happened, even though she seemed so damn certain he was going to somehow mess her life up again. Apparently she thought men like him couldn't handle the type of trouble she was in. Or maybe she thought he was only looking out for himself— just like her father.

So when she found out the secrets he held, she'd be pissed as hell.

Her first instinct would be to push him away. But his first instinct would be to hold her close. Through the worst of her anger, he'd be there at her side. Eventually she'd forgive him. Years had changed nothing on his end. He'd just been waiting for her to come home when she was ready. She'd done that, and she'd brought a shitload of trouble with her.

It was his job to clean it up.

Closing his mouth over hers, he slid between her legs, groaning at the feelings of her skin on his—something he'd craved over the past ten years more than anything else in the world. She wrapped her legs around him, still trembling from the orgasms he'd already given her.

If he had it his way, he'd spend the rest of his life making her scream his name. Making her happy, because, damn it, Chelsea deserved some happiness in her life. It'd only been recently that he'd finally discovered she had disappeared to Miami. Before he could go down there for her, all hell broke loose.

Her replacement hero had turned out to be a villain.

His tongue found hers as he thrust inside her warm heat and they both moaned at the same time. An animalistic hunger took over, and he tightened his grip on her ass as he thrust into her harder, deeper, claiming her in a way he should have done lifetimes ago. With every stroke, every kiss, every caress, he dug deeper into her, until he was sure he'd disappear altogether and cease to exist.

And that was fine with him. He was man enough to admit he needed Chelsea by his side. She made him whole, and that had never been clearer than it was right now.

He moved his hips faster, harder, not even pausing when she came again, her tight walls closing around him. The faster he moved, the more she clung to him. As her nails scraped down his back, leaving scratches in their wake, she cried out as she orgasmed again, and this time, he was right there with her, soaring into the sky before gently drifting down, like snow. Dropping his forehead to hers, he breathed in deep, her scent filling his senses. "Chelsea…"

"You're wrong," she whispered, her hands tightening on his shoulders. "I do trust you."

He closed his eyes, drawing in a deep breath. "Then tell me—"

"Shh," she whispered, shaking her head. "Not now. Don't ruin it."

He felt way too damned good to care that, technically, she was still keeping her walls up. This was Chelsea, and she was the love of his life, and no matter what happened, he wasn't letting go of her again.

Not even when all his lies were revealed.

Chapter 21

I FINISHED DRYING my fake blond hair, staring at myself in the fogged-up mirror. My cheeks were flushed, and I swore I could still feel Jeremy touching me, making my body come alive with his soft, tender embrace. Everything about today had been perfect, which made me want to grin and uncharacteristically dance around in circles, but there was one thing holding me back from being happy.

Our relationship had an expiration date.

I wanted to selfishly spend as much time as possible with Jeremy, before it was all ripped away, but the game I played was a dangerous one. There were only two ways out, and one of them was a body bag.

I wasn't the type of person to focus on regrets, but right now? I had them. I had *lots* of them. If there was a way to go back, to not run away from the things I'd had all those years ago, I'd travel back in time in a split second. I'd stay by Jeremy's side and fight for him. I never would have gone to Florida, or met Richard, or almost lost myself in his abuse. And I never would have had to kill him.

But regrets were as useless as dreams. I stared at myself in the mirror. For the first time in years, I liked what I saw, blond hair aside. I'd done a lot of bad things over the course of my life, but this time, I wasn't just moving forward. I was taking a stand to fix things. I was accepting responsibility for my actions, and I was righting the wrongs I'd inadvertently committed.

For the first time, I wasn't running from anything.

Not even Jeremy fricking Holland.

He knocked on the bathroom door. "You still showering, Chels?"

I lowered my fingers from my lips, eyeing my damp hair and the tiny towel wrapped around my body. My pulse sped up at the sound of his voice. "No, I'm out. You can come in."

Jeremy opened the door slowly, peeking his head through. When he saw me standing there in next to nothing, he tossed the envelope he'd been holding onto the counter, crossing the room with heated green eyes full of seduction. He wore a pair of sweats and nothing else.

He gripped the towel and raised a brow questioningly. I shrugged, and he undid the little knot I'd made to keep it in place. As the towel fell to the tile floor, he pulled me close, his hands resting on my ass, and whistled through his teeth.

I met his eyes in the mirror. A strand of hair fell over his forehead, giving him a rakish appearance. He looked so happy, standing there holding me, that it physically hurt my heart. Looking away from our image, I buried my face in his bare chest and breathed him in like air, digging my fingers into the hard muscles of his back.

He gently tipped my face up to his, staring down at me for a second before he lowered his face to mine and kissed me tenderly. It took my breath away, that kiss. After his lips left mine, he released me, bending to pick up the towel he'd taken off me. "I didn't come in here to strip you, believe it or not."

I wrapped the towel around myself, trembling. "I wasn't exactly complaining," I said dryly.

"I know." He dragged his hand through his hair and reached for the envelope he'd tossed as he came in the room. "This came for you from the DMV."

My heart pounded in my ears, and I took it, feeling the envelope. Sure enough, something hard and rectangular was inside. "Oh."

He locked eyes with me, brushing my wet hair out of my face. "What's in it?"

"Nothing. It's nothing at all."

He frowned. "You're going to talk to me eventually."

"I know. Later." I bit my lip, staring up at him, making sure to hide any emotion. "Okay?"

For a second he looked disappointed, but then he gave me a tight smile and nodded. "All right. I'm going to hop in the shower. Want to go to Ollie's for dinner? We can get some takeout for Paul and swing by the hospital afterward. Then we need to go to Lowe's and pick out a chandelier for the foyer. Were you still thinking the elegant one, with the crystals and silver?"

"Yeah, I think that's the way to go. It'll match the old charm of the house."

He nodded. "And Chels—"

"I know," I said. "Later."

After the shower started, I took a second to grieve for what might have been, and then I tossed the envelope that held my new ID in the garbage, not even bothering to open it. There went my new start, in my inn and hometown, where I'd been planning to live with a real man by my side. I didn't need it anymore.

Because I wasn't getting it.

Chapter 22

WE GOT HOME really late, long after the moon had come out, when the sky had filled with stars. We'd been the last ones to check out at Lowe's after selecting the perfect chandelier that highlighted the comforts of modern style with an old-fashioned flair....

Which was exactly the effect that the inn would eventually have.

I stared up at the wires hanging from the ceiling and pictured the inn, in all its glory, once it was renovated, shiny, and open for business. Fixing up this place had given me a new purpose in life. It was exciting to build something real here in Hudson with my own two hands. I only wished I could finish what I'd started, but at least I had a man I could trust to see my vision through...even if I never got to see it for myself.

And that was fine. Or so I kept telling myself.

I'd run into Tommy McGinnis at Lowe's. I'd gone to school with him, and he'd been pretty thick with Paul. They'd constantly caused trouble, like a pair of thieves... which they were. Last I heard, his wife left him and he was drowning his sorrows in heroin. Word was he was pretty much a lost cause...and that he was trying to drag my brother down with him. All the more reason I was happy Paul had insisted on going into protective custody with me. At least he wouldn't end up like Tommy. He'd be clean. Or as clean as two O'Kanes could get, anyway.

He'd promised when he asked to come along with me.

Jeremy set the chandelier down with a soft *oof*. "That shit's"—he kicked the door shut behind him and locked it— "a hell of a lot heavier than it looks."

"It's perfect."

"I agree." He craned his neck, glancing into the living room. "We totally could have gotten that second one tonight. It'll fit over the coffee table, for sure."

"Pick it up tomorrow for me, after work? Along with the carpet I was eyeing for the foyer."

"Of course." He stopped staring at the living room and focused those bright green eyes on me. He set his phone down on top of the box, his gaze locked on me. "We need to talk."

"Yeah. Okay."

"Don't look so scared. No matter what you tell me tonight, I'm not going anywhere." He smoothed my hair off my cheek. "I'm gonna grab a beer. Want one?"

I let out a soft breath, because *he* wasn't the one going somewhere. "Whiskey. Straight whiskey."

"Damn. That bad?"

I didn't say anything. Just stared at him. That was answer enough.

I knelt beside the chandelier box, looking at the picture on the side. Maybe we could get it hung up tonight before bed, so I could see it before I left. It was weird, but a melancholy acceptance had taken over, and I was almost...*numb*.

"So why are you racing the clock?" Jeremy called out from the kitchen.

I eyed the peach walls and the painted fireplace. "I started the paperwork to give you authorization over the inn and its accounts. Did your boss give the go-ahead for—?"

Jeremy's phone lit up on the box. Out of habit, I glanced down. It was a text message from someone named Vasquez. Need to update you on the Hudson project, call me immediately.

Vasquez…

Richard had employed a man with that last name, and he'd been even more ruthless than Richard. At first, I couldn't put two and two together as to why Vasquez would be texting Jeremy about a project, but some small part of me whispered, *Ha! I knew it all along! He was playing you.* And I couldn't shut that voice up once it came to life.

"For what?" he called out. "For me to take the inn on as a client?"

My heart pounded so hard it hurt. I stared at his phone, my finger itching to open it up and read more of those texts. Why was he getting messages from Vasquez? And why was he so insistent he stay here, by my side, the second I walked back into town? Jeremy didn't fit the profile of a cartel informant…which didn't make me feel better. If anything, it made me feel worse. Because I knew of a few occupations that used last names as much as they did first. Athletes, military…and *cops.* A perfectly respectable profession.

And that made a hell of a lot more sense than Jeremy being dirty.

The answer was blindingly obvious, and yet I didn't want to acknowledge it, because if he'd been lying to me this whole time—if he was a damn *cop*—then every ounce of trust I'd placed in his hands was complete and utter crap. I thought of the way he'd handled the gun the night we'd been shot at. His grip had been so sure, so comfortable, like he was around guns all the time. Like it was his *job.*

When I didn't answer, he came out into the foyer, scanning the room until he found me, sitting next to a box, looking lost as hell. The second we locked eyes, he froze, the smile slowly dying on his charming face. "Chels?"

Ah, the clever use of my childhood nickname, perfectly brought back into play so he could worm his way into my good graces. And the way he looked at me, like I mattered to him. Had he planned that, too? Was it the best way to make me, the gullible girl who was in love with him, jump back into his arms? I'd fallen for it, like the naïve little idiot I'd always been with him. Apparently years of distance hadn't changed that. All he had to do was kiss me, pretend he wanted me, and I became clay in his hands, waiting to be sculpted the way he wanted.

That son of a bitch.

"Who's Vasquez?" I asked, watching him closely for any signs of guilt.

He shifted on his feet, opened his mouth, closed it, and then pressed his lips together, his cheeks flushing ever so slightly as he turned away, hiding his face from me as he tried to come up with an answer I might believe.

Well. There you had it.

The guilt I'd been hoping not to see. It was written all over his damn face.

"Get out," I said, struggling to my feet, pulse racing, heart aching. "Get the hell out of my house *right now*."

Chapter 23

JEREMY STOOD THERE, staring at me, looking confused. What was there to be confused about? I told him to go, so he needed to leave. "What's wrong?" he finally asked.

"You tell me." I crossed my arms, gripping my elbows hard so I wouldn't launch myself at him and take him down. "Or better yet, don't. Just go. Tell your boss you failed to con me. I saw through your lies and kicked you out, *cop*."

He set the drinks down and walked toward me, making me stiffen. I didn't want him close to me. If he touched me… "Chels—"

"Oh, and FYI?" I picked up his phone and hurled it at him. He caught it easily, making me want to punch him even more. It would have been so much more satisfying if he hadn't. "There's an option on iPhones to make the text in a message not appear on the lock screen. Since you're trying to trick women into spilling information while undercover, you might want to use it."

He pinched the bridge of his nose. "I can explain."

"Yeah, I'm sure you can," I said sarcastically. "And I'm sure you're also convinced you can put a spin on this so I'll magically forgive you, and I don't blame you for thinking that, considering our history. Something like, 'I was trying to save you. To help you.'"

His jaw flexed. "It's the truth."

"Yeah. Sure it is."

He reached for my arm, but I lurched back. "Damn it, Chels. You know me. I didn't come here to hurt you. I've been watching—"

"You're a *cop*." I shook my head, backing away from him, my eyes burning. "What the hell, Jeremy? Why didn't you tell me?"

"Actually, I'm not a cop," he said, dragging his hand through his hair. "I'm DEA."

I threw my hands up. "Doesn't matter who signs your checks, you're law enforcement."

"Look, I *am* here to help you." He caught my hand, not letting go when I tried to tug free. His skin on mine, after finding out he'd been using me, felt wrong. "I'm not the enemy. I lo—"

"Tell me, were you laughing at how easy it was for me to believe you came back to me, after all these years, begging to be mine? Did you and all your little agent friends laugh at me when I kissed you in your motel room? Did you strategize together about how to pump me for information? Did they give you shit when you freaking *begged* me to let you in, to trust you? I bet that was a laugh. And when you got me to have sex with you again? Well, that must've been a real bonus."

His cheeks flushed. "Damn it, Chels. You know I wouldn't do that to you, or use you like that."

"Do I?"

"Damn right you do. I was protecting you even though you refused to tell me what happened between you and Richard. Even though you lied to me, time and time again, I stood here, watching your back—"

I laughed. Legit laughed. "You're going to try to lecture me about lying? Seriously?"

"Yes." He grabbed my shoulders gently, his touch burning right through my T-shirt. "And when your brother was attacked, I made sure he had a guard, that he had protection, even though you wouldn't tell me a damn thing about what happened or what you know. Why else would a mugging warrant police protection?"

"Well, that was all for nothing," I said, jerking free. "Why bother pushing me to open up, to reveal all my secrets in the first place? You already know what I did, don't you?"

He remained silent, not bothering to lie again. That was all the answer I needed.

"That's what I thought. You know the truth. I killed a man. I shot him where he stood, and I watched the blood soak the carpet as his body went limp." I pointed to the door, trembling slightly. "Get out before I kill you, too."

Chapter 24

HE REARED BACK, staring at me like I'd punched him in the gut. Which I guess I had, in a way. I'd threatened to kill him—not that I actually would. "Chels—"

"You have no idea how angry I am right now. I killed Richard, is that what you want to hear? I pulled the trigger, and he stopped breathing in front of me. And you know what? I'm not sorry. Things were great at first, but he became an abusive bastard. When I found out he was working with a cartel, compromising cases so their guys would walk, that was the last straw. I was going to leave him quietly, but he came at me and I grabbed the gun, and I—" I broke off, choking back a sob, hating myself for that sign of weakness but unable to take it back. "So you see, bad things happen to people who lie to me."

He swallowed hard, stepping closer despite my threats. "Chelsea, please, let me—"

"You know what the worst part was? I was going to tell you tonight. Tell you everything. I wanted to be honest because I…" The fire of rage inside me transformed into the cold of heartbreak. I wasn't sure I'd ever be warm again. "I was going to be honest. And you've been lying to me, playing me, all this time."

He shook his head, taking another step toward me. "Chels, you have to understand, the DEA had you flagged as a person of interest. Richard had been under investigation and they weren't sure how complicit you were. After the shooting, I got involved to *protect* you. I convinced my superiors that our preexisting relationship made me the perfect person to send in, but it was always my intention to get you clear of this."

"Right." I laughed, but it wasn't a laugh. Not really. I'd obviously been nothing but a damsel in distress to him. Wasn't he surprised to find himself defending the dragon? "And the part about missing me? Wanting me to be with you?"

"True," he said quickly. "I did miss you. A lot."

"Yeah. Sure." I rubbed my face. My eyes burned and my throat ached, unfamiliar sensations for me. "You're a DEA agent, Jeremy. I was a 'person of interest.' You knew where I was. You could've ridden your white horse down to Miami at any time."

"I did look for you, but you'd covered your tracks too well. By the time I found you…" He shook his head, reaching for me again. I shifted back, not letting him touch me. Those days were over. *"Chelsea."*

"Let me guess. You're up for some sort of promotion, once this is over?" I asked slowly. "If you arrest me or I help you get the bad guy?"

He rubbed the back of his neck, shifting uncomfortably. That gave me my answer.

"You really think I'm doing this because it'll benefit me? No, I'm doing it for the seventeen-year-old Long Island girl who overdosed on heroin. For the mother of two in Philadelphia who died when her car was T-boned by a driver high on cocaine. For the family who got caught in the crossfire of a drug war in Boston." His shoulders were hard, and his entire body was tense. I couldn't help but wonder if *I* was his enemy now. "We've been investigating these guys for years, working with local PDs as they scoop up the small fish, but we're after the head. The leader of the cartel has a brother who's a total mess. The only thing he's good at is taking care of people who become problems. When you took out Richard, you became a problem."

"You're hoping that he's such a disaster that he'll turn on his brother. So, what, you leaked my general whereabouts and used me as bait for this asshole, never thinking I might just want to keep my head down and live my life? You put my brother in danger? When exactly were you going to arrest the guy? Before or after he tortured me, too?" I rubbed my throbbing temples.

Jeremy reacted like I'd stabbed him, his body jerking slightly. His hand reached out to me. "I told you, I came here to protect you. I would never let *anyone* hurt you."

I pointedly ignored his hand, and he let it drop to the back of a floral upholstered loveseat. "Should I presume that my arrest would soon follow Javi's? Or is the warrant already waiting, just in case I discovered the truth?"

He pressed his lips together. "I've been authorized to offer you a deal—"

"What was the plan for the inn?" I asked, cutting him off, my voice hard. Frozen solid. "Was it going to be seized? Or would you let me make you a signatory, keep it as part of your cover, and use it as some secret DEA safe house?"

Jeremy went to answer and then paused for a moment. "Wait a second. How did you know Javi's name?"

Oh, look, the DEA agent was back.

I turned away, staring at the divots in the wall where Jeremy had plastered the bullet holes. "I'm the daughter of a con man, Jeremy. Dad always said to have either an exit strategy or a will. I couldn't just break up with Richard; his pride would never allow that. I was preparing to blackmail him in exchange for my freedom. It was easy to gather the proof I needed, once I knew where to look for it, because he never saw me as a viable threat. Sometimes he even took meetings at the house. So, yes, I know Javi, and Gabriel, and David. I know them all. But more importantly, I know where the money goes."

Jeremy moved around that loveseat fast. He stood in front of me, catching himself before he grabbed my shoulders. "Chels, this is huge. With this proof, we could arrest them all now. You and Paul would be safe."

I shifted my head slightly so I could continue staring at the wall. "Funnily enough, I wasn't that concerned with my own safety when I made the deal with Homeland Security. I'll turn over the evidence for immunity and Witness Protection. *I* was trying to protect *you.*"

He instinctively reached for his pocket, as if to go for his phone. "You made a deal with Homeland? I wasn't informed."

"So much for interagency cooperation." I walked over to the front door and finally met his gaze. "Get out."

The last time I saw that expression on his face, it was after Rocco, his dog, passed away. I refused to be moved. "We can figure something out. Witness Protection doesn't have to be the end of us."

"It wasn't. We ended when you decided to play me instead of telling me the truth and asking for my help. I tried really hard to live in your world, Jeremy, to do what's right, but in the end, all you saw was a criminal," I said, my voice cracking on the last word. More weakness. And it was all Jeremy fricking Holland's fault. "I thought you were one of the good guys. Thanks for proving to me that good guys don't just finish last—they don't exist at all."

I knew my words hit home for Jeremy because he rubbed his chest right over his heart. "I'm sorry. I never wanted to hurt you."

"Yeah. That's what they all say." Opening the door, I met his eyes again, forcing my chin up. "Get. Out."

Jeremy headed for the door, looking like a lost puppy being sent back out into the rain. He stopped just outside. "This isn't over. I'm going to go find out the particulars of your deal. I'll be back tomorrow. I let you run from me once, but that's not happening again."

There it was again. That stubborn determination to win me back. It wouldn't work this time. He'd done me dirty, and I wouldn't forget it. "I'm not running anywhere, Agent Holland. Like the O'Kane family motto, I'm gonna keep moving forward. Without you." And then I slammed the door in his face. "Asshole."

I waited till I heard his car start, till the headlights receded down the driveway, and till I felt his absence down to my soul. Then, and only then, I let myself slide down the door into a sitting position. My eyes burned but they were dry. The *one* man I thought who wouldn't break me, who wouldn't *use* me, had done exactly that.

Go figure.

I stared out into the living room, at the half-finished promise of what the inn could be. A respite from stress, an oasis of calm, a sanctuary, never fulfilled. I should have known better. Every time I tried to do something good, it went to shit. I was done fighting, done trying to be better. Being something I wasn't.

I was *me*.

And nothing would ever change that.

Chapter 25

I WENT TO the hospital and told Paul everything, explaining Jeremy's deception. He was not pleased in the least, but he promised to make sure that, before we left town, the inn would be taken care of for me through some legit contacts of his. And unlike *some* people in my life, when my brother made a promise, he kept it. He also promised to have his people make Jeremy's life a living hell, but I told him not to bother. Jeremy had just been doing his job. If he'd really cared about me like he'd claimed, he would've approached the situation differently.

Maybe he'd just never known me at all.

Either way, he didn't deserve my brother breathing down his neck. Witness Protection might make Paul legit, but he would still have friends in low places.

Then I went back to the inn to say good-bye for the last time. The work on the living room was almost finished. The furniture I'd picked out would be delivered Monday, and Paul had promised to have his guy place it according to the floor plan I'd drawn on a napkin, using the fireplace as a focal point. The antique white fireplace stood out against the pale walls, and the hardwood floors shined with the fresh coats of varnish we'd put on after Jeremy had sanded them. The sun shone in the windows, reflecting off the shiny floor, and the room was as bright and inviting as I'd imagined it would be.

I swallowed hard at the ache in my chest that had never fully gone away since the other night. I headed for the kitchen, taking in the detailing on the moldings. Now that the DEA knew everything, things had started to move along quickly. However, the closer I got to the kitchen, the more cautious I grew. The air smelled like spaghetti sauce, and soft classical music played from my bedroom. I hadn't made any sauce, or left the radio on....

"Jeremy?" I called out, my heart racing.

Knowing he was here, waiting for me to come home as if nothing had happened, made me equal parts nervous and angry. When I found him, I was gonna kick his ass. I knew that with one look at him, the chemistry between us would roar back to life, but I'd be strong and resist him this time.

No one answered as I entered the kitchen, staring at the sauce. It bubbled slowly, painting the glass lid with little spurts of red. There was a bouquet of red roses on the counter, and the combination of the red sauce and the red roses set me on edge. Jeremy knew I didn't like roses any longer, and, despite his terrible lies, he'd never remind me of the abusive dead ex-boyfriend I'd killed.

I made my way to the front door, walking slowly, heart pounding with fear. Even though it might seem crazy to think that Javi had broken into my home to make spaghetti sauce and turn on Mozart...I knew, I just *knew*, that something was wrong. I'd never doubted my instincts before, and since they'd saved my life more than once, I wasn't about to start now.

I opened the drawer with my gun inside it slowly, lifting the Glock cautiously as I made my way up the stairs. I could leave, call Jeremy for help, but I was done leaning on other people for support. I'd taken care of Richard all on my own—I could handle Javi, too. Each step I took brought me closer to whatever waited for me up there. Whether it was Javi or Jeremy, there was going to be a fight.

The second-to-last step creaked as I put my weight on it, and I froze. The gun wavered, and I tightened my grip on it, trying to talk myself down. I was probably overreacting. Maybe it was Jeremy in my bedroom, putting together some grand romantic gesture, like sprinkling flower petals on my bed. Maybe this would all be a bad daydream.

There was no way in hell I'd call out his name again...just in case. I crept around the corner of the hallway, keeping an eye out for movement from any other rooms along the way. I passed Jeremy's, which was empty, and sucked in a deep breath at the entrance to my room. The door was cracked open, and I saw a brown-haired male, his head lowered as he sat on my bed. The very sight sent a chill down my spine.

Because that hair...I knew it.

I'd run my fingers through it, once upon a time.

Biting down on my lip, I stepped forward, my knuckles aching and my heart pounding. My weapon wobbled in concert with my trembling body, as I nudged the door open with my foot. It creaked and the man lifted his head, locking eyes with me.

My gaze met brown eyes. Dark, soulless ones. His jaw was hard and unbreakable.

"No," I whispered, staring with horror at the man on my bed as my stomach turned. "You're...you're..."

"Dead? Sorry to disappoint." Richard gave me a small smile. One I recognized all too well. He usually smiled like that before he "corrected me."

No. No, no, no, *hell, no*. He was supposed to be *dead*. I'd killed him. Watched him hit the floor, not moving, as blood sprayed from his chest. *This couldn't be...*

Shaking my head, I aimed the gun at his chest and did the only thing I could do, given the situation. The only thing I could think of that might save my ass.

I pulled the trigger again.

Chapter 26

THE RESOUNDING CLICK of the striker was the only sound that filled the room, somehow managing to seem louder than an actual gunshot. I choked on a half laugh, half sob, because *of course* Richard had taken care of my only weapon. He wasn't about to be taken down by the same weapon, or person, twice.

He tugged on his tie to straighten it. "I wasn't sure if you had the balls to pull that trigger again, but you understand my hesitation to find out firsthand."

"Go to hell. I should have known the devil couldn't be taken down by a bullet."

He laughed, pressing a hand to his flat stomach. He looked so handsome standing there, laughing as if everything were normal. That had always been one of his best weapons. His good looks. He used them well. "I don't know whether to be insulted or flattered."

"I don't care how you feel anymore."

"Tell me, have you been having fun, playing house with that man? What's his name? Ah, yes, Agent Jeremy Holland." When I stiffened, he locked eyes with me.

Shit. He knew Jeremy's name.

"Don't tell me you think I haven't been watching you

with him. Kissing him. Fucking him. Letting him take what's mine."

I stepped forward, muscles tight, fists even tighter. The second I took a step toward him, someone grabbed me from behind by both arms. Of course. Richard was too much of a coward to take me on alone. "I'm not yours. I stopped being yours the second I realized you were nothing but a scared little boy, kowtowing to the cartel so they didn't kill you. Tell me, did you agree to be their bitch before or after you took office? I'm dying to know."

"You little—" He lifted his hand threateningly, the backs of the knuckles facing me, and I flinched reflexively. Being backhanded hurt more than being punched with a closed fist, and he knew it. "You have no idea what you're talking about. *I'm* the one with the power. *I'm* the one who controls them, not the other way around. Why do you think they're here with me, hunting down you and everyone you ever loved?"

I didn't flinch. Just stared him in the eye. "Luckily for you, you never fell in that category."

He snorted. "You loved me. Did you get my flowers? I left the last ones on your bed as a reminder of who you belong to."

Knowing he'd been in my room made my stomach turn hard. "Yeah. I got them. And I threw them in the trash," I said from between clenched teeth.

Running his hand over his jaw, he eyed me, grinning like the calm maniac he was. "I admire your spunk. It's a shame you had to try to kill me. You would have made an excellent wife. But now I have to kill you because if you're not an asset, then you're a liability."

"What makes you think my death will change anything? That I haven't already given the feds everything?"

"I have my ways." He shrugged casually as he rolled up

his shirtsleeves. He did it calmly and without emotion, even though we both knew what was coming. I'd found out first-hand how much he liked playing with his toys before breaking them. "And your lover won't be an issue."

Cold fear struck my heart, sending a shaft of pain piercing through my chest. I knew better than to fall for that shit, but at the same time…this was Jeremy we were talking about. God, if he hurt him, it would be all my fault, and a world without Jeremy wasn't a world I wanted to be in. He might have lied to me and I might be pissed as hell at him, but I loved him with all my heart. And I wanted the chance to maybe forgive him someday, after a hell of a lot of groveling on his part.

I needed him to be okay.

"You're lying," I said with a confidence I didn't feel.

He shrugged again, finishing up with his sleeve. The second it was perfectly in place above his elbows, he took a step in my direction. I jerked hard, trying to break free of my captor, knowing it was pointless to do so. I caught sight of Javi's profile over my shoulder and it was clear there'd be no escape.

"Jeremy will figure out where I hid everything. It's in the hiding place from when we were kids," I said in a rush, lying through my teeth in a futile attempt to buy time. "You're too late."

"We both know that's not true. Let's not diminish your spirit with useless lies and pleas for mercy. You're a fighter, Chelsea. We both enjoy that."

I glared at him silently, heart pounding against my ribs.

"This is going to hurt me more than it hurts you, darling," Richard said softly, his voice like warm butter spreading on fresh-baked bread. "But I need to teach you a lesson. By the time I'm done, you'll wish you never let another man touch what belonged to me. And maybe, if you're lucky, I won't kill you. Maybe I'll take you back, if you promise to never cheat on me again."

The crazy thing was, he meant every word. Richard honestly thought I'd want to be with him, completely ignoring the fact I'd tried to kill him. How had my life gotten to this? How did I become prey to this bastard?

The abuse had started slowly. It had been emotional at first, delivered so craftily I didn't even notice it until it was too late. When that stopped working, he became violent. A push here, followed by an apology. A slap there, followed up with flowers and words of love.

That's when I'd started planning my escape. I'd rediscovered my strength when I came here, to this inn. When I'd pulled that trigger and put an end to the abuse.

I'd be *damned* if I lost that strength again.

"I doubt I'll go back to you," I said sweetly. "After all, you're nothing but a spineless, wormy coward who has no idea what it's like to be a real man. Jeremy knows how to treat a woman, and he knows how to be a man, so I'd never regret being with him. Only you. I wish I never let you touch me, and I wish you had died when I shot you."

Finally, for the first time ever, he lost his cool. Anger flushed his cheeks, his upper lip curled, and he growled. Hauling his fist back, he let it fly, and pain burst in my skull, making me crumble in Javi's arms. Stars exploded into my vision.

"Drop her," Richard said.

Javi obeyed immediately, and I hit the floor hard, banging my head. Suddenly, Richard was on top of me. "Take it back."

Unable to speak, I did the one thing I knew would piss him off, because, God, I wanted to get under his skin…I laughed, spitting out blood with the sound.

Right in his face.

An animalistic sound escaped him, and his eyes bulged in rage as he stared down at me, unable to believe I'd disobeyed him. He lifted his hand and slapped me with his knuckles. I weakly pushed at his shoulders, but Javi pinned down my arms before I could get any leverage. I let out a loud scream, my one last attempt at freedom, but then his hand was on my throat, cutting off my air supply, and I knew with a sinking clarity that this was it.

And then the blackness took over.

Chapter 27

JEREMY WAS STEPS from the front door of the inn when he heard it. A fall leaf crunched behind him, and a soft breath was released. The hair on the back of his neck rose, and every instinct he'd ever trusted told him danger approached. He dropped the chandelier to the ground with a crash and spun with his gun drawn.

The man creeping up behind him froze for a split second, which is the only reason Jeremy didn't end up with a bullet in his brain. Unlike the other man, he didn't hesitate—his finger squeezed the trigger and the guy went down with a hit to his chest. Jeremy stared at him. It didn't take a genius to figure out the man was in the cartels.

"Shit," he muttered. "Fueller? You out there?"

There was no answer from the agent on duty. Jeremy scanned the trees as he picked up the dead man's gun and tucked it in the waistband of his jeans. Finally he saw Fueller. He was on his back in the shadows, blood congealing on the ground from a bullet wound to the head. Cursing, Jeremy made a phone call to request backup and then wasted no time approaching the inn on light feet. Knowing Chelsea might be inside made him want to run up the stairs screaming her name, but that wouldn't do either of them any good.

His pulse pounded. He should have come earlier, damn it, but he'd been trying to give her some time to cool off. She had every right to be angry, but he knew he had to get past that anger and find a way to make her see he hadn't been lying to her about everything. He did love her, and he had no intention of giving up on her…again.

After a few more steps, he was in the foyer. The door was ajar, and he scanned the interior for any signs of intrusion. The table drawer by the door was open, and Chelsea's gun was gone. The second he stepped into the living room, he saw another cartel foot soldier. He stood guard over the kitchen, watching the back door.

Well, that was a good sign.

It meant he was counting on the dead guy out front to stop anyone from coming in, and he was watching the back. Hopefully, there would be no one else to contend with. Tucking his gun away, Jeremy crept up and locked his arm around the man's throat, taking him down effectively and silently. The asshole struggled for a good five seconds, arms flailing, but it was a useless fight. Jeremy wasn't letting go till he was unconscious or dead.

Either one worked for him.

The second he went limp, Jeremy lowered him to the floor. At the same time, Chelsea let out a scream. He bolted up the stairs, not bothering to be quiet anymore, not even debating whether or not to wait for his backup, skidding into her bedroom with his gun aimed for anything that wasn't *her*. He'd seen a lot of messed-up shit during his time as a DEA agent, but the sight that met his eyes was horrifying.

Something he would *never* forget.

Chelsea was on the floor, and someone was on top of her, choking her. She struggled against her assailant, but her movements were slowing. Another knelt at her head, holding her shoulders down as the other man attacked her viciously. The amount of rage that slammed into Jeremy was unreal, and he saw red.

Literally. Blood *red*.

He recognized Javi as the man holding her down. Javi glanced up, spotting him, and cursed. Releasing Chelsea's shoulders, he pulled out a gun and took aim. Jeremy did the same. He didn't hesitate or think like an agent in that moment. He just pulled the goddamn trigger and took the asshole down.

Javi was hit between the eyes, but not before he could squeeze off a shot. Jeremy staggered back, pain ripping through his body, but he didn't take a second to recover. He didn't have time. He turned to Chelsea, who was struggling under her attacker with renewed fervor, and when he glanced at him…

Richard wasn't dead.

This changed everything. If they managed to take him down without killing him, Chelsea would be a free woman. Richard would probably do anything to save his own skin and they could use his testimony to replace whatever evidence Chelsea had. This whole thing could be over.

Chelsea punched Richard in the face with an impressive upper-cut, and the asshole reared back, blood spurting out of his nose. She squirmed out of his arms, struggling to reach the gun lying on the floor. Richard grabbed his nose, cursing. "I'll kill you, you little bitch."

"DEA, asshole. Don't move," Jeremy said, aiming at Richard, who'd been so focused on hurting Chelsea that he'd ignored the gunplay three feet away. "One move and you're a dead man."

Richard froze, watching him carefully, his gaze finally leaving Chelsea. He seethed with a cold, calculated rage. "You're a federal agent. I'm unarmed. You can't just shoot me."

"Try me." His finger flexed on the trigger. "Chels, are you okay?"

"Yes," she croaked. She cocked the gun in her hand and Jeremy stiffened. "But *he* won't be."

Jeremy tore his eyes off the man and stared at Chelsea.

"Go ahead," Richard taunted, holding his arms to his sides. "Shoot an unarmed man. That one's actually loaded."

She stood up on unsteady feet, swaying, and pointed the gun at Richard. Blood trickled out her nose and from the corner of her split lip, and bruises were already forming around her neck. Her eyes held a light that warned that she was close to the edge and not thinking clearly. He'd seen that look in plenty of people's eyes before. She was going to take any chance at freedom she had, and nothing he said was going to stop her.

Downstairs, men came into the house, calling out to one another that it was clear. His backup was here, just in time to witness this. If Chelsea killed Richard now, no amount of maneuvering on Jeremy's part would save her.

Chapter 28

RICHARD WAS JUST staring at me with that goddamn cocky smirk, kneeling on the floor with my blood smeared on his knuckles, so sure I wouldn't do it. That I wouldn't put an end to his pathetic excuse of a life. Right now, there was nothing I wanted more in this life than to end his. Murder hadn't been part of my original plan, but Dad always said that you had to be ready to improvise.

If I didn't kill him now, what would stop him from coming back in a year, or five, or ten, to finish what he'd started? No. Never again.

I tightened my finger on the trigger.

"No!" Jeremy shouted out, holding a hand in front of him as he approached slowly. "DEA is here, right downstairs. If you pull that trigger, you'll go to jail, Chels. Your immunity agreement won't save you. Your hands are clean right now. You didn't kill him before, and you don't have to kill him now."

I didn't ease up, and my eyes burned with the force of the tears I held back. Angry tears that screamed to be released. Tears I'd been holding back for longer than I could remember. "I don't care. He'll be dead. That's all that matters."

"That's not all that matters. There's the inn. And there's…"

He tucked his gun away, waving off the men standing behind me. Clearly they were standing there ready to take Richard away—or take me down. "There's me. I love you, Chels."

I swallowed hard. "Don't lie to me again, Agent Holland."

"I'm not," he said slowly. "I'm telling the truth. Yes, I lied to you about my occupation. Yes, you have every right to be angry at me and to hate me, but damn it, Chels, give me a chance to earn your forgiveness. I'll never stop trying, and I'll never stop knocking on your door, asking you to let me in. But if you're in jail…we don't stand a chance in hell of making this thing we have between us work.

"He wants you to kill him because it keeps him from retribution from the cartel, and it ruins your life. It's a win-win for him," Jeremy said in a rush. He stepped closer, putting himself between me and Richard but not moving to take the gun from me. Blood soaked his shirt at the shoulder. I stared at the spot, watching the red spread across his blue shirt. "Don't give him that satisfaction. Don't give him what he wants."

My grip on the gun wavered, and I sensed men creeping closer behind me, waiting to take me down if I didn't give up the gun soon. I had a feeling the only reason they hadn't yet was because of Jeremy. "But he'll come back if I don't kill him. Just like he did this time."

"No, he won't. He's going to jail."

I heard the words he said, but I didn't have much faith in the criminal justice system to keep him there. I'd seen too much to believe that it would all be okay.

"He's still alive, Chels. If you keep him that way, you're free." Jeremy held his hands up, locking eyes with me, looking a little ashen. "You can rebuild the inn. You can be here, like you wanted, with a new life. And I'll be here with you, helping. I swear to God, I will be here."

I bit my lip, swaying slightly. "Don't think you're off the hook. You lied to me. I'm still pissed at you."

"I know. I swear, I'll make it up to you. Every second of every day, I'll make it up to you." He shot a nervous look behind me. "Just put the gun down."

Chapter 29

I LOWERED MY arm slowly, releasing the trigger and exhaling at the same time, my throat aching because of Richard's abuse. "Take him away."

I didn't even look at Richard. Didn't give him the satisfaction. I just stared at Jeremy as the men who had hovered behind me rushed forward, taking Richard away in cuffs. Once we were alone, I wrapped my arms around myself, my whole body aching from the beating and the fight I'd lived through. But it was over now. It was actually over. "You're shot."

Jeremy glanced down. "Yeah. It's nothing."

I didn't say anything to that because it didn't look like *nothing* to me. "So now what?"

"Now—*Christ.*" He crossed the room, closing the distance between us. He pulled me into his arms, threaded his hands in my hair, and kissed me gently. I was pissed at him, and there were a million reasons why I shouldn't be in his arms like this. But right now? I needed him more than I needed air. When he pulled back, he framed my face with his hands gently. "Now we get checked out by a doctor, and then we come home. I'll tuck you in and stay the night to make sure no one bothers you for at least twenty-four hours. You need to recover from today."

His voice was raspy at the end. Almost broken.

"You think you're staying the night?" I asked. "Hell no. I'm fine on my—"

"It wasn't a request. I'm staying." He ran his thumb over my cheek, smiling gently when I glowered at him. "I meant what I said before all this went down. I'm not going anywhere, Chels. I know this scares you, and you don't feel the same way yet, and I know you're pissed as hell at me, but I love you. I'm going to spend the rest of my life loving you, even if you never forgive me or love me back. And nothing you do or say will stop me."

I stared up at him, heart pounding. For the first time, hearing those words come out of his mouth and seeing him look at me like I was his whole world didn't make me want to run. It made me want to *stay*. We had a lot to resolve between us, but at the end of the day, it had always been…and would always be…Jeremy fricking Holland. I could have it all. The inn. The man. The life I'd always wanted.

And suddenly, it didn't seem too crazy to let myself feel that way.

"I love you, too," I said, my voice more of a whisper than anything.

His eyes widened. "What?"

"I love you," I said again, this time with more strength behind the words. "But I'm still mad at you for lying to me," I added for good measure.

He laughed, and he kissed me again, this time in a promise of forever, and of what was to come. And I believed every single second of it. I'd finally found my home.

It was with him, in Maine, all along.

Sacking
the
Quarterback

Samantha Towle

Chapter 1

BUZZING.

Loud buzzing.

Something is vibrating close to my head. I force open an eye in my dark bedroom, which is now illuminated by the vibrating phone on my nightstand. Reaching out a tired hand, I retrieve my cell, catching a glimpse of the time as I do— *3:00 a.m.*—and see my boss's name lighting up the screen.

Benedict Cross, State Attorney. He became state attorney twenty years ago at the age of thirty-five, youngest ever in the history of Miami. He's a man I respect and admire greatly, and I want to be in the same position he is when I'm thirty-five, which means I have only four years left to make it.

Benedict isn't going anywhere, so if I want to achieve my goal, I'll have to move to a different city. And I'm completely fine with that. I have no ties here in Miami. My career is one of the reasons I keep myself attachment free. And it's also the reason I'm working myself into an early grave, answering work calls at three in the morning. It's nothing new. I've always had to work hard to get everything. Nothing has ever come easy to me. And I prefer it that way. It makes success taste all the more sweet.

"Ben?" My voice is scratchy.

"Melissa, I'm sorry to call so late."

"Or early."

"Yeah," he says with a laugh. He knows I'm usually in the office by six thirty. "I need you to go down to the police station on 62nd Street."

It isn't out of the ordinary for Ben to ask me to go to a police station. Early-morning calls aren't strange either, but they don't usually come in at this time. Being a state attorney comes with its perks—the satisfaction of knowing that I put the bad guys behind bars—but these visits to the police station can be tough.

"Okay," I say, collecting my thoughts. "Who am I going to see?"

"Grayson Knight."

That makes me sit up and wake up a little more. "*The* Grayson Knight?"

"The one and only."

I'm surprised to hear the name. Grayson Knight, quarterback for the Miami Dolphins, is football's golden boy and everyone's favorite player, or at least everyone whose team isn't playing against him.

He's also seriously hot—not that it matters.

I run a hand through my tangled hair. "What's he done?"

"Drug possession."

My brows come up.

"He was arrested at Liv an hour ago."

Liv is an exclusive club at the Fontainebleau Miami Beach, a hotel the rich and famous frequent.

"Grayson Knight is high-profile, and men like him think they're above the law. We need to show him and the rest of the world that celebrities and sports stars are no different from anyone else who is caught with drugs. We need to make an example of him. I want you to go after Grayson with guns blazing. Getting a charge to stick to him won't be easy. It'll take my best. You're my best, Mel."

A burst of pride fills my chest at Ben's compliment. I know he thinks highly of me. I know I'm good at my job—no, I'm amazing at my job—but still, it's nice to hear it. And bringing down someone like Grayson Knight would be career-defining for me. It could be the case to push me up the career ladder sooner than I had hoped.

"I'll get down there now," I tell Ben.

"Call me when you're finished."

"Will do."

I hang up. Pushing back my duvet, I turn my bedside lamp on and put my feet on the floor. I take a quick deep breath and then head for the bathroom to get ready.

Thirty minutes later, I'm ready to go, briefcase in hand. I'm wearing a black business suit and a white silk blouse, but my face is free of makeup and my long chestnut-brown hair is tied back in a knot.

I'm not out to impress here. I'm here to do my job: get the lowdown on Grayson Knight before he lawyers up with some hotshot from a big firm.

Leaving my apartment, I take the elevator down to the lobby. Earl, the night doorman, is sitting at the desk. He smiles at me. "Early start, Miss St. James?"

"Too early." I smile back.

He chuckles. "Can I get you a car?"

"Don't worry, I'll flag a cab down outside."

"Let me do that." He gets up from his seat, coming around the desk.

I follow him to the front door of the building.

"Young girl like you doesn't want to be out on the streets at night alone. You never know what kind of crazy is out there."

The crazy that I fight against every day. The crazy that I'm trying to put behind bars to make the streets of Miami safer for other young women.

I don't say that out loud, though.

I love being an assistant state attorney. There's nothing better than putting away criminals and seeing justice served to up-their-own-ass jocks like Grayson Knight who think that just because they have money and fame, they're untouchable. Yeah, well, I'll show him just how touchable he is.

How touchable his body is.

I banish the thought from my mind. He is my opponent.

Earl flags down a cab. I thank him and climb into the backseat.

"62nd Street police station," I tell the driver as I sit back.

Chapter 2

I PAY THE DRIVER, tipping him well due to the hour, and get out of the cab. With my briefcase in one hand, I make my way up the steps to the doors of the police station. Pushing them open, I step inside to find the reception area reasonably quiet. That isn't strange at this hour. A man and a woman are sitting in the plastic seats off to my left. Cops are milling around in the office behind the desk. I don't recognize the on-duty officer. She's a dark-skinned woman in her midforties who looks far too alert.

I approach her with a smile, noting the name on her badge. "Hi, Officer Santiago, I'm Assistant State Attorney Melissa St. James. I'm here to see Grayson Knight."

She smiles at me. "He's being interviewed at the moment. Would you like me to take you through?"

"Please."

Officer Santiago comes out from behind the desk and I follow her through a door and down the corridor that leads to the interview rooms. She stops outside one of the doors. "They're in here."

"Thanks."

I knock once and open the door. Inside is Sergeant Matt Daughtry.

I dated him for four months and broke it off six months ago, even though he wanted it to continue. And he never makes any effort to hide that fact.

Jason Black, Matt's partner, is sitting next to him. I really don't like that guy. Something about him has always set me on edge, and I'm not feeling any differently about him right now.

Sitting across from them, with his back to me, is Grayson Knight.

Matt's eyes connect with mine. I tip my head back, indicating that I want to have a word with him outside.

"I'll just be a minute," Matt tells Jason.

All the while, Grayson, being the arrogant ass I imagine him to be, doesn't even turn to look at me.

Matt pushes up from his seat and comes out to me. The door closes. I move down the hall and lean my shoulder against the wall. "Melissa," Matt says, greeting me with my first name.

"Sergeant," I say, to remind him of what we are to each other now.

"You can call me Matt."

"And you can call me Assistant State Attorney St. James."

Laughing lightly, he shakes his head. "Is that really where we're at now?"

"Where 'we're at' is at work," I say, folding my arms over my chest. "Fill me in on the night's events." I lift my chin again, this time in the direction of the door, the one Grayson Knight is sitting behind.

"We received an anonymous tip that someone had drugs on the club premises. Sergeant Black and I went down there with a few other policemen. We did a sweep and search. Grayson Knight was found with a large quantity of Schedule II drugs on him."

"Large?"

"Enough to make every person in that club high and happy."

My brow furrows. "He was the only one carrying?"

"We found some small quantities on others there. Nothing substantial."

"Do you think it's strange that he was carrying so much? It's not like he needs to deal for the money."

Matt leans his shoulder against the wall, facing me. "Who knows why these celebs do what they do. Probably doing it for the kick."

"Hmm…yeah." My eyes go back to the closed door. "You were interviewing him without representation."

"He waived his rights. Said he doesn't want a lawyer."

I look back at him. "He doesn't want a lawyer? I guess that'll make my job easy."

"Yup. He said he didn't." Matt shakes his head.

Interesting. And unusual. The first thing celebrities usually do is scream for their attorney.

"You wanna talk to him?"

"Yeah. Give me a few minutes alone with him. Ben wants to throw the book at him."

Matt smiles, then pushes off the wall and opens the door. I walk through it. Jason gets up from his seat and, after brushing past me, leaves. I wait for the door to close before I take a seat in front of Grayson Knight.

He lifts his head slowly. My eyes meet the tired but striking green eyes of Grayson Knight.

Wow. Okay.

I'm a professional and I've dealt with celebrities before, but Grayson Knight is in a league of his own. It's hard not to be a little affected. I know football players are big guys. But Grayson is huge. Big shoulders, all muscle. And he's even more attractive than he is on TV. He exudes confidence and power, even in the tired state he's in. It's easy to see why America loves him.

But I'm not here to adore him. I'm here to stick him with a big fine or put him in jail. So I don my work armor and say, "My name is Melissa St. James. I'm the assistant state attorney on your case."

Chapter 3

GRAYSON STARES AT ME and doesn't say anything.

"Can you run through the night's events for me?"

"I already told the officers," Grayson says. His tone is almost bored, bordering on condescending.

Leaning forward, I rest my forearms on the table between us. "And now I want you to tell me."

He sighs. "I was in Liv. I had some coke on me for recreational use. The cops raided the club. They found the coke. They arrested me and brought me here. End of story."

"You're telling me the amount of drugs you were carrying was just for… recreational use?"

"I'm a big guy. What can I say?" He lifts one of those aforementioned giant shoulders.

When I look at Grayson, I immediately know the guy doesn't have a drug habit. I've seen enough addicts in my career to know the signs. This guy looks as clean as they come. Besides, if he was addicted to drugs, it would have been flagged in one of the many tests they do in the NFL these days. His team might have covered it up, but they also wouldn't have a high tolerance for him if he was a user. Addicts are generally unreliable and unpredictable. Grayson's contract wouldn't have been renewed, or his team would have found a way to get out of it.

Grayson Knight is their star player. And he was found with drugs. None of this is making sense to me right now.

But I don't need it to make sense. He broke the law. I'm here to see that he goes away for it.

"You waived your right to an attorney."

"Yes."

"Why?"

"Because I don't need one."

"You might want to reconsider, Mr. Knight." I stand up and walk to the door. Before opening it, I turn back to him. "Your release papers are being drafted up."

His eyes widen. "I'm free to go?"

"For now. I want you in my office in the morning at ten thirty sharp for your plea bargain. That's where I'll explain the charges against you, and you'll tell us how you'd like to plead in court. And, Mr. Knight, bring a lawyer to that."

He stands and moves to the side of the table. "That's it?"

"For now."

Something flickers in his eyes. Then I watch as his gaze drags up my body until it rests on my face.

I feel a surprising but delightful chill run through my body.

"I expected more." His tone is low and cuts through me, putting me off-balance.

"More?" I ask. My head feels suddenly foggy.

"Yes," he says, taking a step toward me.

He's still staring at me. Something in me wants to step back, yet there's another part that's urging me to go a step closer.

He's intense. And there's a raw magnetism in him that's

drawing me in. I guess that's what makes him famous. That and the fact that he's an unbelievable football player.

There's a knock on the door behind me, bringing me back to my senses.

I give Grayson a hard stare. "There will be more. Because all actions have consequences, Mr. Knight. Irrespective of *who* you are." I yank open the door to see Matt on the other side and then look back at Grayson. Using a hard voice that means business, I say, "Sergeant Daughtry will sort out your release papers."

Since he's still standing there silently, I pull a business card from my briefcase and hand it to him. His fingers touch mine in the exchange. I steel myself against the jolt I feel. "My office details are on there. My office, 10:30 a.m. And don't be late." I turn on my heel and march out of there.

Chapter 4

GRAYSON HASN'T TURNED UP. It's 11:00 a.m., and he was supposed to be here a half hour ago. His lawyer is here—George Simpson, a man who works for the best law firm in Miami. No surprise there. Of course Grayson got the best lawyer in town.

At least he bothered to get an attorney. Shame he couldn't be bothered to show up for his plea bargaining.

Asshole.

"I can try calling my client again," George says, picking up his cell phone.

"No, it's fine."

It's not fine. I'm really pissed off. I don't like being stood up for anything. And I don't like when people make a mockery of me and my career. I get up from my chair.

George Simpson follows suit and stands. "How do you want to proceed?" he asks.

"I'll be in touch."

He nods and leaves my office.

I sit back down in my chair, my hands in fists. Who the hell does Grayson Knight think he is? *Asshole.*

But why am I really so pissed off by this?

Because I'm an assistant state attorney, for God's sake,

and Grayson Knight thinks he can stand me up because he's what? A stupid football player. Well, guess what? I'm the law. He doesn't know what he's got coming.

Furious and unable to let this snub go, I make a quick call to Grayson's agent. I'm so angry that I let my emotions get the better of me and pretend to be his lawyer so that the agent will tell me where he is.

At a training session where his team practices.

The arrogant asshole went to practice instead of coming to his plea bargaining.

Armed with fury, I grab my bag and cell. I head out and catch a taxi on the street, telling the driver to take me to the Bubble, at Nova Southeastern University. That's where the agent directed me.

The taxi pulls up and I climb out. I make my way to the reception area, which is manned by a security guard. "Hi," I say. "My name is Melissa St. James. I'm here to see Grayson Knight. Harris Jones, Grayson's agent, said he would call ahead to let you know I was coming." Yes, I had pulled that little trick with Harris as well. Not my most ethical moment, but my anger is clouding my judgment, so I'm rolling with it.

"He did. I just need to see some I.D."

I pull my wallet from my bag and produce my driver's license. The security guard checks my I.D., then hands it back to me. I fill out the sign-in sheet and take the visitor's badge he hands me. I clip it to the lapel of my jacket.

"The team is training outside today on the main field. Take that door there," the security guard says, pointing. "And walk all the way down the hallway. There's another door to the field at the end, on your right."

"Thank you," I say, smiling at him.

I make my way through the corridor until finally I'm outside. The Miami Dolphins are on the field in the middle of a training session.

Now that I'm here, I'm not really sure what to do. It's not like I can just walk onto the field and interrupt the training session to demand to know why Grayson didn't turn up for our appointment this morning.

It takes me a minute to find him on the field, which is filled with big, sweaty men.

"Can I help you?" a male voice asks.

I turn around and see a guy in his midthirties who's wearing running shorts and a t-shirt. He has cropped blond hair and is attractive. But he's no Grayson Knight.

"Hi, I'm Melissa St. James. I'm Grayson's…attorney." There, I've lied again. "I have an appointment with him."

"Ellis Mitchell. I'm the team's conditioning coach," he tells me as he shakes my hand. "Grayson shouldn't be much longer. They're almost done here. Why don't you take a seat while you wait?" He gestures to the bleachers.

"No, I'm good, thanks," I say, giving him a polite smile.

"I should get back to it," he says, returning my smile. I have a feeling mine doesn't look nearly as warm as his. "Nice to meet you, Melissa."

"You too."

Ellis leaves and my eyes go to Grayson. In spite of myself, I can't deny that he looks really hot out there. And I don't mean hot in a sweaty way, even though he is. He's hot in the sexiest way imaginable. Grayson looks like the epitome of male out there as he throws the ball to his teammate. His jersey tight over his biceps, showing off the muscles in his arms. And don't even get me started on his legs. I'm pretty sure he could crack walnuts with those thighs.

Or me.

Jesus, where did that thought come from?

Of course Grayson is undeniably hot. But he's a criminal, and I'm intent on making a guilty charge stick to him like glue. A criminal who thinks he can ignore a plea bargain appointment with an assistant state attorney.

And he's a criminal who has just noticed I'm here. I see his head turn toward me, and I watch as he hands the ball off to his teammate before he starts to walk those powerful legs over to me.

And for some strange reason I feel a tremble in my own body.

Chapter 5

GRAYSON STANDS BEFORE ME with a frown on his face.

It makes me frown in return. Even though I'm angry at him, I can't help but notice his size and how hot he looks with sweat trickling down his neck.

"What are you doing here?" he says in a low voice.

What am I doing here? The nerve of this guy!

"You stood me up." I practically spit the words out.

All he does is raise a brow in return.

"Remember the plea bargain? To discuss your charges?"

Why am I so flustered right now?

He folds his arms over his chest. "I never said I would come."

I feel my eyes widen at first, so I narrow them quickly and say, "You don't get a choice in the matter. I tell you to come—you come."

He glances around at his teammates as they start to move in our direction. Then he takes hold of my elbow and starts steering me away.

I snatch my arm back. He opens the door I came through, giving me a look as if he's demanding I go through it. It makes me want to dig my heels in and stay where I am, but he's right. The field is not the place to have this conversation.

I follow him down the hall and stop behind him when he opens a door. I walk through it. He closes the door behind us and turns to face me. "What's the problem?"

"Seriously? You think I don't deserve your time. That you're such a big shot that you can just brush off your arrest. Do you think it'll all go away as if nothing ever happened?"

He takes a step toward me. "I don't think it'll all go away. I didn't turn up because I had to be at training, so I sent my lawyer in my place. The lawyer you told me to get."

"Funny. He seemed to think you'd be attending with him."

"Then he's an idiot."

"And you're the one who hired him. Wouldn't that make you an idiot, too?"

His lips turn up into a smile. I'd like to say it doesn't affect me, but it does. And I'd never let him see that.

"I told you to be at my office, Grayson. If I tell you to do something, you do it."

Something flashes in his eyes and he takes another step closer to me. The room suddenly feels a lot smaller. "I like a woman who takes charge."

"I don't care what you like in a woman."

He steps closer. "The thing is, I think you do care. That's why you're so pissed that I didn't show up. That's why you've come all the way here...."

"You're very close to crossing a line," I tell him.

"Maybe I like crossing lines," he says, taking another step. He's close now. Too close.

My heart is beating hard in my chest. My breathing becomes quicker.

Take control of this situation now, Mel, before it gets out of hand.

Lifting my chin, I look him square in the eyes. "I came here," I say, "because you didn't show for an appointment"—*that's not exactly true; I came here because I was pissed off*—"and it was an important appointment at that. I was trying to do you a favor, but that was clearly a mistake. You can kiss the plea bargain good-bye. I'll see you in court, Mr. Knight."

Chapter 6

I PULL A BOTTLE of wine from the fridge and pour myself a glass. Carrying the wineglass and a large bag of chips over to the sofa with me, I put them down on the coffee table and turn the TV on.

After a long, shitty day and zero sleep, all thanks to Grayson Knight, I'm ready to relax for an hour before I hit the hay. With my remote in hand, I channel-hop while sipping my wine. I settle on a rerun of *Friends*. It's exactly what I need right now—some light humor.

I'm still chewing over Grayson's behavior earlier. I can't believe he was hitting on me like that. And I'm still trying to ignore the fact that it affected me.

That he affects me.

I stretch my legs out and rest my feet on the coffee table. My phone starts to ring. I reach over and pick it up from the table. The call comes up as a private account, and for a moment I consider ignoring it, but then I decide to answer. It could be a client. Always the lawyer.

"Hello?"

"Melissa?"

"Yes."

"Melissa, it's…Grayson. Grayson Knight."

Why the hell is Grayson Knight calling me at 9:00 p.m.? Actually, why the hell is he calling me, period?

Whatever his reason, I'm not going to make it easy for him. "How did you get my home number?" I ask. My tone is accusing.

"I, um…if I tell you, will you have me arrested?"

"Probably."

He laughs, but I'm not entirely kidding about having him arrested. I won't put him behind bars for this call, but it's my job to put him there for drug possession.

There's a distinct pause. I feel the tone in the conversation shift to serious as he blows out a long breath. "Can we…talk?"

"About?"

"Earlier."

I take a deep breath and let it out. Then I say, "You have one minute."

"One minute. Got it."

I hear him exhale loudly down the line. Again. But then he says nothing.

"Minute's ticking," I say, taking a sip of my wine.

"Right. Look, I'm calling to apologize for my behavior earlier. I acted like a total dick. Not showing up for our appointment, and for the way I behaved…I'm sorry."

"Okay."

"Okay…as in, okay, you forgive me?"

This guy is actually charming when he's not acting like a total tool. A smile is fighting its way onto my lips. I'm just glad he can't see it.

"Who helped you realize you were being a jerk?"

He laughs again, this time knowingly. "My dad might have chewed my ass out after my idiot lawyer told him that I hadn't shown up for our appointment."

There's another pause. Charming he may be, but I'm going to make this guy work for it.

"So…am I forgiven?"

"Maybe."

"Maybe. Okay. I'll take that," he says, chuckling softly. "And now this is the part where I ask you to keep that maybe-forgiven part in mind, and agree to meet with me tomorrow to discuss that plea bargain you wanted to talk about this morning."

I sit up, put my glass on the coffee table, and say, "I don't know."

"Please." When he says the word, there's a plea to his tone, and that starts to weaken my resolve. "I won't screw around. I'll be there whatever time you say. I swear."

I pause, thinking. I can hear him breathing.

Ben wanted me to throw the book at him, but I have this nagging feeling that I don't know the whole story here. And the lawyer in me has to know what it is.

"Okay, be at my office at 10:00 a.m. tomorrow morning."

"I'll be there. Thank you, Melissa."

"You're welcome. And, Grayson?"

"Yes?"

"This is your last chance. Don't screw it up."

Chapter 7

"GRAYSON KNIGHT IS HERE to see you," my assistant, Jill, says over the intercom.

I press down on the button and say, "Send him in."

I grab Grayson's case file and my notepad and pen and take them with me to the small meeting table I have in my office. Putting the file on the table, I take a seat on the chair that faces the door.

When the door opens, revealing Grayson, I have to hold in a breath to stop from gasping.

Holy shit, he looks amazing.

He's incredibly handsome. Like, out-of-this-world handsome. He's wearing a closely fitted black suit. And as I take in his size, I assume that it must have been tailored to fit him like that.

"Hey," he says, smiling at me. His teeth are dazzling.

I force my brain to function. "Hi. Great. Uh, take a seat," I say, gesturing to the chair across from me.

"Can I get you anything to drink?" I ask as he sits. This gives me time to compose myself.

"Water would be good."

I go over to the mini-fridge I keep in my office and grab two bottles of water. "Bottle okay, or would you like a glass?"

"Bottle's fine," he says, giving me another smile.

Jesus, stop smiling at me. And stop looking so damn hot.

I hand him his water and take my seat. Grayson unscrews the cap and takes a drink. I can't help but watch as he swallows that water down. The way his strong neck works on the movement. He lowers the bottle from his lips, catching me staring. Then his tongue darts out to catch the drops of water on his lips.

Holy mother of God.

That tongue…I wonder how it would feel to have his tongue on my…

I press my thighs together.

Stop it, Mel.

I force myself to look away and down at my file.

"Let's discuss the events that led to your arrest on the night that you were at Liv." I open my file to the police report detailing the arrest and pick up my pen, ready to take notes.

Grayson still has the bottle of water in his hand. He screws the cap back on and leans back in his seat. "I'd had a hard day training," he says, "so I went out with some buddies to let off steam. We ended up in Liv. We were drinking and having a good time. Then the cops showed up. I was searched and they found the drugs on me, and then I was arrested."

"Okay, let's start with the first part of the night. You say you went out—to some bars?"

"Yes."

"Which ones?"

"Can't remember."

"Where did you get the drugs? Did you already have them before you left home, or did you buy them while you were out?"

"While I was out."

I make note of that. "Which bar did you buy the drugs in?"

"I don't know."

"You don't know?" I ask, looking up at him.

"I don't remember," he says. His hand curls around the water bottle.

"Who did you buy the drugs from?"

He gives me a look and says, "A dealer."

"And his or her name is…?"

"I don't know," Grayson says again, unscrewing the cap of his water bottle and taking another drink.

I watch him again with my attorney eyes and see how uncomfortable he looks right now. I know he's at least looking at a big fine and all the negative publicity that goes with it, but there's something else going on here. Something he's not saying.

It isn't my job to save Grayson from a guilty charge—it's my job to give it to him. But I'm also not someone who will charge blindly. More than that, I like to know all the facts before I try someone. And I feel like I don't know all the facts here. Grayson's clearly hiding something.

"So, you're telling me you don't know the name of the person you bought that large quantity of drugs from?"

He lowers the bottle to the table, looks me in the eye, and says, "I told you, I don't know. He was some guy in the club that I bought drugs from. End of story."

"But you said you bought the drugs from a dealer in a bar, not the club."

"Club, bar. They're the same thing."

"No, they're not."

"Whatever. Jesus. Look," he says, leaning forward, resting his forearms on the table. He stares me in the eye as if that will make me back off. "I was in a bar. I went up to the guy because I knew he was a dealer—"

"How did you know he was a dealer?"

"Because I just knew."

"How?"

"Because he looked like a dealer."

"He looked like a dealer? How do dealers look?"

"Jesus! I don't know!" He's getting flustered. And he'd only be flustered right now if he were lying.

"But you just said you did. You said he looked like a dealer."

He clenches his jaw, and a frustrated breath leaves him.

"Grayson, I can't help you if you aren't truthful with me."

His eyes flash to mine. "I thought it was your job to put me inside—not to help me," he says, and I have to admit that he has a point.

So why do I feel the incessant need to do it?

"You're right. And based on what you're telling me, there's no plea deal that I can offer you."

"So we're done here?" he says without meeting my eyes.

I put my pen down, sigh, and say, "Yes. We're done."

Grayson stands. I feel a weird pull at the thought of him leaving right now. Once he reaches the door, he stops and looks back at me over his shoulder. "Thank you for your time. See you, Mel."

His words and stare hit me in the gut. And then Grayson Knight is gone, my door closing softly behind him.

Chapter 8

"PASS THE SALT," Tori says to me.

"Who puts salt on pasta al forno?" I say, frowning.

"I do," she says, giving me a cocky smile. "Now pass it over."

Tori is my best friend. I met her at law school. She works at a private practice, specializing in family law. Honestly, I don't know how she does it, dealing with people getting divorced, fighting the custody battles.

As a child of divorced parents who hated each other and fought over who got to see me the most, I've had my fair share of that pain. No way would I want to deal with it on a daily basis like she does.

Give me criminals any day. But I'm not really sure what that says about me.

I hand the salt to her and say teasingly, "Does my cooking not taste good enough for you?"

I had made dinner, and though I'm not the best cook, I can rustle up some decent al forno. Tori and I make sure to have dinner together at least once a week. Tonight we were supposed to go out, but I didn't much feel like being social, so I changed our plans and said that I would cook.

"It tasted just fine," she says with a grin, bringing a forkful of some salt-covered pasta to her mouth. "But now it tastes even better."

Picking up my wineglass, I give her a sly middle finger, grinning as I do.

"So classy," she says, laughing.

"I learned from the best."

Then it's her turn to flip me off, causing us both to laugh. And it feels good to laugh, after the past few days I've had. After the laughter has settled, I tuck back into my pasta.

"So why didn't you want to go out tonight?" Tori asks.

"Just didn't feel up to it," I say, lifting my shoulders.

"Work getting you down?"

"You could say that." I put my fork down on my plate.

"Wanna talk about it?" She forks more pasta into her mouth.

"No—" I pause. I can tell Tori anything. Anything within legal parameters, that is. "Yes."

She laughs.

"It's just this case I'm working on...I feel conflicted."

"Conflicted?" Her brows rise.

"I just...I think the guy is hiding something. I don't think the case is as clear-cut as everyone else thinks it is."

"You mean as clear-cut as Ben thinks it is."

"Yeah." I sigh.

"So, you think this guy is what? Innocent?"

I chew on my thumbnail. "Maybe not innocent. Just not as guilty as he appears."

She studies me for a minute, then says, "Go with your gut, Mel. You have great instincts. You think there's more to this, then find out what it is. What if Ben makes you put the guy in prison? You give jail time to an innocent man and find that out after the fact...I know you, it'll eat away at you forever."

Chapter 9

I'M JUST SHUTTING DOWN my computer when Ben comes into my office.

"Hey. Everything okay?"

"Yeah," he says, but he doesn't sit. He stands behind the chair on the other side of my desk, hands resting on the top of it. "I've just been reading over the Grayson Knight case."

"Okay," I say, waiting to hear what he's going to tell me. My heart starts to beat a little faster. I don't know why. "What do you think?"

"I think your proposal of charging him with possession of a Schedule II drug is too light. I was reading over the police report, and the amount of drugs he was carrying…I think we should push for possession with intent to supply."

"You do?"

"You don't?" he says, his brows pulling together.

"It's just…he's Grayson Knight. Superstar football player. Squeaky-clean record. Incredibly wealthy. Arguing for possession with the intent to supply will be a hard sell. It's not like he needs to deal drugs to make money. I think a judge would more likely accept a charge of possession of a Schedule II drug. That way, we still have a good chance of winning the case in front of the public."

"I disagree," Ben says, and his words are biting. I'm surprised, because Ben rarely disagrees with me, and when he does, he does it respectfully. "He won't get enough jail time with a Schedule II felony. With a good lawyer, he'll only get probation and a fine. Maybe community service. I told you that I want to make an example of Grayson Knight. That charge won't make an example of him."

"Okay," I say, unsure which tack to take right now. "So…you're saying you want me to…?" I let my words drift so he can fill them in.

"Up the charges to possession of a Schedule II drug with intent to supply. Let's make him look at a felony in the second degree."

I nod once in assent.

"Okay, then," Ben says. He pushes off the chair and takes a step away. "You're leaving for the night?"

"I was heading out, but I can stay. Do you want me to draw up the charges tonight?"

"No, go home. Do it in the morning."

"Okay."

"Good night, Mel."

"Night, Ben."

I watch him leave my office, my door closing behind him.

His words rattle around in my head.

Why is he so insistent on putting him in prison? I know that putting a high-profile celebrity like Grayson away would look good for him. But there are no elections till next year. And Ben is highly respected in Miami. It's not like he needs to pull tricks to get reelected.

Ben's words, mixed in with Tori's from last night, swirl around in my head.

What Tori said was right. If I prosecute Grayson without knowing the whole truth and he ends up going to jail as an innocent man, it'll eat away at me. Especially now, since Ben wants me to up the charge so that Grayson will be looking at some serious jail time.

I got into this job to do good. I want to be the best assistant state attorney, and to me, that means being honest. I don't want to put people in jail to better my numbers—I want to do it because those people deserve to be in jail. I want to do it to make my city a safer place—not just to get good publicity. And that's why I find myself dialing Grayson Knight's number.

He takes a while to answer the phone, and when he does, he sounds out of breath. "Mel," he huffs.

I love the way he calls me Mel. But my stomach sinks as thoughts flash through my mind as to what's causing Grayson to be out of breath. *Is he…with a woman?*

God, I hope not.

"I'm not interrupting anything, am I?"

"No. I'm just in my gym, working out."

"Oh." *Sweet relief.*

I shake away my thoughts. I want to get to the truth, not bone the guy.

"Is everything okay?" he asks.

"Yes…I was just wondering if you have time for a chat."

"Sure." He doesn't ask why. And honestly, I feel a flutter of content that he's so quick to answer yes. "Do you want me to come to your office?"

I don't think it's a good idea to meet Grayson here—Ben could find out about it. But there's a coffee shop I really like that's on the other side of town, not far from my apartment. And I never see anyone from work there. Grayson and I will be able to talk in peace.

"Can you meet me at the Hideout instead? It's a coffee shop on—"

"I know where it is," he interjects. "I love that place. What time did you want to meet?"

I glance at the clock. "How long will it take you to get there?"

"I just need to grab a quick shower. I'm all sweaty from the gym."

A nice image pops into my head. *Grayson is all sweaty, naked, and hovering over me as he…*

Stop it, Mel!

"It'll probably only take me ten to shower and change, and another ten to drive over."

I clear my throat, but when I speak, my words still come out ragged. "I'll see you in twenty, then."

"See you soon," he says, and hangs up.

I leave my office and head for the elevator. Downstairs, I flag a cab on the street.

The entire time, I desperately try not to think about the fact that Grayson is probably naked right now. Naked and wet, in the shower.

Holy God.

I need to wipe these images and thoughts from my mind so that I have a clear head when I see him. I'm meeting him to discuss his criminal charges, and all I want to do is take off his sweaty clothes.

Chapter 10

I'M THE FIRST to arrive at the Hideout, so I order myself a latte and take a seat in a booth at the back of the shop to give us privacy. It's a good table because I can still see the door when Grayson arrives.

I don't have to wait long—only a few minutes. From the doorway, Grayson scans the coffee shop. His eyes land on me and he smiles.

And I feel that smile deep inside me, curling my toes.

I try to shake the feeling off, but it's not easy when he's walking over to me, his eyes clearly fixed on mine. Okay, so I'll admit it now: I'm definitely attracted to Grayson Knight. But I'm also the assistant state attorney on the case, and my job is the most important thing to me.

I need to push this attraction down and ignore it.

"Hi," he says. "I'm gonna order a coffee. You want anything else?" He nods down at my latte.

"I'm good, thanks."

I watch as he walks over to the counter, orders his drink, and pays for it. He comes back over empty-handed. "Waitress said she'll bring it over."

He sits down across from me and there's a moment of

quiet. I curl my hands around my cup, unsure what to say. How to open the conversation. It's very unlike me.

"So, you wanted to talk?" Grayson says, his voice soft.

I lift my eyes to him. "My boss wants me to up the charge against you to possession of a Section II drug with intent to supply." I see a flicker of something in his eyes, but his expression doesn't change. The words hang between us as the waitress comes over and puts Grayson's coffee on the table in front of him.

He breaks his stare and looks at her. "Thank you," he says. His eyes scan the coffee shop after the waitress has left our table.

Finally, he looks back at me. "Okay," he says.

"Okay. That's all you have to say?"

"What do you want me to say? The State Attorney wants you to up the charge. He's your boss. I'm assuming you do as he says. So…okay. Thank you for telling me."

I stare at him, perplexed. "How can you be so calm about this?"

"Why do you care so much?" he fires back. His words almost knock me out of my seat.

But he's right—why do I care so much?

The question is almost like truth or dare.

I say the truth, I'm done for. I don't and he takes on the biggest dare of his life.

"Because…" I lift my shoulder as I drag out the word and play for time. "Maybe I think you're not telling me everything about what happened that night."

"Even if I wasn't, why would that matter to you?"

"Because I don't want to put innocent men in prison when I can do something to avoid it."

I watch his hand tighten around the cup. His eyes stare down into his drink.

"Tell me what happened that night in Liv," I say softly, coaxing him.

He doesn't speak for a long moment. When he lifts his eyes, I hope to see something in them. The truth, maybe. But what I see is nothing. His eyes are blank. "I told you what happened," he says. "I got the drugs from a dealer in a bar. Then I went to Liv and the cops busted the place. I was arrested. End of story."

He's hiding something. His expression might be blank, but the small shift he just made and the way his eyes darted to the left—both movements tell me differently. I had a hunch that that was the case in my office the other day. But here in the coffee shop, I can see it clearly. And I'm not willing to let it go this time.

"How long were you in Liv before the cops showed up?" I ask. I want to question him to see if I can learn anything new.

"An hour, maybe."

"And the search, how did it go down?"

"They came into the VIP area. We were one of the first to be searched."

"'We'?"

"My friends…and my brother."

Interesting. I didn't know he had a brother. I wonder if he looks like him.

"And you didn't think to try to dispose of the drugs at any point?" I ask. Of course I don't condone that type of thing, but I see it time and time again—dealers disposing of drugs before the arrest can be made. It's hard to make a charge stick if the drugs can't actually be found on the person. Especially in a public place like a nightclub.

I hold my stare and watch Grayson shake his head. I don't know how else to push this, even though I know there's something he's not saying.

So I shift the conversation elsewhere—to football. He relaxes immediately, and we spend the next hour drinking coffee and talking sports.

One could call it a date. But it's not. It's definitely not.

But I won't deny that I like talking to him. He's smart and fun, and charismatic. He's also nice to look at, which is always a bonus.

Once I get him relaxed, I try to swing the conversation back to the charge, but even then, he doesn't give me anything to work with. After a few hours, my second coffee cup is empty. "I should go," I tell him. "I've got an early start in the morning."

Drafting up his new charges.

I feel my mood drop down like a rock in water.

"Yeah," he says.

I note the flicker of disappointment in his eyes, and I wish it didn't, but it lifts my spirits a little.

Okay, a lot. And, yes, I know how screwed up this is. I'm about to charge this guy with possession of a Schedule II drug with intent to supply, and some people could say that I've just been on a date with him.

Not a date!

Shit.

We both stand and leave the coffee shop.

"I'll walk you to your car," he says when we're out on the sidewalk.

"I took a cab here," I tell him.

"Then I'll drive you home," he says.

And I don't argue.

Chapter 11

I FOLLOW GRAYSON over to a shiny black Range Rover. "Nice car," I say as he unlocks it.

"Thanks." He opens the passenger door and I climb inside. He shuts the door behind me and makes his way around to the driver's side.

I put my seat belt on as Grayson climbs in the car, buckles up, and starts the engine. He pulls out into traffic. I can't help but watch him drive. There's just something so incredibly sexy about watching a man like Grayson drive. Looking at his strong hands around the steering wheel has my mind wondering what his hands would feel like wrapped—

"So where am I going?" he asks, snapping me out of my reverie.

"What? Oh." Flustered, I fire off my address to him. Then we slip off into silence. It's not uncomfortable but definitely filled with tension on my part.

It doesn't take us long to reach my place. I can't deny that I'm disappointed that my time with him is over—until I see him in court, anyway. You know, since I'm trying to put him in prison and everything.

Grayson pulls into the parking lot to my building and kills the engine. The tension between us feels so much heavier now in the dark and silence. I'm very aware of the fact that we're alone.

"Thanks for the ride."

"Thanks for inviting me to coffee. Even if it was to deliver bad news," he says. He glances over at me and smiles.

"I'm sorry."

"Don't be. I was the one who made the decision to carry those drugs with me. I wasn't going to sell them. But I had them. A lot of them. I have to face the consequences for what I've done."

I shift in my seat, facing him. "See, you weren't going to sell them. So why did you have so much on you? It doesn't make sense to me."

He looks away, his hands curling around the steering wheel, gripping. "It…I…it doesn't have to make sense to you. It's just the way it is."

"But it doesn't have to be this way. If I knew the truth, I could maybe—"

"You're not my lawyer, Mel." He turns to me, his eyes blazing. "It's not your job to fix this. You're the one charging me. Why does this matter so much to you?"

"I told you why it matters," I say, keeping my voice even and low to show him that I mean every word. "I don't like to put innocent men in prison."

"I think it's more than that. Tell me," he demands.

"Tell you what?" I fire back. And we're inches apart now, eyes locked together.

"This."

His mouth slams down on mine.

Chapter 12

HE'S KISSING ME.

Oh, God, he's kissing me.

Heaven. And hell. It's the only way I can describe what's happening right now.

The feel of Grayson's lips against mine, his tongue in my mouth, his hands in my hair…heaven. But then there's the message in my brain, screaming at me that I shouldn't be doing this. I'm the assistant state attorney on his case. I'm going to be standing on the opposite side of the courtroom, across from this guy, as I charge him with a crime. This is so very wrong. It's hell.

Just one more second. I'll kiss him for one more second and then I'll stop.

Grayson groans into my mouth. It's a sound that can only be described as sweet ecstasy, and I nearly come right there on the spot.

Holy shit. I'm so screwed.

I don't want to stop. He tastes so damn good…*feels* so damn good. His hands leave my hair, skimming down my shoulders, my arms, coming around my waist as he pulls me closer to him. My hands slide up his biceps, curling around the back of his neck. His tongue slides along my lower lip, then he sucks it into his mouth.

"You feel so damn good, Mel," he says, and his voice rumbles against my lips, before he captures them savagely in an even hotter kiss.

I'm going to lose my job.

"Stop." I press my hand into his chest, pushing myself back and away. "We have to stop."

"Why?"

"Because!" I throw my hands up in the air and move back to my seat. I grab my bag from the floor and put it in my lap as a barrier. "I'm the assistant state attorney on your case! And you're a drug dealer up on a charge, you realize. I could get fired from my job for this!"

"Hey, it's okay," he says, reaching for my arm.

I dodge his move. "No, it's not okay. I'm the one who's prosecuting you."

Grayson doesn't say anything. What can he say? It's the truth.

I'm in so much trouble.

"I have to go." I pull away from him, reaching for the handle.

"Mel. Wait," he says. His tone is imploring, but I can't stay. I have to go.

I jump out of the car and slam the door shut behind me. I hear him get out, too, and then he's calling my name, but I'm practically running to my building.

I'm relieved to find that the lobby is empty. I furiously press the button for the elevator. When it arrives a few seconds later, I practically fall into it. I lean back against the wall as the doors close in front of me and the elevator begins to ascend slowly.

Jesus Christ, what was I just thinking! Clearly I wasn't. Otherwise I wouldn't have been making out with the defendant in the front seat of his car.

I can't believe I did that. That's not me. I don't do reckless things like that. Especially not things that would put my job at risk.

I let myself into my apartment and drop my bag on the counter. Just as I do, my cell starts to ring. I go through my purse and pull it out.

Grayson's calling.

I stare at his name for a long moment. And for the first time in a really long time, tears well up in my eyes.

I reject his call, leave my cell on the kitchen counter, walk through to my bedroom, and undress. Falling into bed, I let the tears flow. *How did I make that mistake?*

But that's when I realize that my tears are about something else, too.

Because I can't have what I want.

And right now, that's Grayson.

Chapter 13

I'VE SHUT DOWN my computer. I need to talk to Ben. Though I've been putting this off all day, I can't put it off any longer. I want off this case. In all honesty, I also have to tell him that there's a personal conflict. I'll have to deal with the consequences, whatever they may be. My stomach roils with unease. Forcing strength, I get up from my desk and leave my office, heading down the hall.

Ben's door is ajar, and I hear him talking to someone. It takes me a moment to realize that he's on the phone. I'm just about to walk away when he says something that catches my attention.

"—Dolphins versus Browns, next month. Yeah, put fifty grand on the Browns." Silence, and then he laughs. "Yeah, well, maybe I've got a good feeling about this one."

Feeling sick, I take a step back, my hand pressed to my stomach. I glance around to make sure no one has seen me and hurry back to my office.

I close the door behind me and lean against it, feeling off-balance.

What the hell did I just hear?

Ben wouldn't be pushing up Grayson's charge just to win a bet, right?

Grayson is the star quarterback. If the team loses him, they'll probably lose most of their games. Even against a team playing as poorly as the Browns are this season.

Ben wouldn't do that.

Would he?

I slump down in my desk chair. My cell rings on my desk. I pick it up, answering on autopilot as I usually do during the workday, and don't even look at the caller display.

"Melissa St. James."

"Mel," Grayson says. His deep, masculine voice hits me square in the chest.

It takes me a moment to speak, and all I manage to say is: "Hi."

"Hey," he says.

There's a beat of silence between us. An unspoken word, filled with everything that happened between us last night.

I shut my eyes. But behind my lids, all I see is him. Kissing me. Touching me. Wanting me.

I can't do this. I open my eyes and say, "Why are you calling? Because if it's—"

"Wanted to hear your voice."

With that one utterance, Grayson knocks the wind out of my sails. I lose my resolve.

He wanted to hear my voice. I feel like crying in frustration. He's being so sweet and I want him so very badly.

And my boss is trying to put him in prison. Actually, he wants me to put him in prison. I'm royally screwed. I have no clue what to do. For the first time in my life, I don't have the answer to this. I really hate the universe sometimes.

"You shouldn't say things like that to me," I tell him.

"You think I shouldn't. I think I should. One thing you should know about me is that I always tell the truth. So I'll keep saying those things until you start listening to them. I want to hear your voice, I'll call you. I want to tell you that I want you, I will. And, Mel, I do want you. Whether you want to hear that or not, I'm still going to say it. It doesn't make it any less true."

Oh, God. Now he's being all forceful and alpha, and it's so goddamn hot. He's got me spinning in circles.

"Now, I'm going to tell you that I want to see you. That I *need* to see you." His voice is low and deep, almost a growl, making me shiver.

"That's…that wouldn't be a good idea," I say, because it's true. It would be the worst idea ever. But also probably the best idea.

It's only because he's forbidden, I tell myself. We all want what we can't have, right? It makes it all the more desirable.

Even as I think the words, I know they're not true.

I would want Grayson even if he was readily available to me.

There's just something about him…something that has gotten under my skin and embedded itself deep inside me.

"The best things usually come from the worst ideas," he says seductively.

"I…can't."

God, I want to punch myself in the face. *Just end the call. Get off the phone. Tell him no, and stop torturing yourself.*

But then his tone changes and he says, "I really do need to see you. Just to talk. About the case. Nothing else. I'll keep my hands to myself, I promise." His voice sounds soft and sweet. And just like that, all bets are off.

Because, goddamnit, I *want* to see him, too.

"Where are you?"

"I'm at the Bubble. Come in through the field entrance. I'll tell security to let you in."

"I'll be there in ten."

Chapter 14

I IGNORE THE TREMOR of excitement that I feel in my stomach as I walk toward the entrance of the Bubble, knowing that I'm going to see Grayson very soon.

When exactly did I turn into a fangirl for him?

Probably around the time he stuck his tongue in my mouth, making my body come alive for the first time in years.

Yep, that was the exact moment.

I can see that the main entrance is all closed up. The lights are out, but Grayson said that I should come in through the field entrance.

If only I knew where the field entrance was. I look around for a sign, see nothing, and decide to walk around until I find it. I'll give it ten minutes before I call Grayson and have him come get me.

I begin walking down the length of the Bubble. The area's well lit, so it isn't completely scary. But I am relieved when I round the side and see a guard standing by a door. He looks up at me.

"Hi," I say. "I'm here to see Grayson Knight. He's expecting me."

"Yeah, he said to let you in when you arrived," he says, and stands aside, opening the door he was guarding.

I step through and hear it clang shut behind me. And then I'm on the edge of the football field. Floodlights all the way around illuminating it.

And there's a solitary figure in the middle of the field, facing away from me.

Grayson.

I can tell that it's him from the line of his broad shoulders and the way he holds himself. Proudly, but like he's got the weight of the world sitting on him. His hand comes to his side and I can see a football in it.

I take a step onto the grass, and he turns to face me as if he's sensed my movement.

I can't see his expression because he's too far away. But I can definitely feel the heat and electricity that seems to connect us. It travels across the field and right into the very core of my body. And the pull is begging me to race in Grayson's direction, right into his arms. Or bed.

Crap. I'm so screwed.

On wobbly legs, I start to walk slowly toward him. *Thank God I wore fluts today.*

Grayson doesn't make a move. He stands there, watching me walk to him. I feel like he's slowly undressing me with his eyes. It's torture. And it puts me on edge. God, I'm so nervous. My stomach is rolling, and my heart is doing jumping jacks in my chest. I don't know what I'm going to say when I finally reach him.

All I do know is that Grayson makes me feel out of control. And I'm not used to being out of control. Control is what shapes me, keeps me moving forward in the safe life I've created for myself. Grayson seems to strip all of that away, leaving me vulnerable and bare. Yet I can't seem to stay away from him.

Finally I reach him. I stop a few feet away. "Hi," I say, my voice sounding small in the expanse.

"Hey." He flashes a smile at me, and I almost swoon.

Jesus Christ.

"Are we alone? Apart from the security guard." I tip my head in that direction.

Grayson puts the ball down on the ground by his feet. He takes a step toward me. "Yeah."

I step back. "We shouldn't be seen together. Not with the way things are at the moment."

He frowns, his brows drawing together. "So why come at all?"

I wrap my arms around my stomach, looking at my feet. I shift on the spot. "Because…"

"You wanted to see me."

I lift my eyes back to him. "I did. But I shouldn't. This—" I say, gesturing between us with my hand. "What happened last night. Can't happen again. I'm the assistant state—"

"I know," he snaps. "You've already told me a hundred times."

"I'm saying it because it's true."

He closes the space between us by reclaiming that step. "If things were different?"

"But they're not."

"If they were?" he asks, keeping his eyes firmly on me.

I hold my thoughts for a while, lips pressed together. "Grayson, I can't…"

Disappointment flashes through his eyes. He turns away from me. "I'm sorry that I kissed you last night," he says, and his voice is quiet and it breaks my heart. "I was out of line. It won't happen again."

"Okay," I say. What else can I say? I'm glad that he isn't looking at me right now, because I know that the disappointment that's lancing through me is showing on my face.

He turns back to me. His expression is fierce as he says,

"When I say I'm sorry, Mel, I mean I'm sorry for the way I made you feel when I kissed you. The last thing I ever want to do is make things hard for you. But…" He takes a large step in my direction, his long legs eating up the space between us. He's so close now that I have to tilt my head back to look in his face. "*I'm* not sorry it happened. I'll never be sorry it happened. Because I wanted to kiss you. Goddamnit, did I want to kiss you." His eyes go to my lips. "I always want to kiss you. I have from the first moment I saw you."

He lifts his eyes from my mouth back to my eyes. My body starts to tremble.

Holy crap. I'm so screwed.

"I…" I part my lips to say something. What that is, I have no clue. So I close my mouth again.

Grayson pushes a hand through his hair. "I know you don't want things to be that way between us, so I'll back off. I just wanted you to know how I feel. Now that I have, I won't bring it up again."

My heart sinks so hard I'm pretty sure it's in my foot.

In my heart I'm screaming, *I do want to be with you!* That's the problem. I want him and I can't have him.

How do I tell him how I feel without actually telling him?

I rub my forehead with my fingertips, frustrated. I take a breath and say, "Grayson, my job is everything to me. *Everything*. I've worked really damn hard to get where I am today, and I'm still not where I want to be. I want to go further. I want to be state attorney someday. And I won't do anything that will risk that happening."

He leans down and picks his ball back up. Holding it between his large palms, he stares down at it while he says to me, "I get that, Mel. I do. I really wish I didn't, but I do understand." His eyes come back up to mine. "But I have to know. If things were different. If I wasn't up on this charge. And we were just who we are, and I kissed you—"

I cut him off. "If you weren't up on this charge then we wouldn't know each other. We don't exactly run in the same social circles."

"Stop evading and just answer the damn question."

My mouth goes dry. He knows the truth. He knows I'd be with him in a heartbeat. I don't know why he's forcing me to say it.

Saying it out loud will do neither of us any good. It'll just remind us of the reason we can't be together. So I choose not to say it. I choose to remind him of why we can't be together.

"I'm the assistant state attorney who's prosecuting you, Grayson. Outside of that, nothing else matters. 'What ifs' and 'maybes' are pointless. What matters is the here and now, and that means that what happened last night will never happen again."

Chapter 15

GRAYSON'S FACE DARKENS. Anger and frustration and sadness all flicker through his eyes. It's a hell of a combination to see. His jaw is clenched tight and the muscles in his face work angrily. "I don't accept that," he says, and throws the ball to the ground. Just like that, my face is in his hands, his body is pressed against mine, and he's kissing me all over again.

This time I don't stop him. I couldn't if I wanted to. My body is weak to him. He kisses me with a passion and intensity that I've never before known.

Breaking from my mouth, he presses his forehead to mine. "How can you be sorry for kissing me when it feels like this?" he asks, brushing his lips over mine. "I want you. You want me. We can make this work."

I open my eyes. "How? Because I can't see a way we can work."

"Take yourself off the case. If you're not the one prosecuting me, then there's no problem."

"I can't do that," I say, shaking my head. I have to see his case through. And if what I overheard earlier is true, then Ben, my boss, whom I once admired, might be trying to set Grayson up for a big fall for his own gain. Financial and political. And if I'm not there, I don't know who will stop him.

"I'm the assistant state attorney," I tell Grayson, pretending that's the only reason. "I don't get to pass off cases."

Exhaling, he brushes his lips over mine and says, "I want this with you."

I wrap my hand over his wrist. "I know." *I want this, too.* "I don't see—"

"Don't say it." He cuts me off with his lips. "Just...don't say it."

I murmur my assent, letting him kiss me softly.

When we break apart, I take a small step away, needing space to try to clear my muddled thoughts. Grayson catches my hand, like he's afraid I'm going to run away.

I let my eyes drift over the field.

"Have you been training all day?" I ask, trying to lead us away from this thing that's happening between the two of us.

"Yeah. I've been out here all day, practicing. I love being on the field. Having a ball in my hand."

I understand that feeling. Except I love being in court, putting the bad guys away.

Pulling his hand from mine, he picks the ball back up from the ground and throws it clear across the field.

"Wow. I can see why they pay you the big bucks. You have a hell of an arm on you."

"Football is the only thing I was ever good at. If I can't play anymore...then I don't know what I'll do," he says, and there's a sadness in his tone that pulls at my heart.

"So why risk it all and take drugs to the club that night?" The words are out before I can stop them.

He doesn't look at me. Doesn't say anything. Just stands there, motionless. And even though my question was valid, I feel like a bitch. A little part of me feels like I'm using him— but of course I know I'm not.

I want to know what he's hiding, because nothing about

him being caught with those drugs makes any sense to me. I want him to open up to me. Too bad the direct-attack tactic doesn't work with Grayson. I'm learning that very quickly.

I step up close behind him. "I could never throw a ball that far," I say softly. "I've watched you play in games and I don't know how you do that, get it all the way down the field with your accuracy."

"Years of practice. Hours spent on the field, in all weather." He picks up another football from the ground. "Here, I'll show you how to throw."

"Oh, I don't know." I take a step back. "I'll be terrible at it."

He chuckles low. The sound makes me smile. "You won't be terrible."

"I'll embarrass myself. I've never been good at sports."

"I'm going to teach you how to throw a football." He holds the ball out to me. No argument in his voice. It's a demand.

"Fine. But you'd better not laugh at me," I say, taking it from him.

"I won't laugh, I promise," he says as he comes to stand behind me. I'm aware of every inch of his nearness. My whole body is on alert. "Okay, so this is what you have to do to throw a perfect spiral."

"What's that?" I ask, glancing at him over my shoulder. He's a lot closer than I had realized. So close that I feel his breath on my cheek as he speaks.

"It's the type of pass the quarterback throws. The ball moves through the air, spinning like this," Grayson says, as he turns the ball in slow motion. "The whole game revolves around the perfect pass. This is it."

"Okay."

"So, hold the ball with a good, firm grip. Place the tips of your fingers on the laces. That's right," he says, guiding me.

"You need a little gap between your hand and the ball." He moves it into position.

My breath catches at his touch.

"Perfect," he says. "Now lift the ball high on your chest. That's right. Relax your shoulders and let your arms hang loose." He presses his hands down on my shoulders.

Having him touch me like this, while standing so close to me…it's torture.

The best kind of torture.

"Okay, now put your feet shoulder-width apart. Good, that's right." He praises me as I move my feet into position. "Now put seventy-five percent of your weight on the back foot."

"Seventy-five. That's very specific."

"I'm a specific kind of guy," he says, grinning.

I feel that grin like a soft caress between my thighs.

"Now," he says as his hands go to my hips, "as you move through your throw, shift your weight from the back of your foot to the front."

He rocks my body forward, demonstrating, and his hips press into my ass.

I feel something very significant prod me in the butt and I have to hold back a moan.

"You got that?"

"Mmm-hmm." I dare not speak because I'm afraid I'll say something I shouldn't.

He moves to my side. I almost sigh with relief. "Okay. Now," he says, "when you throw, you'll draw a circle with your elbow like this." He moves my arm, keeping his hand on my arm while he shows me. "Let the ball roll off each finger, starting with your pinky, so your wrist rotates. Your index finger should be the last thing to touch the ball as it leaves your hand. That's what generates the spin. Got it?"

"Got it," I say.

"Okay, so come back on your heels. That's it," he says, standing behind me. "Now, bring your weight forward, drawing that circle with your elbow, and then rotate your wrist as you throw."

The ball leaves my hand, going farther than I can normally make it go. It's even spinning, though it's a little bit wobbly. I admire my throw, but it's nowhere near as perfect as Grayson's was.

"I did it!" I shout as I turn to face him, beaming.

"You did good," he says. He reaches up and tucks a stray piece of my hair behind my ear. His fingers linger on my cheek.

I'm around 99 percent sure that he's going to kiss me again. And I really want him to. But then I hear the ringing of a phone.

Grayson lets out a frustrated sigh. He reaches into his pocket and pulls out his cell.

He frowns at the screen and then answers the call.

"Tyler... wait, what? Hold on. You're where? Jesus Christ, Tyler!" There's a sigh before Grayson says, "I'll be there in ten minutes. Yeah. Yeah. Just wait until I get there.

"Shit!" he curses, slamming his cell back in his pocket.

"What happened?" I ask, touching his arm to bring his attention to me.

"It was my brother, Tyler. He's been arrested," he says, meeting my eyes. "Drug possession."

Chapter 16

SUDDENLY THINGS START to make sense to me. I heard Grayson say those words and instantly knew, in no uncertain terms, that the man in front of me is in the position he's in because of his brother.

"I have to go to the police station," he says urgently, interrupting my thoughts. "I need to bail him out."

"That's not a good idea."

"Well, I can't just leave him there."

"I'm not saying you should leave him there. I'm just saying it's not a good idea for you—currently out on bail—to turn up at the police station to bail out your brother who has been arrested on a similar charge."

He steps back from me, thrusting his hands through his hair.

I want to tell him that I think I know what's been going on. That I know what he's been hiding from me. But I know that now isn't the time to confront him on that.

Later, I definitely will. Right now, I need to help him.

With a fire in my belly and adrenaline racing through my veins, I take my cell out of my bag and dial Ben's number. Grayson opens his mouth to speak. I hold my finger up and stop him.

Ben answers on the third ring. "Mel."

"Ben, I'm just going to get straight to the point here—I want off the Grayson Knight case."

"That's not possible."

"I won't prosecute a man who I believe to be innocent." My eyes meet Grayson's. I see the flare of surprise in them. There's something else in them, too, something that makes my stomach flutter and tighten.

Ben laughs. "Grayson Knight is definitely not innocent. And you will continue with his case. If you don't, you're fired."

"You don't have to fire me. I resign," I say, and hang the phone up before he can respond.

I'm staring down at my phone when Grayson's hands touch mine. "Mel."

"Did I just quit my job?"

"It sounded that way." His voice is gentle, his grip on my hand tightening.

"Holy shit." I breathe out.

I just quit my job.

My job.

I love my job, and I just quit it.

"Are you okay?" Grayson asks.

I stare at him blankly. "No…I'm not sure. I think…I can't believe I just did that," I say, shaking my head.

"Not to seem like an insensitive asshole, but I have to go bail my brother out of jail."

That snaps me back to the present. To one of the reasons that I called Ben in the first place. Then I say, "I'll go to the station and get your brother out."

"Mel…I can't ask you to do that."

"You're not asking. I just know that it's not a good idea for you to be going to the police station right now. Not when you've been arrested for a similar charge. And honestly, Grayson, I think I know what's going on here."

He frowns at me and says, "I don't know what you mean."

"I mean, you're a guy who has never even had so much as a parking ticket. You have everything to lose if you face prison time for supplying drugs. Now your brother, who was there on the night you were arrested, is also sitting in a jail cell because he's been arrested for drug possession. It doesn't take a genius to figure it out."

His expression tightens. "You can throw whatever you think you've uncovered out the window, because you're wrong."

"Grayson—"

"You're wrong," he says with determination. "Whatever theory you've conjured up is wrong. And I don't need you to go get Tyler. I'll go bail him out myself."

Grayson turns to leave, but I touch his arm, stopping him. "Please…I'm on your side here. I quit my job because I'm that far on your side. I know you're holding something back from me. You don't havè to tell me right now…but you should tell me, and soon. Now I'm going to help you by going to get your brother out of jail. Then maybe you'll believe that you can trust me."

He's staring at me like I've grown another head.

I step forward, closer to him. "Let me help."

"Okay." He softly breathes out the word. "Thank you… for everything." Then he leans close and presses a kiss to my cheek.

Chapter 17

I TAKE A CAB to the station. During the whole ride, my mind is working overtime. Why is Grayson taking the fall for his brother, who doesn't have as much to lose? Tyler doesn't have the media spotlight on him or the high-profile career that his brother has.

Sighing, I rest my head back against the seat. I really need to see Grayson's brother's rap sheet. If I can see that, then all my questions will probably be answered. I take my iPad out of my bag and log into the criminal database. I'm sure Ben hasn't gotten my access removed this quickly. I see that I'm right as my login works and I'm in straightaway.

I type in "Tyler Knight" and wait for the results to load.

My screen fills with enough information to tell me that everything I was thinking is correct.

Tyler Knight has a rap sheet dating back to juvy. But nothing as an adult.

From inside the system, I can see that he's been charged for small things like shoplifting, driving without a license, underage drinking, and criminal damage, but then for bigger things, like drug possession, as well. They were all things that Grayson could probably hide with his money. But if Tyler's caught with drugs as an adult, and with the intent to sell, then he'll be looking at serious jail time in an adult prison since he has a rap sheet like this.

But if his brother, the all-American football star, a guy who doesn't even have an unpaid parking ticket to his name, is found with the drugs on him, then we're looking at no jail time. A slap on the wrist, maybe a fine.

Until a crooked state attorney ups his charge to possession with intent to sell.

I call the station holding Tyler. It's the same one that had Grayson a few days ago.

"Hello, my name is Melissa St. James. I'm a…lawyer… and you're holding my client Tyler Knight."

So, he's my client now? Apparently so.

"Can you tell me if his bail has been set?" I ask.

"One second." I hear keys tapping on a keyboard. "Yes, bail has been set."

"I'll be there soon to pay it."

Chapter 18

MY LIFE HAS CHANGED a lot since I came here for Grayson's interview. I can't believe that was only a handful of days ago. I make my way inside, pushing open the door, and approach the desk. The officer on duty looks up at me. "Hi, I'm here to pay bail for Tyler Knight," I say.

"Sure thing."

"Can you tell me what he was charged with?"

The officer turns to the computer on the desk beside him, taps a few keys, and says, "He's charged with felony possession of the second degree. He was caught with a Schedule II drug with intent to sell." He glances back to me.

"How much is bail?"

The figure he tells me gives me pause. I mean, I am now unemployed. But I hand over my credit card and put up the money.

"He's in cell two at the moment," the officer tells me. "I'll call through and have him brought out to you."

I'm sitting on the waiting room seats, halfway through a game of Candy Crush, when Matt Daughtry comes out through the door. He takes the seat next to me and I put my phone back in my bag. "You're here bailing out Grayson Knight's brother?" he asks.

"Yes."

"Do I even want to know why the assistant state attorney is bailing out the brother of the man she's currently prosecuting?"

I meet his eyes and say, "I'm not an assistant state attorney anymore."

I see the shock reverberate through him. "Since when?"

"About an hour ago."

"Jesus, Mel. What happened?"

"It's…complicated. I don't really want to talk about it right now."

He blows out a breath, staring ahead. "When I was told his lawyer was out here bailing him out, I thought they'd made a mistake when I saw you sitting here. So I guess…you're his lawyer now?"

I sigh and say, "I guess so."

I hear him exhale again, but I can't meet his eyes.

"Look," he says, placing his hands on my shoulder. "Just…be careful. I know Grayson Knight is a big celebrity, but…be careful, okay?"

I nod.

Matt stands, abruptly changing the conversation. "I'm having Knight processed. He'll be brought out to you soon."

"Thank you, Matt."

"Since you're his lawyer, you should know that his arraignment is set for two days from now. I don't consider him a flight risk, but he'll still need to turn in his passport tomorrow."

I know the process, but I nod my head and thank him again.

"Mel," he says, stepping close and lowering his voice. "I don't know what the hell has happened…but I do know how much your job means to you. You need someone to talk to, call me. Okay?"

"Okay."

Matt disappears back through the door he came through.

Fifteen minutes later, a disheveled, younger-looking version of Grayson Knight comes through the door. Matt is leading him forward with a tight grip on his arm.

"Thanks," I say to Matt, getting to my feet.

Tyler looks at me and then back to Matt. "Who's she?" he asks, jerking his chin in my direction.

"She's your bail money and ride home," Matt says to him, definite contempt in his voice.

I take a few steps toward Tyler and say, "I'm Melissa St. James. Your brother asked me to come and get you."

Tyler stares at me. "Why didn't he come himself?"

I glance at Matt and then back to Tyler. "He wanted to, but…it's…difficult, with his…situation. So I offered to come."

"You got this, Mel?" Matt says, heading for the door. "I need to get back to it."

"Yeah, we'll be fine from here. Thanks again, Matt."

Matt pins Tyler with a stare. "Remember I want you back here first thing tomorrow to turn in your passport."

"Yeah, yeah. I got it."

Matt gives a frustrated look and shakes his head. "I'll see you later, Mel," he says to me. Then he disappears behind the door, leaving me alone with Tyler.

"Well, thanks for coming to get me out," Tyler says as he heads for the exit. "Tell Grayson I'll call him."

"Tell him yourself."

He stops at the exit and turns to face me.

"You'll be seeing him soon. I'm taking you to his place."

"And if I don't want to go?"

"I'm not giving you a choice. You don't come with me, I'm taking you right back in there to Sergeant Daughtry and telling him I'm rescinding bail."

"You can't do that."

"I can do anything I want," I say, and put my hands on my hips. "So what's it going to be?"

He tilts his head to the side. "You're not like Grayson's other girlfriends."

"That's because I'm not his girlfriend."

Though I'm not really sure what I am right now.

"Fine," Tyler says as he walks out the door. I follow quickly after him. He's waiting near the side of the road for me. "You got a car, then?" he asks.

"No. We'll catch a cab to Grayson's place," I say. Then I stick out a hand to an approaching cab. It pulls over.

Tyler opens the back door and waves me in first. "I do have some manners," he says after I give him a surprised look.

The driver pulls up outside Grayson's house ten minutes later. Tyler and I haven't really spoken during the ride over. I thought it would be best to wait until he and Grayson were together before I started questioning them.

I find Grayson in his living room, standing by the fireplace, a tumbler of whiskey in his hand. A flash of relief passes over his face when he sees Tyler. But then the relief is gone and anger settles in.

"What the hell were you thinking?"

"Nice to see you too, bro," Tyler says as he throws himself down onto one of the plush couches. "You know, you look just like dad, standing there by the fire, glass in hand, pissed-off look on your face. I feel like I've just gone back ten years in time."

"Screw you," Grayson snaps, putting the glass down on the mantelpiece. He pushes his hands into his pockets and steps closer to Tyler. "How could you do this? You promised me that it wouldn't happen again."

"I didn't exactly have a choice," Tyler snaps.

"What do you mean you didn't have a choice? There's always a choice," Grayson says.

"Maybe in your perfect world there is. But in my world"—Tyler gets to his feet—"there isn't."

"I don't know how to help you anymore," Grayson says, sounding lost and frustrated.

"I never asked you to help me in the first place," Tyler says quietly.

"You're my little brother…I couldn't just…" Grayson's words die out and his eyes come to me. It's as if he's remembering I'm still here.

Tyler turns to look at me, too.

"Don't stop on my account." I wave a hand toward Grayson. "I mean, I think I've pretty much figured it out myself, anyway. Tyler has a history of criminal offenses. The cops raid the club. He has a sizable amount of drugs on him. Enough to put him away for a long time.

"Grayson, you tell him to give the drugs to you, so if they get found, neither of you will go to prison, because your record is clean and you're a notable figure in entertainment. You'll probably get a slap on the wrist—at the worst a fine and be put on probation. Only when it comes to laws about drugs, you don't know that Tyler was carrying enough to up the charge to possession with intent to sell.

"Because that's what you were doing, right, Tyler? You were going to sell the coke. Grayson took the drugs from you, got caught with them, and now he's looking at possible jail time. And I'm taking it the people you work for were not happy you lost those drugs that were seized from Grayson. Were they looking for their money back? Maybe you were out tonight, selling to try to make the money back to pay them off. Am I on the right track here?"

Tyler opens his mouth, but Grayson holds up a hand, cutting him off.

Grayson turns to me, his expression weary. He moves over to me, puts his hands on my arms, and says, "Mel...I need to talk to my brother...alone. I appreciate everything you've done for me and Tyler. But just give me tonight with him to talk."

Even though his voice is gentle, I feel stung by his words.

He wants me to leave.

"Trust me," he adds.

I step out of his hold.

"Sure," I say, as if everything is fine.

Chapter 19

I'M AT HOME, making myself some lunch, when my cell rings. I don't recognize the number but decide to answer it. Maybe I'm hoping it'll be Grayson, calling me from a different line. I haven't heard anything from him since he asked me to leave his house last night.

"Hello?"

"Is this Melissa?"

"Depends who's asking."

"Tyler—Tyler Knight."

"Oh," I say, surprised.

He pauses for a moment before he speaks. "I was just calling because…I wanted to say thank you for bailing me out last night."

"It's fine."

"Not many people would do that. You must care about my brother a lot."

"I…" I only get one word out because I don't really know how to answer that.

"I'm sorry about last night, with Grayson asking you to leave. He does appreciate everything you've done."

"Okay."

"He just…he thinks he's protecting me."

That gets my attention. "Protecting you from what?"

There's a pause on the line. "Can we meet? I don't want to talk over the phone."

"Does Grayson know you're calling me?" I ask. I don't want to go behind his back on this…whatever it is that Tyler wants to talk about. But then, if it helps Grayson, maybe he should be left in the dark.

"No, he doesn't know I'm calling. But I need help and there's no one else I can ask."

"You can ask Grayson, too. Talk to both him and me. Don't you think that the three of us should approach this together?"

"No. I…look, I'm just gonna come out and say it. I'm in trouble and Grayson…well, he's in trouble, too. But the thing is, he doesn't know it. I really need your help, Melissa."

"Okay," I say.

"You'll meet me?"

"There's a coffee shop on Ninth. I'll meet you there in twenty minutes."

"Thank you, Melissa."

I grab my purse and head for the door, my stomach twisting in knots. It's not that I don't trust Tyler or think he's out to hurt me. But he's definitely involved in something with some dangerous people.

I make a ten-minute trek to the coffee shop. I've been to this place a few times before with Tori. They do the most amazing carrot cake. And I could really do with some cake right now.

When I get there, Tyler hasn't arrived, so I take a seat near the window and order a coffee and a slice of my favorite dessert. The waitress brings over my order as Tyler pushes open the door. He looks harried and a little nervous. His eyes are darting everywhere. I lift a hand to get his attention. He spots me and comes over.

"Something to eat or drink?" the waitress asks Tyler.

"Just a black coffee," he says.

"Is coffee a good idea?" I joke.

"What do you mean?" he asks as his gaze darts to mine. He takes his jacket off and hangs it on the back of the chair.

"You look on edge. Like you've already had a bucket of caffeine."

"I need something hot."

We sit in silence until his coffee arrives. "Thanks," he says to the waitress when she puts it down in front of him.

"You sure you don't want something to eat? The cake here is really great." I cut a piece off with the fork and put it in my mouth.

"No, thanks," he says.

"Okay, so we're here. What did you want to talk about?" I put my fork down and pick up my coffee, blowing on it before taking a sip.

"What you said last night, at Grayson's place…about the real possibility of him getting jail time for the drug possession? Was that true?"

I put my cup down and lean back in my seat, staring at him. "Yes. Grayson isn't a drug user. The police took a look at the regular tests that athletes take. Grayson has taken these tests for the past twelve months, and since he's always showed up as clean, a hundred percent of the time, the police know the drugs weren't for personal use. And the amount he was carrying…well, even without the clean testing, they have enough evidence to pin an intent to distribute charge to him."

"I didn't know," Tyler says as he shakes his head, putting his cup down and staring into it.

"Grayson is hanging by the skin of his teeth onto the life he's living, and that's only because the press hasn't gotten wind of his arrest yet. The moment they do, his endorsements will go. He might still be allowed to play until his case goes to trial. But if he's found guilty, the team will drop him. And it wouldn't matter anyway, because if he goes to jail on the felony possession of the second degree charge, he'll be too old to go back into the pros when he's out, even if a team agrees to take him after he's damaged his reputation this much."

"I didn't realize."

"You knew how many drugs he had on him, and you had to know the police wouldn't think it was for personal use."

"But I thought with him being who he is…they'd just let it go."

I let out a dry laugh. "Police and judges love to make examples out of famous names—sports celebrities especially. With my old boss on the case, there was no way Grayson was getting off clean from the moment they found the drugs on him."

"But he said—"

"It was Grayson's idea."

He stares me in the eye. Then breaks contact and blows out a breath. "He won't be happy I'm telling you this."

"He'll be less happy if he ends up living in a prison cell."

"That night I was out with Grayson. I had that stash on me. I wasn't actually selling yet. I would never do that around Grayson. But I was out and he called me—asked me to come meet him for a drink. So I went along for one. I was planning to leave and hit up some clubs after, sell the shit on me."

"But the cops showed up?"

He nods. "I panicked and told Grayson I was carrying. I

knew that if I got caught with the drugs, I was going down. Grayson told me to give them to him. That he wouldn't get searched because of who he is. I followed his orders. But then they searched him and carted him off." Tyler meets my stare and says, "I didn't mean for any of this to happen. And now I'm totally screwed. *We're* totally screwed."

"You're not screwed. All you have to do is tell the truth. I can help you."

"You don't understand," he says, picking up his coffee and taking a big drink of it. "It's gone further than that now." He meets my eyes again. "You were right about what you said last night, about my bosses...not being happy. Shit." Tyler covers his face with his hands.

"Calm down. Talk to me."

He drops his hands and stares at me. "I got involved with the wrong people. The drugs...they're cartel drugs. I've been dealing for the cartel."

"Holy shit." The words came out loud, so I adjust my voice down to a whisper. "You're working for the cartel?"

Tyler nods. "The drugs that were seized from Grayson were part of my second run for them. I was supposed to sell them and bring back the money. But then Grayson was arrested. I didn't want to ask him for the money to pay them on top of everything else. So, I...damnit. I stole some drugs from the stash, hoping they wouldn't notice, so I could sell those to pay them the money I owed them."

"You took drugs from the cartel and were planning to pay them back with that money you made off of stolen goods? What were you thinking?"

"Clearly I wasn't!" he snaps. "I panicked. And now those drugs are gone, too, and I don't have any money to pay them. And when I got home from Grayson's late last night...my place had been shot up. And there was a note pinned to my wall…a warning. They knew I'd been arrested. They're telling me to keep my mouth shut. I don't think they know about Grayson's arrest or the missing drugs yet, because if they did, then they wouldn't have shot up my place as a message. There would have been someone waiting there with a bullet for my head."

"I still can't believe that you're involved with the cartel," I say, putting my elbows on the table, driving my fingers into my hair. This feels way out of my league.

"What do I do, Melissa? How do I fix this?"

I lift my stare to Tyler. I can see how afraid he is when he says, "I don't want anything to happen to Grayson because of me."

"Let me think about it. I'll figure out what to do. But first I need to talk to your brother. He has to know what's been going on with you."

"No," he says.

"Yes. I have to tell him everything—about the cartel and what happened to you last night. I don't think it's a good idea if you're there when I tell him. I need to have Grayson thinking rationally, not trying to kill his little brother. Once I have him thinking straight, I'll bring him around to talk to you."

"What do I do while you do that?"

"Don't go back to your place. Just in case the cartel wises up and comes looking for you. Do you have anywhere to go that they don't know about?"

He shakes his head. "No."

I pull the keys to my apartment from my bag. "Go to my place. You'll be safe there." I give him my address. "Don't call or speak to anyone. I'll try to be as quick as I can with Grayson. Then I'll come home and we'll figure this out—the three of us. Don't worry."

I get up, hanging my bag on my shoulder.

As I walk past him, Tyler touches my shoulder. "Thanks— for everything."

"Don't thank me yet. Thank me when this is all over, when you and Grayson are safe."

Chapter 20

I ARRIVE AT the Bubble and have an easy time getting in to see Grayson. The security guy from last night is on reception today and he recognizes me and leads me straight through. I head out to the field, knowing that's where Grayson will be.

He's scrimmaging with his teammates, so I take a seat up in the stands. Watching him out on the field is really something special. He's magical out there. His teammates are great, but Grayson shines especially bright.

Once the scrimmage comes to an end, he sees me sitting up in the stands. I watch him move toward me, removing his helmet, so I start to make my way down the steps. "Hey," I say, stopping on the bottom rung.

"Hey," he says, holding his helmet in both his hands. He stares down at it. "I was going to call you."

"You were?"

"Yeah," he says, shifting the helmet into one hand and running the other hand through his wet hair. I know that he's just run around the field, but I can't stop imagining that I've made that hair sweaty in bed instead. "I was going to call you as soon as practice was over." He steps closer to me—so close I smell the sweat on him. It's a primal male scent and

I can't get enough of it. It does funny things to my stomach and makes my legs feel weak.

"I'm sorry," he says in a low voice. Reaching out, he wraps his large hand around my wrist, drawing my eyes to it. "I was totally out of it last night."

I lift my eyes from where we're joined and stare at him and say, "You don't need to always be at your peak performance with me, Grayson."

He lets out a soft laugh and says, "Using sports terminology now, are we, lawyer?"

I laugh, shaking my head. But then I take the humor out of my voice. "I'm serious. I want to be with you, and that means being with you when you're acting like yourself. All the time."

His hands move down from my wrist, and he takes hold of my hand.

My eyes fix on his.

"I'm still sorry."

"I know you are," I reply softly. Then I slide my fingers between his.

I see the surprise in his eyes and then watch them soften. He curls his fingers around mine, gripping them tightly. "Let me take you home," he says. And I know he means to use his time alone with me well.

"We need to talk."

"I know," he replies. "We can do that at my place."

"I do mean talk, Grayson. That isn't code for sex."

"Talk," he says, laughing. "I got it."

"Seriously. It's going to be about things you probably won't like and you have to promise not to throw me out of your house again."

His brows push together. "I won't ever do that again. That was a terrible idea, and I don't make the same mistake twice."

"I'm glad to hear it."

"Let me take a quick shower first. Then we can get out of here. I'll drive us back to my place."

For all the times I've fought it, I know that I want Grayson more than ever right now. More than I've wanted anything in my life.

And I'm tired of fighting it. Fighting him. So I settle on letting him take the lead so we can see where we end up. But I pray that I didn't just make a terrible decision.

Chapter 21

I STEP INTO Grayson's house, remembering my visit there yesterday. That was the first and only time I had been here. And it didn't go so well. I'm hoping this one turns out better.

"Can I get you something to drink?" Grayson says. He takes off his jacket and hangs it on the coatrack in the hallway.

I remove my own and hang it up, putting my bag away with it. "Water would be good," I say, and follow behind him, my heels clicking on the wooden floor. I really should have taken them off at the door.

"You don't want something stronger?"

I'm standing with my hand against the wall, reaching down to remove my shoes. When I look up, I see Grayson's eyes slide down my body to the foot I just freed from my heels. Something that smolders like lust ignites in his eyes. And it sets off a heat inside of me. Swallowing, I place my first shoe down and then quickly remove the other.

"Water's fine." I don't think alcohol would be a good idea around him, especially if one look is already setting me on fire. We have a big problem on our hands right now. And we have to address it first if we want Tyler to stay safe.

I head into the kitchen, where Grayson is already at the

fridge. He pulls out two bottles of water, walks over to me, and hands me one.

"You're a lot smaller without your heels," he says, a hint of something like humor or sex in his voice—or both, I think. Without my shoes, he's towering over me and the feeling is thrilling.

"I'm normal-sized," I say with a grin. "You're just weirdly tall." Then I make the mistake of meeting his eyes.

The air crackles between us with lust so thick it fogs up my vision. All I can see is him.

"I, er…" I stumble back a step. Seeing the breakfast bar, I move over to it and prop myself up on a stool. Feeling flushed, I unscrew the cap on my bottle and take a long pull of water.

Grayson moves around to the other side of the breakfast bar. He puts his unopened water down on the countertop and curls his hands around the marble edge. I put my water bottle down and keep my eyes on it as I slowly screw the cap back on.

I know he's staring at me, but I'm nervous to meet his eyes again. The more I look into his eyes, the more I get caught in their hold. It's easier for us to control ourselves when there are other people around, but when it's just me and him…it's impossible.

And my willpower is weakening by the second.

"So…" he says, voice low and decadent.

"I saw Tyler earlier," I say, cutting through the tension. We need to focus on his brother. "He called and asked me if I would meet with him, so I did."

The silence is palpable. I risk a glance at him.

Grayson's jaw is tight. But he doesn't look angry, he just looks closed off. It's a look I've seen on him before. "And what did he have to say?"

I squeeze the bottle tightly. "He told me the truth—that the drugs found on you were actually his."

Grayson doesn't move or speak. But I see his grip on the counter tighten, his knuckles whitening.

"Why didn't you tell me?" I ask, looking him in the eyes unafraid, because I know sex is the last thing on his mind right now.

"Because he's my brother." He says this like it's a given. Like there isn't anything he wouldn't do for him.

Emotion overwhelms me. I find myself wondering, again, what it'd be like to have someone who cares about you so deeply that they would literally do anything for you—put their own ass on the line, risk going to jail for you, potentially lose everything—just like Grayson is doing for his brother. I find myself envious of Tyler in this moment.

"And he told me that he's…" I bite my lip. I'm actually nervous to tell him this part.

"What?" he asks. His tone is impatient, as is the look on his face.

"He's involved with the cartel. That's where the drugs came from. He's working for them."

Grayson doesn't speak but his eyes say it all.

"This is serious, Grayson," I say, my voice nearly a whisper. "You could lose everything—seriously, *everything*."

"You think I don't know that? Damnit!" he says, pushing off the counter and stalking away from me to the other side of the room. He slumps down in a chair at the large glass kitchen table. He puts his elbows on his knees and his head in his hands.

I hesitate for a moment before I go to him. I slip off the stool and I move over toward him, my bare feet padding on the wood. He doesn't look up as I get close. He stays there with his head in his hands.

I lift a hand to touch him, then pause, hesitating once again. With my hand hovering in the air, it feels like I'm touching him. Like I'm making the decision to erase that line between us. I stare down at him, my heart beating wildly.

Then I press my hand to his head. His hair is much softer than I was expecting. I slide my fingers through it.

He lifts his head and his dark-green eyes meet mine.

"We can fix this," I whisper.

"How?" he asks, and for the first time, he sounds vulnerable. And that's what cuts me wide open. He's finally allowing me in.

"I know people who can help…all you have to do is tell the truth—you and Tyler."

He lifts a hand and wraps his fingers around my wrist. His eyes drift down from me.

There's a beat before he lifts them back to me. "Okay," he says softly. "Do what you need to do, and I'll talk to whoever you need me to talk to, just…Tyler…"

"I'll make sure he's safe," I say quietly. Our eyes are locked. My thumping heart skips, beating erratically. "You'll have to let George Simpson go so I can represent you and Tyler. I should, um, make some calls…" My hand is still on his head, his fingers still wrapped around my wrist.

"Yeah," he says. But neither of us moves or looks away. "Look, Mel. I can't tell you how much I appreciate what you're doing. My brother means the world to me and now you—you've quit your job, you're sticking your neck out…you're an amazing person."

Then he stands and my hand trails away from his head. But he doesn't let go of my arm as my eyes follow his body as it rises. Suddenly, we're face to face.

My mouth feels dry. I wet my lips with my tongue.

It's right then that I see it in his eyes, the exact moment

he makes the decision to consume me. He yanks me into his body, my chest heaving into his, and his mouth crashes directly onto mine, and he kisses me.

And, boy, does he kiss me.

Hands in my hair, tongue in my mouth, he kisses me. And it's hot as hell. My hands are gripping his huge arms for support and my legs feel like they're going out from under me.

God, the man can kiss.

He's kissing me like it's the only thing he needs—like I'm all he needs. There's no aphrodisiac like it. He presses into my hip and the feeling of how much I turn him on does all kinds of crazy things to me. I slide my hands up his arms and wind them around his neck. He makes a deep sound of pleasure into my mouth. It ripples through me, hardening my already erect nipples and teasing my clit like a featherlight touch of his fingers.

His hands leave my hair and slide down my back, grabbing my ass through my pencil skirt. His mouth leaves mine, and the sensation leaves me panting, and then he kisses down my neck, his teeth grazing my skin and making me shiver. "I want you so bad," he rasps against my skin.

I'm sure I mumble something incoherent back. All rational thought has left my mind and I'm a mess of hormones. But more than that—I'm his completely. In this moment, he can do whatever he wishes to me.

His fingers find the hem of my skirt and pull it up, over my hips. Then his hands are back on my ass and he's lifting me, then placing me down on the table.

He stares down into my eyes as his large hands cup my face. "I've never wanted anyone the way I want you, Mel. You make me crazy—seriously, it's unbelievable how it feels so good and so right when I'm with you. I can't even sleep because I'm always thinking about you."

"I…" I swallow. "I feel the same—and…I want you. I want you, too." As I speak, I'm pretty sure my face is the color of a tomato because for some reason, I can barely get the words out. I might be falling for him.

His lips break into a smile that could dissolve the panties I'm wearing and his eyes darken with lust. Then his mouth crashes back down on mine, kissing me, taking greedy pulls on my tongue as he sucks it into his mouth.

Jesus, that feels good—amazing. He feels amazing. And I need more of him. All of him. Reaching my hands down, I fumble for the button on his jeans. I pop it, then slide the zipper down and slip my hand inside. I barely get my fingers inside his pants when he catches hold of my wrist, stopping me.

I blink up at him in surprise.

He lowers his forehead to mine, his breath gusting over my mouth as he speaks. "I want to make love to you in my bed. But if you touch me here, it's game over, Mel. I will take you right on this table."

Sweet baby Jesus.

"Maybe I want you to give it to me on the table," I say, hardly sounding like myself at all. I sound kind of…husky and sexy.

"Christ," he breathes, and I take it as an invitation. I slide my hand inside his jeans, and he doesn't stop me. My fingertips make contact with skin. The fact that he isn't wearing boxer shorts sends me over the edge.

Holy God.

I curl my fingers around his cock, gripping him.

"Shit," he hisses. His hand comes down so he can shove his jeans down to the floor. He wraps his big hand around mine and moves my hand up and down, so we're both driving him wild. And, damn, it's hot.

"That's it, harder—grip me harder."

I tighten my grip, giving him what he needs. His hand leaves mine, and I keep working him up and down. He wraps my hair around his hand, and then takes my mouth in a hot kiss.

The hottest, wettest, dirtiest kiss I have ever experienced in my life. The kind of kiss that could make a girl come. And honestly, with his tongue in my mouth and his cock in my hand, I feel like I could at any second.

His hand drops from my hair and pulls my silk shirt out from the confines of my skirt, kissing me all the while. He unfastens a couple of the buttons, and after he breaks away from my mouth, he pulls the shirt over my head.

His eyes drop to my breasts, which are still covered by my white, lacy La Perla bra.

Moving back from him, I take my hand out of his pants. I reach back and unfasten the clasp on my bra. Sliding the straps down my arms, I drop it on the table.

When I look back to Grayson, his eyes are on fire.

His large hands come up and cup my breasts, and he brushes his thumbs over my nipples, making me shiver. His lips lift at the corner and he bites down on that smile. Then he lowers his head, taking one of my nipples in his mouth. He swirls his tongue around and in less than a moment, I'm squirming. His mouth feels exquisite.

"God, Grayson," I pant. I'm burning up, desperate for his touch. I push my hips forward, needing contact… needing him.

He must have read my body language, because he drops to his knees before me. With his hands curling into my skirt, he tugs it off me. I lift my hips. Skirt gone, he yanks my panties down, tosses them over his shoulder, pushes my thighs apart, and puts his mouth on me.

"Oh, my God!" My head drops and my hands press to the table as they try to grip the flat surface. "Grayson!" I cry.

There, on Grayson's kitchen table, I have my first orgasm from him. *God, don't let it be the last.* It explodes out of me in a toe-curling, mind-blowing release. I'm still trembling when he gets to his feet.

"Do you know how hot you are?" His voice is a rasp, exuding pure sex. I feel it shiver through me.

"I know how hot you make me," I whisper.

His eyes flare with need. Then, his hand goes down and wraps around his impossibly hard cock. "You make me crazy," he says, sliding his hand up and then down slowly. My eyes are fixed on his hand, riveted. "I'm going to show you exactly how crazy you make me."

He reaches his other hand into his back pocket and pulls out his wallet while he keeps working his hand up and down his shaft. He flips his wallet open and pulls out a condom. After he rips open the packet with his teeth, he slowly rolls the condom on.

When his cock is sheathed, his eyes lift back to mine.

I tremble from the look in them.

He moves in between my legs and takes my face in his hands, kissing me deeply. His tongue slides over mine in a mind-blowing, drugging kiss. He breaks away from my lips, his eyes burning into mine, and drops his hands from my face to grab my hips.

He pulls me forward so my ass is perched on the edge of the table, and he slowly pushes himself inside me.

The feel of him sliding inside me so deep is like nothing I've ever felt before. And the look in his eyes…I feel like he's staring right into the very heart of me. The parts of me that I keep hidden from everyone else.

I feel exposed, vulnerable, but also…safe.

While he's inside me with his hips pressed against mine, his hands come back up to my face. Cupping it, he kisses me again. Gently this time.

He starts to move, slowly at first. I moan into his mouth, and that's when his control seems to snap. Our tempo instantly picks up. He's driving into me and the feeling is beyond incredible.

Grayson starts moving with an animalistic need. My hands are on his back, nails digging into his skin. The only sound is the rasp of our heavy breaths. No words are needed because our bodies are saying everything.

And mine is saying a lot. The second orgasm hits me and I'm crying out Grayson's name, my nails digging deeper into his back. My orgasm seems to set him off, because he yells out a string of expletives, my name mixed in among them, as he comes right after me.

With his forehead pressed against mine, he closes his eyes and his breath comes out labored.

"Jesus," he says. "That was amazing. You're amazing."

I slide my hands down his back. "I didn't do a lot. It was all you."

"But you're what I needed—all I need, Mel—it's you."

Then he brushes his lips over mine, kissing me softly. He pulls out of me carefully and takes the condom off. I can't keep the smile from my lips, because this gorgeous man…the hottest man I've ever met…he just told me that the only thing he needs is me.

"You're smiling," he says as he reaches me, moving back between my legs. He slides his hands around my waist.

"I am."

"I like when you smile."

Then he lifts me, and instinctively I wrap my legs around

his waist and my arms around his neck. He starts walking through the kitchen.

"Where are we going?" I ask.

His smiling eyes meet mine. "To my bed, so I can make you smile some more."

Chapter 22

IT'S DARK OUT and Grayson has fallen asleep beside me. I take a moment to look at him. He looks relaxed and at peace. It's a look I've never seen on him before. Something pulls at my heart. I knew I had feelings for the man, but in this moment, I realize how strong those feelings are and have the potential to be.

But I have a lot to do—a man's life is on the line—so I quickly slip out of bed. After the week that Grayson's had, I know that he needs his sleep, so I move carefully. I don't want to wake him. More than anything, I want to stay here with him, but I need to go. I need to help him fix this mess that Tyler has gotten them into.

I look down at Grayson, tempted to kiss him before I leave, but I resist. I tiptoe out of his bedroom and downstairs to retrieve my clothes. After I grab my cell from my bag, I go into the downstairs bathroom. I fire off a text to Tyler telling him that everything is okay and that he should stay put at my place. I have a few things to do and then I'll be home.

My phone beeps with Tyler's reply immediately: Cool. I've eaten the entire contents of your fridge—hope that was okay? ☺

Chuckling, I reply: No problem. I'll be in touch soon.

I climb into a cab and give the driver my address. I stare out of the window at Grayson's house as the cab pulls away. I can still smell him all over me. The scent of him sends memories from the night screaming through my brain. My body shivers from those thoughts and then aches to be back with that man.

Closing my eyes, I breathe through the moment. Then, I turn on my work brain and fish my cell out of my bag. It's late, but I'm sure the person I need to call will be awake. I search through my contacts until I find his number. I press Call and put the phone to my ear.

"Mel?"

"Hey, Matt," I say carefully, noting the surprise in his voice. I can't say I blame him for it, since I haven't called him in a long time.

"Are you okay?" he asks with genuine concern in his voice. It makes me feel like a jerk for all the times I've been standoffish to him and for using him now. But, like I said, a man's life is on the line.

"I'm fine…but I need your help."

"I'm looking over some reports at the coffee shop near my place, the one we always used to go to."

"I'll be there in five minutes," I say, and end the call. Then I ask the driver to take me to the new location.

Five minutes later, I'm walking into the shop. The scent of coffee sends my nerves into overdrive as soon as I push the door open. It feels weird to be here with Matt, but I push that aside, because I know I'm here for Grayson. He and Tyler need help, and Matt will be the one to provide it. He might be a pain in the ass at times, but he's a damn good cop.

I order my coffee and head to his table.

"Hey," I say, hanging my bag on the back of my chair.

"Just like old times, being here with you," he says with a smile, tipping his mug at me.

I don't chastise him for the comment, even though he knows better than to act like that's the reason I'm here. I don't want to get into a battle with him, especially since it's best if I stay on his good side right now.

"So, what can I do for you?"

I glance around and my eyes catch on a guy sitting over by the back, who's glued to his cell phone. I'm going to have to take my chances.

The barista brings the coffee over. I wait for her to leave before I start talking in a low voice. I tell Matt everything about Grayson's situation from start to finish—how he covered for his brother by holding the drugs, where those drugs came from, how Tyler was threatened by the cartel.

Matt doesn't say anything the whole time. He sits there and listens to me talk, taking it all in. When I'm done, I sit there staring at him, waiting for him to say something.

"Well, that's an absolute mess, Mel."

After everything I've just told him, that's what he says. And he is right. It's a huge disaster.

"I know, and that's why I need your help—Grayson and Tyler need your help. We're talking about the cartel here, Matt. The minute they find out those drugs are missing... Tyler's as good as dead. And Grayson..." I trail off, because I can't bring myself to say the words.

Matt blows out a breath. It's a resigned sound and I'm not sure what it means. "I have a contact in the DEA," he tells me. "I can call him, see what we can do to get them out of the mess they've got themselves in." He reaches for his cell, and

I reach over and put my hand on his arm. He pauses, his eyes meeting mine.

"Thank you, Matt," I say earnestly. I move my hand away and into my lap.

"You don't have to thank me, Mel. You need help, and I'm there."

Chapter 23

IT'S LATE AFTERNOON and I'm heading back to my apartment. I spent most of the day with Matt at the police station, meeting his DEA contact, Paulo Dresden. We were mapping out a deal with him. Dresden is a short guy with a receding hairline who smells heavily of smoke and drinks way more coffee than I knew any one person could. He seems like a good guy and Matt trusts him. They went to the academy together.

Most importantly, Dresden has pulled together a good deal for Tyler—well, as good a deal as a person can get in these circumstances. Things won't be easy for him, since the DEA is proposing a plan that will turn his life upside down—he'll have to get a new identity and move into the Witness Protection Program.

Everything rests on Tyler agreeing to do this, and I would like to think that's a possibility, especially if he feels the same way about his brother as Grayson feels about him. I would hope he'd also do anything to keep him safe.

I walk toward my door, a little apprehensive about seeing the guys. Grayson joined Tyler at my place after I called to tell him it'd take me a while to sort things out at the police station. I'm sure they're going a little stir-crazy. They've been hunkered down all day.

My stomach flips at the thought of seeing Grayson. Grayson, who drove me wild last night. I force deep, steadying breaths to calm myself.

He's just a man. One you've spent half the night getting hot and sweaty with, but still just a man.

I open the door and let myself in. My eyes connect with Grayson's instantly. Seeing someone for the first time after you've had sex with him is always nerve-racking, but I didn't expect to feel the way I do looking at Grayson right now. Like my whole world is centered around this one man.

But suddenly my world gets flipped again. There's nothing in Grayson's face or eyes. They're emotionless and cold. And I don't know if he's angry with me for leaving before he woke or just indifferent about what happened between us last night.

My heart sinks. Grayson said a lot of things last night— telling me how much he wanted me—but men generally say those kinds of things when they've got their cock deep inside you. It doesn't necessarily mean they want you forever.

I force a polite smile and gesture for them both to sit in the plushy couch in my living room. "Thanks for your patience," I say, dropping into a chair across from them. I look at Tyler as I speak because it just seems easier to do. Looking at Grayson right now would be like staring at the sun—it'd blind me. I can smell his cologne, teasing and taunting me. I take a breath and decide to just go straight into it. "I spent the last fourteen hours or so with Sergeant Daughtry—"

"The cop who arrested me?" Grayson demands. His words force me to look at him, and when I do, I swear to God I see jealousy burning in his eyes.

Why would he be jealous? Grayson isn't looking at me like he cares about me. And he doesn't know Matt is my ex, anyway…does he?

"Yes. I went to Sergeant Daughtry—Matt—because I trust him—"

Grayson snorts.

I ignore him and focus on Tyler, who is giving Grayson the side-eye. "I told Matt everything both of you told me. I thought it'd be easier to work with Matt on this, since he was the arresting officer in both of your cases. There's no reason to bring a third party in. Also, Matt has a contact in the DEA named Paulo Dresden. He called Dresden, brought him in, and the three of us hashed out a deal for you, Tyler."

"What's the deal?" Grayson asks.

I look at him. His expression is still blank.

"The deal is that both of you make a statement that says that Grayson had nothing to do with the drugs the police found on him that night in Liv. You tell them the only thing Grayson did was hide them for you, Tyler. Even though the police found the drugs on Grayson, Matt is willing to let the charge drop so long as"—I focus on Tyler, because this affects him the most—"you give up names of the main players in the cartel who you work for, and you testify against them—"

"No," Grayson says, cutting me off.

"Gray…" Tyler says his name in a gentle warning.

"No, Ty. You take this deal, you know what that means? If you testify in a trial, your life will be in danger. You—"

"It's already in danger," Tyler cuts him off. "The second I got involved with these people I was putting my life on the line. I got involved and now I have to face the consequences by myself. I can't let my big brother face them for me." Tyler turns to me and says, "I'll be protected, right? By the DEA?"

"Yes. Full protection. Then…" I bite my lip, pausing, because I can guess how Grayson will react to this piece of information. "After the trial, you'll go into witness protection and be given a new identity."

"Hell, no," Grayson says, getting off the couch. "Tyler, you're not going into witness protection. If you go, I'll never see you again."

Tyler gets to his feet, turning to Grayson. "I have to do this. There's no other choice."

"I'll take the rap on the drug charge," Grayson says, turning to me. I can see the panic in his eyes. "I'll go to jail. Call Daughtry, tell him that's the way it'll be."

"No," Tyler says in a firm voice. "I'm not letting you mess up your life for me. I should have never let you take those drugs from me in the first place. This is on me. I screwed up. You have a life and a great career—I saw how hard you worked, all your life, to get into the NFL. And now you have Mel. I won't have you lose that because of me."

He puts his hands on Grayson's upper arms, looking him in the face. His voice drops lower and turns more serious. "Even if I was selfish enough to let you do that, it won't make any difference anyway, Gray. The cartel knows I was arrested—they left me my first warning when they came to my apartment. Once they realize that there are charges against you that match mine and that I stole those drugs from their stash, they'll put everything together and I'll be as good as dead. You too, man. I won't let that happen."

Tyler swivels his head toward me and says, "This offer from the DEA is the best chance I have. Right?"

I see fear in his eyes and a desperate need for support, so I give it to him. I push up to my feet and say, "He's right, Grayson."

Grayson looks at me and I see the moment he accepts the plan. Hurt fills his eyes and defeat slumps his shoulders. He pulls his eyes from me and back to Tyler. He takes Tyler's face in his hands, looking him in the eye. "I'll be there for you the whole way. I won't let you down."

"I know, Gray. I know. You never have."

Then Grayson wraps his arms around his younger brother, and I turn away to look out the window and give them their moment. It also gives me the chance to discreetly wipe away the tear that decided to show up and escape from my eye.

I hear Tyler clear his throat. Then he says, "So what now?"

I turn back to the brothers. "Now we go see Matt Daughtry."

Chapter 24

THE THREE OF US go to the police station. Grayson and I go in first, so he can give Matt his statement about what happened the night he was arrested. Next, it's Tyler's turn to give his statement. Then Matt brings Grayson back in and tells him that the charges against him are officially dropped.

I've got to say, even though I knew it was coming, it's still a relief to hear. Matt tells Tyler that he should expect a call from Paulo Dresden within the hour, since the DEA agent will now be in charge of Tyler's case.

Since Tyler is advised not to go back to his apartment, we decide that he'll go to a safe house until the DEA gets in touch regarding the next step. That's when they'll collect the names of the key cartel players that they need, and then they can start making plans for their arrest.

Even though the cartel doesn't know that Tyler is talking to the police or the DEA, there's still a distinct possibility that they could find out about the missing drugs. Tyler's apartment is definitely a dangerous place for him to be right now.

Matt walks us all out. Tyler is up ahead, Grayson is glued to my side, and Matt is on my other side, at a slight distance from me. I'm starting to get the distinct impression that Grayson knows that Matt and I have a history.

Grayson's been off whenever he deals with Matt. I mean, I know the guy arrested Grayson once, but Matt has helped him today—and he's helped his brother. Grayson should be grateful for that. But his snide comments and attitude haven't shown that. When he made a crack about my "best friend Matt" to me, I cottoned on to the reason for his problem with the guy.

He was definitely jealous.

Superstar Grayson Knight was jealous of Matt Daughtry. All because of me.

I won't deny that I got a little thrill from knowing that the green-eyed monster was at work on Grayson. Some things just make a woman happy.

But Grayson's jealousy confuses me, because he's been so incommunicative ever since last night. Not that I've rushed to talk about things either, but I think that I've been cordial. It's strange that this morning and around Matt…well, I'm half-expecting Grayson to pee on me, so he can mark his territory.

I guess Grayson and I do need to talk about what happened between us. I'm worried about what last night was for him.…What if he was just chasing the unobtainable? Maybe I was something forbidden to him. Something he couldn't have. Now he's had that something—*me*—maybe the thrill has worn off and he's just not interested anymore.

Maybe the jealousy thing with Matt is more about male pride than anything else.

I guess the only way I'll know is if I talk to Grayson about it. Have a proper conversation with him. And I will talk to Grayson, once we've got Tyler settled at the safe house.

"Thank you for all of your help, Matt," I say, offering a smile and also my hand. Even though shaking Matt's hand seems too formal after everything he's done, I don't think hugging him would be the best idea with Grayson standing right beside me like some sort of animalistic predator. Who knows what he would do.

Matt stares down at my hand in his. A chuckle escapes him as he shakes his head. "Anytime, Mel. I told you earlier: You need help, you call me first."

"I know. Thanks again."

Matt is still holding my hand, even though he's stopped shaking it.

Grayson clears his throat. I take that as my cue to move. I ease my hand from Matt's, giving him one last smile of thanks before I leave. I walk through the door that Tyler is holding open. Grayson is on my heel, his hand possessively on my lower back.

His touch surprises me. It's the first time he's touched me since last night. The skin that his hand presses against feels like it's on fire. Even though there are layers of clothing between his hand and my back, I can still feel the heat of his fingertips.

I lift my eyes to him. The look in his face is heated with anger and lust. The combination is one hell of a sight, and my needs flare to life. My need for him.

I break eye contact so I can breathe. This isn't a moment we need to be having now. But it's one we need to have soon, if my libido has any say.

We've just hit the sidewalk when suddenly I hear the screech of tires. I look up and see a car moving down the street toward us. Panic stiffens my spine.

The car is a black Escalade with full blacked-out windows and no license plate. I feel completely paralyzed as I watch it. Those windows lower, almost as if in slow motion. I see the guns poke out from behind them.

Matt yells something.

Tyler turns and yells, "Get down!" His words hit my ears, but it sounds like I'm hearing them underwater.

Everything seems to slow right down, almost to a stop. I'm frozen and the guns are pointed in my direction.

I'm going to die.

Out of nowhere, someone grabs me and throws me to the ground. A large body lands on top of me, covering me, just as the earsplitting shots are fired.

All I can hear is the sound of screams and bullets spraying everywhere.

My eyes are closed and my heart thunders in my chest. I have never felt fear like this in my life. It seems like the gunshots go on forever.

The deafening noise stops as quickly as it started. My breath is caught in my throat and I'm afraid that a second spray is going to be aimed at us. But then I hear the distinct sound of tires screeching away.

They've gone.

I almost cry in relief.

There's only silence for a long second, as if someone has hit pause on the world around me.

Then the yelling begins as everything instantly comes back to life. Grayson's voice is loud and clear as he speaks to me. He keeps it surprisingly calm as he says, "I got you, baby. Are you okay?" He doesn't move his body off mine.

"Y-yeah, I'm fine," I say, my voice trembling. "They didn't"—I mentally check my body for pain, but there's nothing—"I'm okay. Are you—?"

"They didn't get me. I'm fine."

"Thank God." I breathe a sigh of relief. I couldn't bear it if anything had happened to him.

Grayson lifts himself up slightly but doesn't move off me completely. It's almost like he's afraid to leave me.

"Tyler?" I ask, my voice still trembling.

"He's fine."

I follow his line of sight to see Tyler sitting on the ground, looking completely shocked but physically okay. Matt is with him, and seems uninjured. He's checking over Tyler.

I shift, turning my face so I can look at Grayson. He looks fine, calm, but I see the fear and disbelief in his eyes. And I know how he feels, because I'm right there with him. I've realized, in this moment, how much he's come to mean to me. I knew I cared for him. Now I know how much.

Grayson's looking deeply into my eyes.

There's this moment where something intimate passes between us. He cups my cheek in his hand. "Mel, I—"

But he doesn't get to finish whatever he was going to say. Police officers come swarming out of the building, ready to help. The wail of an ambulance gets louder until the vehicle pulls up close to us, and paramedics jump out to check over our injuries. Whatever Grayson was going to say to me gets lost in the mire.

Chapter 25

THE CASE STARTED to move faster once the cartel tried to take Tyler out. A shooting in front of civilians at a police station is a much more serious crime than some warning shots fired in an empty home. I sat with Tyler and the DEA agents while he gave his statement to them. Then I checked over the written report with him before he signed.

Grayson was on the phone with his father in another room. I didn't want to bother him, so I waved good-bye and left. I needed to be home to take a moment to collect my thoughts in the safety of my apartment. I wanted to take a hot shower and wash the day off me. Then I had plans to curl up on my sofa and drink a large glass of wine.

Besides, I thought that Grayson would want to be with Tyler right now. Someone tried to kill his brother today, and I know how important Tyler is to him. Talking to me about what happened between us last night is probably the last thing Grayson wants to do right now.

I was shot at today.

It feels surreal. I can't even think about what would have happened if Tyler and Grayson hadn't reacted as quickly as they did. Especially Grayson…when he threw me to the ground and put himself on top of me like that…he saved my life. And I haven't even thanked him for it.

Suddenly, there's a knock at my front door. I freeze with my wineglass halfway to my lips. I carefully put it down on the coffee table and get to my feet. I secure the belt on my robe since I'm naked underneath. Taking a deep breath, I tuck my damp hair behind my ears and quietly pad across the wooden floors in my apartment.

I've just made it to the hall when there's another knock.

"Mel, it's Grayson."

My heart sputters to a stop.

He's here.

Moving quickly, I reach the front door, and after checking the peephole, I throw it open. His eyes lift to mine. He looks tired and his hair is messy, like he's been running his hands through it. But he looks hot. So very hot.

"What are you doing here?" I say, and I don't mean it to sound as harsh as it does, but it comes out that way because I'm surprised.

"I needed to see you. And I wanted to make sure that you were okay."

"I'm fine."

His gaze drops, and I realize that the belt on my robe has loosened a little when I rushed over, exposing my cleavage to him. Green eyes lift back to mine, causing shivers to break out all over my body.

The next thing I know, he's stormed through the door and slammed it behind him. Then I'm in his arms and his mouth is on mine.

"Grayson!" I gasp.

He swallows up his name with a kiss. Then he backs me up against the wall. His hands go to my thighs and he lifts me, putting himself between my legs. I wrap them around his waist and start kissing him back.

We're all tongues, teeth, and deep moans. There's nothing finessed about this kiss. This is happening out of pure need. Grayson's hand goes to his jeans. I hear his zipper pull down, and a condom package tear open. He stops kissing me. Lips still pressed to mine, he stares into my eyes, a question in them.

"Yes," I say, more a breath than a word.

In one movement, he thrusts his bare cock up inside me.

"Oh, my God!" I cry.

He starts making love to me there, against my hallway wall, while he's still fully dressed and I'm wearing only my robe. The feel of him inside me…it's amazing.

He starts to move, his pelvis hitting my clit each time he hits home, driving me wild.

"You saved my life," I pant between thrusts.

He pauses, staring into my eyes. "I did what anyone would have done."

"No," I say. "Not everyone would risk their own life to protect me."

"I would never let you get hurt, Mel. Never," he tells me, and I know he means it.

"Thank you," I whisper, brushing my lips over his. "Thank you so much."

Grayson captures my mouth again in a hot kiss, sucking my tongue into his mouth and making me moan. Then he starts moving again, driving into me harder with each thrust, making me crazy with desire.

My orgasm is quick, hitting me with a powerful force, and I scream out his name. He thrusts up inside me, once, twice, and then I feel him start to climax. He groans my name as he comes undone. We stay there, panting, trying to catch our breath. Grayson's face is pressed into my neck, his mouth soothing hot on my skin. My arms are wrapped tightly around him.

"I want you," he says softly. His lips brush over the skin of my neck as he speaks. He lifts his head and stares into my eyes. "Not just this—sex—but *you*."

"I want you, too," I say breathlessly.

"No—that's not what I'm trying to say. You told me that I should always be myself around you, that you want to be with every part of me. And that's what I want. I want more. I want something good and real with you, Mel. When I woke up this morning and you were gone, I...felt empty. And I've never felt that before. Then I realized the emptiness was there because you weren't." He cups my face with his big hand, threading his fingers into my hair. "I don't want to wake up like I did this morning, wondering where you are."

"I didn't want to leave like that either, but I had to help—"

"I know. And I'm thankful that you helped my brother. But now this is about you and me. And I like you."

"I like you, too. A lot. A whole lot," I say with a smile, and it reflects in his eyes as they light up.

"So, we're doing this—you and me?" he asks softly.

"A...relationship?"

"Yeah, Mel, I mean a relationship." He grins. "You and me together. I want you to be my girlfriend. And I'm not just saying that because I'm still inside you."

My smile widens as I giggle. "Oh, well, I'm glad to hear it. But—"

"But what?" he says, frowning.

"Well, we haven't even been on a date, Grayson—unless you count trips to the police station and getting shot at on the street corner as dates."

"Sounds like I better take you on a real one tomorrow,

then. First thing in the morning, let's go out to breakfast. That can be date number one. Then lunch for date number two. Then dinner—"

"I get it," I say, laughing. "But how about right now, you take me to bed and screw me until it's time to take me out."

Smiling, he moves off the wall, carrying me with him as he starts walking down the hall. He presses a soft kiss to my lips, then whispers over them, "Take my girlfriend to bed and screw her all night? Yeah, I can definitely do that."

Epilogue

Six months later…

I HEAR A KNOCK at my office door, and then Grayson's beautiful head pops over the threshold. "You ready to go, babe?"

"Yeah," I say, and smile at him. "Let me just finish this article—it's about my case."

"It's in the news already?"

"Yup. I'm so glad that the world is seeing the great Benedict Cross, State Attorney, for the scum he really is."

And all because of me. After the DEA had set the wheels in motion for Tyler, I approached Internal Affairs to report Ben. I couldn't sit with what I had heard him saying on the phone and what he had been trying to do to Grayson. What if he was going to target other arrested athletes in the same way?

As it turned out, Internal Affairs had been looking into claims about an illegal gambling ring, packed with tons of high-powered people, but they'd never had anything concrete to go on before. I worked with them to help bring it down, and Ben is no longer the state attorney. He's facing charges.

Grayson, Tori, and Matt suggested I run for his position, but I didn't want to. Instead, I've been busy setting up my own practice. After I'd met Grayson, I realized that I had my career goals set in the wrong place. Now I want something different. I don't want to be a big fish in a sea of sharks who are more worried about politics and publicity than justice. I want to be a big fish in my own little pond, helping out the little guys who wouldn't get help anywhere else. I'm happier than I have ever been.

Working on the other side as a defense attorney took a little getting used to, but it helps that I have the luxury of only defending clients I truly believe to be innocent. And Grayson has been such a huge help and support throughout the process. It was scary setting up my practice and going out there on my own, but slowly, my business is starting to build. Since my first case assisting Internal Affairs was such a big win, I'm hoping word of mouth will help me pull in a decent client base.

"I just got off the phone with Tyler," Grayson says as he walks into the room and leans against the wall.

"Oh, yeah?" I ask. After Tyler had left, Grayson told me that he had slipped him a phone so he could call him. They were breaking the rules about witness protection, but I didn't say anything about it. My boyfriend can't let his brother go completely, and I understand that.

"How's he doing?"

"Really well. He has a job and he's dating someone."

"That's awesome," I say, and I mean it. Those weekly check-in calls from Tyler are everything to Grayson. He doesn't know where Tyler is living, but that's for the best. I don't want anyone going after Grayson, and the cartel would if they thought he had information on his brother.

The trial itself was hard on everyone, but thankfully, some dangerous people were put in prison for a long time due to Tyler's testimony. He managed to make it through that stressful period without any more attempts made on his life. We had minimal contact with him in the run-up to the trial, and when it was over, Tyler went into witness protection right away. The whole thing has been very hard on Grayson.

I look up at him waiting for me. His smile lights up his face, giving me butterflies in my stomach.

God, he's so gorgeous.

Sometimes I still can't believe I'm dating *the* Grayson Knight. I never was one for the jocks in high school. But I didn't know what I was missing out on back then. Serious stamina and lots of muscle, and in this case, a beautiful heart and mind.

"Ready to go?" I ask him. And for the first time, I notice that he's being awfully quiet. Maybe a little jittery. "You wanted to grab dinner out, right?" I ask him.

"Sure. But first…" He pushes his hand into his pocket and pulls out a key.

"What's this?" I ask.

"A key to my place."

A smile breaks out on my face. "You're giving me a key to your place?"

"I am."

My smile gets wider. Walking over to him, I curl my hand around the key, taking it from him. "Wow. This feels like a big step. A great step, though. Thank you so much. Do you want a key to my place?"

"No," he says.

My smile drops. "No?"

He takes my hands in his. "I don't need a key to your place…because, well, I'm hoping that I already have one."

"Okay…" Confused, I furrow my brow.

"Babe…I'm not just giving you a key to my place. I'm asking you to move in with me."

Oh. Wow. An even bigger step than I expected.

"You want me to move in with you?" The words rush out of me, my heart quickening.

He smiles softly and says, "More than anything. Question is…do you want to move in with me?" I can hear the nerves clearly in his voice.

There's no hesitation in my answer. I part my lips and say, "More than anything."

His face breaks out into the biggest and most beautiful smile I've ever seen. "Good," he says, "because I love you and I think that we have something good going on here. And I can't wait to live with you to explore it." Then he kisses me, and it feels like a lifetime of kisses to come. Grayson leans his head back, staring down into my eyes, and asks, "So. Are you ready to go home?"

Smiling, I hold up the key he just gave me and say, "Our home? Can't wait."

Seducing Shakespeare

Tabitha Ross

Chapter 1

"NICO!" THE TERROR in Marietta's voice made street vendors jump out of her way as she tore through London's East End, falling over herself. Damn her petticoats—and, for that matter, her corset. She could hardly breathe well enough to run. And she had to get to the tavern as fast as she could.

She bore through the stifling summer heat, and raced across Whitechapel Street, barely avoiding a horse-drawn carriage. The wheels clattered on cobblestones, the horse whinnied, and the carriage driver cursed her to the heavens.

But she didn't look back. Her long dark hair came loose from its pins and fluttered behind her as she flew.

Marietta's brother, Nico, had bragged about playing the odd hand of cards with the playwright Christopher Marlowe, but she'd thought the source of that bragging had been the bravado of a young man. Until now, she hadn't understood what a large debt Nico owed. What if she was too late?

She tore past the stall of a clothing vendor, batting away brightly colored scarves, and ignored the shouts of a few drunks who swayed as she sped by them: *M'lady, why do you run from me?…come back to me, princess…*

Only a little bit farther, and…there it was: the White

Hart Tavern. The place where Nico had been gambling away what little money they had earned, and then some.

Marietta burst through the door and squinted in the bright room. There was a deafening sound of chatter; men were gathered around a spectacle of some sort. For a moment, she felt disoriented, and then she knew. With a strength she didn't realize she had, Marietta shoved two burly men out of her way and forced her way through the crowd. There he was.

"Nico!" Her little brother, barely seventeen and with hardly a hair on his chin, had his back to the wall. He was cornered by another man. The crowd backed away, leaving Marietta in the middle of the circle with the two of them. The other man turned around, revealing his youthful countenance. He wore an expression of wry wit. Nico's mouth, on the other hand, was set in a thin, brave line. He looked terrified to Marietta.

"Pray tell, is this who has come to your rescue, Nico?" Marlowe said. "Ask the broad if she has any money."

Nico stammered. "Sir, she doesn't. But with just a little more time—"

The room fell silent as Marlowe drew a knife from its sheath on his hip. The sharp blade flashed in the light. He took another step closer to Nico. "You've had enough time," he said.

Chapter 2

"STOP!" MARIETTA CRIED, and before she even knew what she was doing, she was in between the two men. The knife point was only inches from her face.

Behind her, Nico's breathing came in gasps. "What are you doing?" he whispered.

Marlowe lowered the knife. "Get out of the way!" he said roughly. "I shan't harm a woman, but a mouthy one does not warrant my good graces. You're only postponing what I'm going to do to this lad."

"Don't hurt him!" Marietta pleaded. "He's my younger brother, and he's but a child. I will find a way to pay you back for everything; but for today, leave him be."

At this, Marlowe let out a short bark. "Dear lady, your passion is to be admired, but your brother here owes me more than you can ever give."

Nico grabbed one of Marietta's wrists in an effort to move her out of harm's way. She wriggled it out of his grasp and looked Marlowe in the eye. The man was young, with pale, smooth skin and not a wrinkle on his face. He couldn't be so hardened and cruel as not to care whether he killed a man, could he? After all, he was only a playwright. *Though a good one*, Marietta thought, because she had witnessed his players at the Rose Theatre. With relief, she felt his threat was nothing but the well-played bluff of someone trained in the dramatic arts.

"How can you be so sure?" she asked.

Marlowe was taken aback by her gall. "I beg your pardon?"

"Are you sure my younger brother owes you more than we could possibly give you? There are things more valuable than gold to be won at cards."

At that, the bar erupted in laughter. Marietta couldn't help but blush as men in the crowd shouted their lewd suggestions for her repayment. Marlowe threw back his head and laughed at first, but after a moment, he looked at her thoughtfully. She saw the gleam in his eye and felt relief.

Ignoring the jostling around her, she said, "I can sew anything you like, or Nico can work for you—we can clean and run errands. You only need to tell me how my brother and I can barter away these foolish debts."

Marlowe grabbed Marietta by the arm, gripping her a little more tightly than she would have liked. "Come this way," he hissed. He led her through the crowd, beckoning Nico to follow.

The men in the tavern dispersed to their various tables when they realized there would no longer be a fight.

Marlowe brought them to a table in the back corner. He pulled out a plain wooden chair and roughly maneuvered Marietta into it. She took a deep breath. Her upper arm felt sore where Marlowe had grabbed it, but she ignored the pain because she didn't want him to know about it. Nico sat beside her, eyes downcast. She was aware of his shame, but at the same time, she was too angry to look at him. Across from them, Marlowe beckoned the pretty barmaid over with a finger.

"A drink for the lady?" he asked Marietta, ignoring Nico.

"Nay, thank you. I don't believe we'll be staying," she said. She didn't frequent taverns. In fact, she'd never been inside the White Hart. She'd only heard tell of her brother's visits to this lowly place full of drunks and cards. She wrinkled her nose. It smelled strongly of brew.

The barmaid brought Marlowe a pint of ale and he took a long pull of the drink before setting the pewter tankard aside and leaning his elbows on the table. "There is something you can do to absolve your brother of the debt he owes me," he said. "However, it will not bode well for your reputation." He smirked. "Although for you in particular, that should matter naught."

Marietta kept her features neutral. It was well known about town that she and Nico had been orphaned at a young age, and that she supported them with her work as a seamstress, while he worked as a stable boy for a wealthy family and ran odd jobs on the side. Unfortunately, it was also a well-known fact that Nico frequently gambled their money away. Her brother had always been impulsive, but otherwise, she would not be shamed for a faultless situation or her honest work.

Nico reacted with less composure. "How dare you insult my sister?" He jumped up, ready to leap across the table, but Marietta already had him by the wrists.

"Sit down!" she hissed.

"Knives wound; words do not!" He thumped his fist against the table and glared at Marlowe, but he stayed sitting.

Marlowe ignored Nico and continued speaking to Marietta. "As you know, I am known for putting on plays at the Rose, but another playwright is adored as well—William Shakespeare."

Marietta nodded. She had heard of Shakespeare's plays,

of course, though she had never been to see one. She loved the theatre, but attended only on special occasions, when she had a little money to spare.

"You know of him?" Marlowe asked her, impatiently.

"I've heard tell of his wit, but I haven't yet seen his face," she answered carefully.

Marlowe studied her while he took another swallow of his drink. "You're a beautiful woman," he observed.

Marietta stiffened.

Beside her, Nico fidgeted, but this time, said nothing.

Marlowe continued, "Shakespeare is notorious for romancing many beauties. I need you to find him and get into his good graces. He is working on a new play. As soon as you convince him to trust you, steal the play and bring it to me." His lip curled. He had a persistent, watchful expression, like a cat who had spotted a mouse in the corner.

Marietta didn't hesitate. Tricking a playwright out of some pages was far less of a crime than allowing her little brother to be stabbed over a game of cards. She felt nothing but contempt for Marlowe, whose collar appeared to be stained with ale and who admitted to stooping so low as to secretly rely on the writings of others to serve his own vanity. But she would perform his dirty work if it meant protecting sweet Nico, her dear brother and only family member.

"I'll do it," she said.

Nico could no longer contain his outrage. He leapt up. "Rogue!" he shouted at Marlowe. "You shan't use my innocent sister as your pawn! I'd sooner duel to the death!"

The tavern fell silent. Heads turned. Marlowe stood and put his hand again on his knife, but Marietta grabbed Nico by the arms.

"He will not duel," she said firmly to the playwright. "I will do as you say," she added in a whisper.

Then she turned to Nico and said, "You've done enough already. Go before you get both of us killed, or so help me." She pushed him toward the door, amid the jeers and laughter. The men ridiculed Nico for being saved by his sister.

He stumbled out into the last light of evening and turned toward her, his face contorted with shame and anger. "Marietta, you shouldn't have come. I won't let you take part in this sordid affair."

She felt her chest tighten, as though the wind had been knocked out of it. "You won't let me? How's that for thanks!" she said. "Do you think you'd not be bleeding all over the dirt of this alley if I hadn't arrived at this tavern?"

"It's not your affair!" he shouted.

"Keep your voice down," she said. "It has become our affair now. We must get you out of trouble." She began walking in the direction of their small cottage. Nico followed.

"I forbid it," he said. "I forbid you to meet with Shakespeare."

Marietta stopped. Nico's lip trembled. For all his bravado, he looked like the scared little boy she had once rocked back to sleep after his nightmares. And yet he had never raised his voice against her this way, acting as though he had the authority to control what she did.

Marietta steeled her spine and eyed him coolly, though it pained her to fight with him.

"I have no choice but to protect you however I can, and if that's not to your liking, you should consider your choices before you play cards with the devil." She spoke the words sharply because she could see in her brother's eyes that he was still full of fire.

She would have to find a way to seduce the playwright Shakespeare without her brother's knowledge, and quickly, before Nico did anything rash.

Chapter 3

THE NEW GLOBE Theatre was noisy and full of people from all walks of life. The aristocrats gleamed in their finery from the balconies, and the many people standing in the courtyard jostled each other for a good position. Marietta and her friend Celia had purchased seats in the gallery for a penny more, but Marietta was thankful to have a little rest.

She drank in the excitement. She loved the theatre. It was invigorating: all that chatter before the curtains lifted, and then the hush as the audience escaped together into a fantasy.

"Have you seen the Lord Chamberlain's Men before?" Celia asked. Marietta had managed to convince her to take a few hours away from chores. She sat next to Marietta, fanning herself as beads of sweat appeared on her porcelain skin. Marietta knew that Celia fancied that using the fan made her look like a fine lady, but it only made her look like a seamstress who was sweating. The humidity caused the tendrils of her thick blond hair that had escaped from her braid to curl around her face.

"I haven't seen them, although I've heard they're quite good," Marietta answered. "Have you?"

"Oh yes; I saw a historical performance, *Julius Caesar.*

I stood that time and it was terribly long. But this is a comedy?"

"*A Midsummer Night's Dream.* I do hope it's funny. I could use some levity," said Marietta.

A quartet started to jig onstage, signaling the beginning of the show. Judging by the noise, most of the crowd seemed to ignore the jig, and so did Celia.

"Where is that wild brother of yours?" she asked, with a sidelong glance at Marietta.

"He's helping to construct a wall—paid labor," said Marietta, with her eyes fixed on the stage. Perhaps she should have come alone and not invited Celia to the theatre. Not because Celia had called Nico wild—Celia was honest to a fault, and as Marietta's closest friend, she had earned the right to be—but because she was already fishing around for details from Marietta. It was clear that Celia suspected something was going on.

Marietta couldn't tell her that she had come here to see the Lord Chamberlain's Men because she needed to get closer to the playwright, William Shakespeare. She needed to keep her dealings secret if she was going to deliver the play to Marlowe. And besides, if Celia knew, she'd be disappointed in Marietta. She would think her a common thief, and her brother a wastrel. And she might try to dissuade Marietta from her task at hand.

"Speaking of paid labor, you ought to be finishing repairs for the Countess. Haven't you a pile of sewing at the shop for her newest set of dresses? You'll be working all day tomorrow to catch up." Celia said. She and Marietta were both employed by the same tailor's shop in London.

"I'm quite ahead of it, truly."

Celia was right again. Marietta should have been working, but wasn't saving Nico more important? She flashed her friend a smile and changed the subject. "Oh, here, the jig is ending!"

With gratitude, Marietta watched the dancers leave the stage. The crowd quieted as several players walked on in their costumes of royalty. Marietta forgot all about keeping secrets from Celia. The theatre and the people surrounding her floated away; she was in the woods outside of Athens, where fairies dwelled.

For hours, she remained transfixed by the music of the words, laughed at the clever jokes, and felt for the humans caught in fate's web. When at the end, Puck stood alone onstage and recited his farewell, Marietta found that she had tears in her eyes. She was struck dumb. Perhaps this enemy of Marlowe's was not so unworthy after all. Before, Shakespeare had been her target. He had been a distasteful man she must endure so that she might restore balance for her brother. Now, the thought of meeting the playwright who had composed such a fantasy made her heart beat a little faster.

"Marietta? Marietta?" She realized that Celia was standing over her, ready to leave. Throngs of audience members were already exiting the theatre.

"Oh! I'm sorry, Celia. What did you think?"

Celia grinned. "It was a laugh, wasn't it? That whole bit with the ass."

Marietta nodded and let out a chuckle, but she didn't move.

Celia's brows knit together. "Shouldn't we be getting back to the East End? It's close to evening, and Southwark is no district for two women like us, especially not in the late hours."

"Yes, yes…" Marietta had to somehow meet Shakespeare tonight. She cast about for an excuse she could use to separate herself from Celia. Then she planned to make her way to the Lord Chamberlain's Men, who she hoped would be flattered enough by her attentions to help her. But here loomed Celia, alert as ever to Marietta's shifty behavior. Oh, why hadn't she come alone?

"Celia, why don't you go and wait for me by the entrance? I want to pay my respects to the actors." Marietta stood up.

Celia looked mildly annoyed at this. "Let me go with you, then."

"No!" Marietta said, then softened her tone at Celia's startled look. "No—it's an embarrassment, but I'm so full of emotion that I must say what I have to say alone. I'll meet you outside."

"If you insist," Celia said, looking bemused. It wouldn't have been the first time Marietta had become emotional. She often showed more emotion at a song or a word than Celia did, and Celia often teased her for her displays of passion. Marietta's friend made her way out of the galleries toward the exit.

Slowly, Marietta walked against the crowd toward the stage, where some of the actors still stood in the courtyard. She made her way toward one of them, the young man who played Quince. He was still half in costume, looking the part of a carpenter.

"My compliments," Marietta said to him. "That was the finest show I've seen in quite a while."

Quince looked her up and down and then took her hand to kiss it. "Compliments accepted." He grinned and winked. "I'm Henry Condell. And you?"

"Marietta DiSonna," she said, and then regretted that she had given her real name, and full name at that. Perhaps it would have been stealthier of her to come up with a false name with which to seduce Shakespeare. In any case, it was now too late.

"Marietta, what a pleasure. Please, come again to the theatre to watch us perform sometime." Henry looked as though he was about to move away toward the other theatregoers.

"Wait!" Marietta said, startling him. "It's only…I loved the play so much that I should like to meet the writer himself. Is he here?"

Henry laughed. "Few request to meet a playwright at the playhouse, and even fewer are granted the wish, but for a woman so beautiful I'll make an exception. William Shakespeare is here tonight. Follow me, and be quick."

Marietta looked to see if anyone was paying attention, but the crowd had all but dispersed, and the few remaining commoners weren't concerned with her. She allowed the player to lead her backstage.

She felt a little giddy, seeing all that was hidden from the audience's view: the props and signs, the ropes and pulleys, and the pieces of costume strewn about.

The door of the dressing room was left ajar so that she could see the young boys bandying about, and the men in states of half-dress. She cast her eyes down, knowing what Celia would say: the theatre was no place for a woman. Celia, who was waiting at this moment by the entrance, would probably leave by the time Marietta emerged. And Marietta would have to lie later, making an excuse about not seeing Celia outside.

Looking up, she saw that she was in a different room. The actor who played Bottom had the wooden head of a donkey on his lap as he drank from a flask. He sat next to a handsome man with a straight nose and a slight mustache. The man turned toward Marietta, revealing warm, intelligent brown eyes that locked on to hers. A shiver ran through her body.

"Marietta," Henry said. "Here is the playwright you so admire: William Shakespeare."

Chapter 4

MARIETTA WAS ONLY vaguely aware of her own curtsy as Shakespeare stood up and bowed to her. The noise of the other actors around her faded into the distance. She was no longer aware of Henry by her side or the actor who played Bottom, still sitting in the corner drinking from his flask. She was already lost in those brown eyes, that mellifluous voice…

"I said, did you enjoy tonight's performance?"

With a start, Marietta realized that the owner of those deep, chestnut-colored eyes had already asked her the same question twice.

"Oh!" She brought her hand to her mouth in embarrassment, but recovered quickly. "Yes, I enjoyed the play much more than I could even tell you. I'm afraid my words fail me in a way that yours would never fail you. It was, truly, like falling asleep into a lovely dream."

Shakespeare smiled. Though his features were handsome, something in Marietta hardened at the sight of that smile. She feared it might be the self-satisfied grin of a man who was used to accepting praise. Especially from adoring women.

"Why, thank you," he said, and bent to kiss her hand.

She couldn't help it—a thrill ran through her when his lips touched her skin. Rising, he added, "I've heard many a compliment for *A Midsummer Night's Dream,* but none from one so fair."

Marietta paused and drew a breath. Marlowe had said that Shakespeare wooed many women. She should not be surprised by his arrogance. She fought the urge to snatch her hand back, remembering how Nico had looked when he was held up at the mercy of Marlowe's knife with his face so full of fear. For her brother's sake, she had to do whatever she could to get that play.

She put on her warmest, most inviting smile. "You flatter me," she said. "I daresay women more lovely than I have enjoyed this masterpiece of yours."

"Oh no, not so many women," he answered. "And certainly not women with such…mysterious eyes."

He moved closer. She could smell the musk of his cologne. If he was a rake, he was a dashing one at that.

She tucked a stray piece of hair behind her ear and let out her most charming laugh. "When you say it with such sweetness, I must believe you," she said.

He laughed along with her and she liked the sound of it—unselfconscious and infectious in its joy.

"Ahem," the sounds of a clearing throat nearby caused her to jump back a little, away from Shakespeare. Henry tugged nervously at his hair.

"Shall we get on to the pub, sir?" he said, addressing the playwright. "I believe many of the fellows are there already."

Shakespeare drew himself up tall, tugged at the bottom of his leather vest, and pulled his rolled-up sleeves down to his wrists, where he buttoned the left cuff.

"Yes, of course, Henry," he said. "And Bottom!" he added gaily, turning with a grin toward the actor who still sat, pouring the contents of his flask into his mouth as the wooden ass's head still lay in his lap. The actor set the head on the floor and lifted his flask in agreement, nodding once at Marietta before standing to join Henry.

Marietta noticed that Shakespeare was fumbling with the button on his right cuff. Without thinking, she reached for his sleeve and buttoned it herself. She felt his arm stiffen in surprise at her touch. Then he softened.

"Thank you," he whispered. She thrilled at the touch of his breath on her neck. She had fixed shirt cuffs for countless men at the tailor's shop, but never with her heart pounding in her chest like that of a bird. His skin was so warm to the touch, and he had strong, lean arms.

She stepped away, more quickly than was necessary, and in her awkwardness, she curtsied again. Heaven help her.

You're supposed to be seducing him, *Marietta,* she reminded herself. *Stop acting the fool.*

Shakespeare, looking amused, took her hand to lift her from her curtsy. The other men turned to go.

"Would you be so kind as to give the cast the pleasure of your presence at our gathering tonight?" he asked, rather formally.

Marietta regained her senses. "I wouldn't dare refuse such an invitation from the famous playwright Shakespeare," she said. "I would be delighted to accompany you."

"Please, call me Will." He gestured toward the door, where Henry and the nameless Bottom were already making their exit. "Shall we?"

He took her arm and held her rather close as they treaded carefully through the candlelit shadows of the backstage area, strewn with half-illuminated props and wigs.

"I'm afraid," he said, "that the establishment my men have chosen is of rather ill repute for a young maiden of your bearing. Nonetheless, its repute is not as ill as that of some."

She affected her lightest tone, though it pained her to do so. "It matters not to me, long as the company is fair."

"Right then," he said, leading her out onto the stage where she could see the theatre in the round, from the perspective of a player. "It is called the White Hart."

The White Hart. Marietta's heart filled with dread. For that was the very pub where she had encountered Marlowe.

Chapter 5

MOST OF THE Lord Chamberlain's Men were already rowdy and thick with beer by the time Marietta arrived at the White Hart Tavern on William Shakespeare's arm. Shakespeare—*no, Will*, she reminded herself—had insisted on paying a carriage driver to take them across the Thames, since no good could come of walking in Southwark at night. She had to agree with him on that, and had considered him a gentleman for thinking of her safety. But he hardly talked at all during their time in the carriage, and she found herself filling the silences with idle chatter and London gossip.

"Are you familiar with the Countess of Pembroke?" she asked, searching for something—anything—that would open him up to her. Perhaps they could find similarities in the people they knew.

"She and I are acquainted, yes," he said, but then he said no more. A list of similar names yielded just as little response.

Marietta was not used to spending time with such mysterious, introspective men. She was rather intrigued by his pensive manner. In the past, her beaus had been boastful and talkative, leaving her without much room to speak. She liked being the one to lead a conversation, and yet she worried that she was boring Will. But this was a man she had to seduce. She would need to find out what he liked in a woman.

As soon as they entered the tavern, the Chamberlain's Men stood and let out a great cheer, clinking their pewter tankards together to celebrate their performance and play-wright. Shakespeare, laughing, led Marietta over to the table and ordered two pints from the barmaid.

Out of their various costumes and wigs, Marietta noticed that many of the men were quite handsome. It wasn't every night that she found herself carousing with a group of lively young actors. Even the younger men, who played women, had long since washed off their rouge and were now drinking with their elders at a seemingly foolish pace.

Henry Condell, his blond hair tousled, raised his pint to Marietta and winked.

He's a cheeky one, she thought.

The actor who played Bottom leaned forward. Marietta couldn't help but notice his piercing blue eyes. "We haven't yet met, officially," he said. "I'm Richard Burbage."

"I wondered!" she said. "A pleasure."

He gestured toward the other men around the table. "And this is Robert and George," he said, pointing to his comrades.

The taller of the two men, Robert, leaned forward grace-fully. "I played Lysander."

"And I was Demetrius," said George. He was jovial and stout.

"A pleasure to meet you as well," she said.

"Rogues and rakes, all of you! I see you're vying for the at-tention of fair maiden Marietta!" Shakespeare handed her a pint of ale. She took the heavy pewter tankard and attempted a ladylike sip.

"We wouldn't dream of it, sir," said Henry, knocking back

the rest of his drink. Again, he gave Marietta another cheeky wink.

"Excellent, excellent," Shakespeare joked. "We found her in the audience. She admired our most recent theatrical production. I daresay she may even be our next patron!"

Marietta blushed at his comment. As if she, simple Marietta, could be a member of a wealthy patron's household. Yet she was pleased that Will perceived her to be a lady. Her playacting must be working. He must think her a young lady who was only living a little wildly for the moment.

But before she could come up with a witty reply, her companion was setting her pint on the table and leading her to the center of the tavern. The band had started playing a folk song and they were suddenly surrounded by dancers.

To her surprise, Will was a talented dancer. She wasn't sure why she would have assumed otherwise, but perhaps it was because he was simply so quiet. As they moved together to the music, Marietta thought about attempting conversation once again, but she felt intimidated. It was probably because he was so intelligent that he spoke so little.

An accomplished playwright, and poet, and now a dancer? Was there anything the man could not do?

Marietta was fond of dancing. She gave herself fully to the jig, her skirts whirling as Shakespeare led her around the steps. Between the scent of his cologne and the grace of his movement, perhaps she could easily enjoy the task of seducing him to steal his play.

She almost stopped cold when, from over Shakespeare's shoulder, she saw a familiar face. He had a steady, unnerving gaze and a little beard—of all people, Christopher Marlowe was watching them!

Seeing her expression shift, Shakespeare glanced over his shoulder as well. He and Marlowe exchanged a stiff nod, then he turned back to Marietta and they moved to the center, where they were surrounded by others and less visible to his rival.

"Do you see that man over there?" he asked.

"The one in the high collar?" she said innocently. She shouldn't have looked so startled upon seeing Marlowe. If she were a smart woman, she would have prepared herself for this interaction, knowing he frequented the tavern. She couldn't let Shakespeare begin to suspect a plot, or all would be lost for Nico.

"Him, yes, the weasel-countenanced scallywag. He's my nemesis."

"I beg your pardon?"

"My nemesis—the Scot to my Englishman, the fox to my hound, the raven to my dove."

She played coy. "I'm afraid I still don't understand."

"Christopher Marlowe: he's a competitor. He writes plays for the Rose. I can feel the heat of his jealous gaze even from over here."

Marietta glanced again at Marlowe and then searched Shakespeare's face as if this entire story were new to her. Shakespeare's eyes smoldered.

"It seems his mere presence truly angers you!" she exclaimed.

"Yes, I have to admit that it does," he said, softening. "But let's not waste a perfectly good evening on anger when it's better spent on merrymaking. If we stay occupied, he will not disturb us."

"I have seen his plays at the Rose," Marietta said. "They cannot compete with yours." Her job was to flatter and seduce him. And yet, she felt she would have needed to say this anyway, for it was the truth. Marlowe's plays couldn't hold a candle to Shakespeare's masterpieces. Even now, hours after tonight's performance, she could look around her at the players and still imagine that fairy woods. She could still hear his dreamlike words.

"Your compliments are music to the ears of a vain man," Shakespeare laughed as he twirled her around him. She glimpsed, out of the corner of her eye, at Marlowe, who kept watching the two of them.

Though she tried to avoid it, her mind drifted toward what she would say to Nico tonight. He didn't know where she was. At least, since Marlowe frequented the White Hart, her brother would know better than to come here.

"Will, you are a terrific dancer," Marietta said, smiling her most coquettish smile. He grinned, and she was shocked to find him launching into a story—this one about his days as a boy in Stratford-upon-Avon, where he became the best dancer and was a coveted partner for all the girls, of course. Marietta tried not to roll her eyes.

She spent the rest of the night on William Shakespeare's arm, flirting with him and laughing with the players. Twice, she could have sworn she saw Shakespeare winking at the barmaids and remembered how Marlowe had reported his reputation as a rake. Will was so charming when one had his attention. But perhaps he was boorish when one didn't.

She could not help but think of Jacob Gibbs, the first man she ever loved. Ruggedly handsome, Jacob had cared for the horse stables of a member of the court. When Marietta was all of sixteen, he had flirted with her on his frequent trips into London and instantly won her heart. Only months later did she learn that he kept several women in the city, all of whom thought they were his one and only love.

Now, in the tavern, Marietta recalled the despair she had felt when she had learned of Jacob's habits. She had sobbed herself to sleep for days. With Shakespeare, she knew she would need to be of two minds: the Marietta who seduced, and the Marietta who knew better than to let her heart get involved in this farce.

Meanwhile, across the bar, Marlowe and his players drank and pretended not to be aware of the Chamberlain's Men, as the Chamberlain's Men were aware of them but said nothing to them either. Marietta hoped her performance was convincing enough for her brother's tormenter.

It must have been past midnight when she found herself walking with Will along the cobblestone streets to her home. A crescent moon and a clear sky full of stars lit the way. She leaned toward him as she talked, though she was aware that she no longer had an audience to impress. Twice, she jumped at shadows, because of the private belief that Marlowe or one of his players might be following them to see that she was making good on her promise. She feared their watching because tonight she would not find the new play; instead, she must return home before Nico began to worry.

Yet Marlowe had not said how much time he expected this to take…

The second time Marietta jumped, Shakespeare teased, "Mouse! Are you afraid of the dark?"

Marietta forced a giggle and said, "Not as long as you're with me."

When they arrived at the door of the false address she'd given Will, they stood for a moment to take in the night sky. The cool air smelled of spring.

"William," Marietta said, looking up at his handsome face. "I'm quite glad we met."

"So am I, Marietta." He brushed her hair from her cheek with his finger. "It's been such a pleasure to meet an admirer as beautiful as you."

He leaned in for a kiss. He was so handsome. His intelligence was shining through those eyes and his unblemished features. But who was he really? She felt she couldn't possibly penetrate his depths. Before she knew what she was doing, Marietta pulled away. She could not kiss a man when she knew so little about him. When it came to displays of physical affection, Marietta was unable to take action simply because a man was a good playwright. Or even because she had been asked to steal his new play. Fear kept her from following through on her plan for seduction.

Will's face registered surprise. *With all likelihood,* she thought, *few women had refused a kiss from the great William Shakespeare.*

Marietta turned to go in the door.

"Good night, William," she said.

"Good night, fair Marietta," he answered softly.

Chapter 6

"NICO, I'M TELLING you the truth: last night I was with Celia, and I came home after you had gone to bed," said Marietta.

Nico gave her a long, shrewd look.

"Truly," Marietta said, feeling guilty. But, she reminded herself, this wasn't a lie, only an omission of the truth. She had been with Celia, and she had returned home while her brother was asleep. It mattered naught what she had been doing in between.

Nico relaxed his shoulders. "I am sorry, Marietta," he said. "Of course I believe you."

"It's quite all right," Marietta said, swallowing a lump in her throat. Oh, how she hated to disagree with her brother under any circumstances, let alone when she was lying.

"It's only that I'm upset about this agreement you've made with Marlowe," Nico explained. He started to get worked up again, his face filling with color. "You must let me duel him! This seduction plan is a fool's errand, and far beneath you." Once again, Nico became full of the swagger of a young man, ready to charge through the door and risk his life on a point of honor.

"Dear brother," Marietta said, desperation making the

edges of her voice sound ragged, "you must not fight. 'Tis only a trick until we have the play. My reputation needn't be at risk. And so if it is, it's a better thing to lose than your life."

Before Nico could speak again, there was a knock at the door. Marietta was startled. It was still morning and they weren't expecting company.

Angrily, Nico strode toward the door and pulled it open with more force than necessary.

"Yes?" he said impatiently, to a messenger on the other side.

Marietta realized with a gasp that the messenger was the young Henry Condell. There was a flicker of recognition as their eyes met. She smoothed her plain, rust-colored skirt and touched the loose braid of hair that fell over her shoulder. She hoped so desperately that Henry would not call her by name or betray in any other way that he knew her.

"I'm looking for a woman named Marietta DiSonna," said Henry. Sunlight bounced off his hair and revealed a face full of tired lines from a night at the tavern. Nico fixed Marietta with a look of suspicion.

Marietta took a deep breath before stepping forward. "I am she," she said, trying to sound timid.

"I have a message for you," Henry said, as he pressed a roll of parchment into her hand.

A message from the playwright himself! Marietta's heart skipped a beat. She would never have admitted it, but though Will may have been a rake, she could hardly sleep last night for thinking of him.

"Thank you," she whispered. Louder, so that Nico would overhear, she said, "And where is the fabric? This is only the list and the sizing."

Henry looked confused. Then, he must have read Marietta's meaningful look, because he said, "How unfortunate. I've forgotten the fabric. I shall have to return with it, Miss."

Nico, calmer but still visibly ruffled, pushed past Henry and went out the open door.

"Good day to you both," he said, tipping his hat. "Marietta, I will see you this afternoon?"

"Yes—I mean, no—" Marietta said, changing her answer as Henry pressed her with a meaningful look. "This afternoon I shall be at the tailor's," she added.

"On what business?" Nico snapped.

"The countess. Her…trousseau."

"Very well. We shall discuss the matter again when I return."

Marietta waited until her brother's form had all but disappeared at the bend in the road before she turned back to Henry.

"My brother," she said, by way of explanation.

"Ah," said Henry. "I might have guessed your jealous husband."

Marietta laughed a little and he turned to go.

"Wait!" she said. He turned back.

She pressed the roll of parchment into his hand.

"It's from William Shakespeare, is it not?"

"The very one," Henry agreed. "May I read it for you?"

At her nod, he unfurled the parchment at both ends and read from it a poem, as if onstage:

> *"How can my muse want subject to invent*
> *While thou dost breathe, that pour'st into my verse*
> *Thine own sweet argument, too excellent*
> *For every vulgar paper to rehearse?"*

Marietta found that her hand was at her throat. Tears pricked at her eyes. His muse—Shakespeare thought of her as his muse? Her? Her! Marietta! And so, she realized slowly, her plan for seduction was working.

"How beautiful," she said eventually, because Henry seemed as though he was waiting for a reaction. He beamed.

"A playwright and a poet, eh?" he said, as proud as if he'd written it himself to woo a woman. "But wait, there is still more: he says he wants to meet you in front of the Birkwood house when the sun is three-quarters of the way toward its evening rest."

He handed her the parchment. She took it carefully, feeling its edges as though it was made of fine silk and gold. It may well have been, for all she knew—it was made of the finest words.

"Thank you, Henry," she said. "Please tell him I will meet him where he says."

He grinned and bowed. "I will take your message back, miss. A pleasure to be of service."

As the actor walked away, Marietta stood in the door, noticing the dew on blades of grass in the morning sunlight and the pleasant cluck of chickens as they pecked at dirt in the courtyard. She was the muse of William Shakespeare! Twenty-four hours ago she had been only Marietta DiSonna, seamstress, orphan, and sister to the gambler Nico DiSonna. Now she felt special. It was as if she were touched by a divine hand. Now she was not only Marietta DiSonna, but a muse to a great playwright.

But only until the play was in Marlowe's hands.

Chapter 7

MARIETTA DONNED HER best dress for her meeting with Will later that day. It was a gold-colored skirt with a cream bodice, as new as anything she had ever owned. When she arrived at the tailor's shop that morning, Celia was already there, busily sewing garments for the Countess.

"Where did you leave to, last night?" Celia asked her, seeming peeved. "I waited outside the theatre until I thought it almost too dangerous to travel home."

"Oh, Celia, I'm so glad to see you!" Marietta said. "I searched for you after I gave the actors my compliments, but I could not find you and had assumed you'd left."

"I would never leave without you," Celia said quietly.

"Then the fault is mine," Marietta said in a soothing tone, kissing both of Celia's cheeks. "Please, forgive me, dear friend. I shan't separate myself from you the next time we go to the theatre."

Celia pouted for a moment, then patted the chair next to hers. Marietta sat. Celia leaned toward her. For a moment, Marietta thought she knew the truth, but she only said, "I had dreams last night of the man who played Lysander. Handsome, was he not?" She let out a girlish giggle and covered her mouth.

"Oh!" Marietta picked up a dress that required stitching at the hem. "Yes, he was, quite," she said, smiling.

Celia looked her over in a way that suggested disapproval for her manner. Marietta had known her since they were girls. If anyone would suss out the secret she was keeping, it was Celia. And yet, Marietta could not tell her. At least not until she had completed the deed and Nico was safe. Marietta turned her attention to the sewing in her lap.

"I thought the actor who played Quince a handsome one," she added, remembering Henry's blond hair and quick laugh this morning. Of course, none could match the deep and brooding good looks of the Globe's playwright, but Celia could not know about her true feelings yet.

Luckily, Celia seemed to take Marietta's observations at face value. "Ah yes, so he was," she agreed. "Though we have so much sewing to do now, I'm glad we attended the theatre last night. It is always a relief to have a laugh." Then, glancing up from her stitches at Marietta's skirts, she added, "Pray tell, why are you wearing your Sunday best?"

"What, this?" Marietta feigned disinterest in her clothes. She ought to have known that Celia would catch her in a detail. "This is not my best."

Celia let out a short bark of a laugh. "Marietta DiSonna, how can you expect to deceive your fellow friend and seamstress? It is your best. I take it you're meeting a fellow?"

"This afternoon," Marietta said conspiratorially. She knew better than to protest when Celia insisted. But she could not tell her friend the truth about the "fellow" in question.

"Go on," Celia said, reaching for more thread.

"Well, speaking of…it's the actor who played Quince, after all."

"Oh!" Celia seemed delighted with this reveal of information. "'Tis no wonder you were so desiring to go alone and meet the actors yesterday."

Marietta smiled. She wished she could tell her friend everything. Though she trusted Celia to keep such a secret, she couldn't ensnare her in this dangerous task. Nor could she take even the slightest risk that word would get to Shakespeare before she managed to follow through on Marlowe's plan. She needed to save Nico's hide.

"If Nico stops by the store," Marietta asked, "will you tell him I'm making a special delivery to measure for the Countess? I don't think he will come, but he has been rather on edge of late."

Celia's face looked grave. Nico's rash behavior worried her, Marietta knew, but she didn't like to hear about it. She stabbed her needle through the hem rather harder than was necessary.

"For you, I will tell him that," Celia said.

Marietta's heart dropped further in her chest.

Chapter 8

MARIETTA STOOD AT the stone wall, feeling certain that she must have the wrong place. She walked into the London neighborhood of Tudors, taking in the sights. She felt she didn't belong in her plain dress that had seemed so lovely this morning. The streets abounded with ladies and gentlemen, walking on foot and riding in fine carriages. Was this where Shakespeare lived? She had thought him an impecunious artist, but perhaps he was an eccentric nobleman after all, who chose to spend his nights at the tavern. Oh, what did she care? All she needed was the play for Marlowe. It shouldn't matter what she thought of Will.

Just as she was about to turn and walk all the way back to the tailor's in the East End, he rounded the corner. His hair was mussed, as if he'd only just woken, and his vest flapped open, untied. His shirtsleeves were pushed haphazardly above his elbows, as they had been in the room where they'd met the night before, when she had buttoned them for him. He bounded toward her with uncharacteristic enthusiasm.

She had to remind herself to breathe.

"Marietta! You came," he said. She was almost taken aback by his excitement. Had he seemed so smitten last night? She didn't believe so. After all, she had refused to kiss him.

"Will!" she said warmly. "Your poem was so unexpected."

He grabbed both of her hands in his, and in spite of herself, she felt a thrill at his rough touch.

"Did you like it?" he asked. "I couldn't sleep last night for thinking of you. You don't know what a block I've had with my new play. But now it's as if the floodgates have opened. Truly, you are my muse."

They appeared to be alone on the street. "Why did you have me meet you here, so far from the theatre?" she asked.

"Ah!" He was still vibrating with an exuberance that, had she not known otherwise, she might have attributed to a madman. He withdrew a sizable iron key from his breast pocket and held it for her as though it were a trophy. "I have something beautiful to show you, something that might *almost* be worthy of your fair countenance."

Marietta couldn't help the pleasant feeling of anticipation she felt, even as she knew that she was the trickster here. It was because of her misleading flirtations that Will was attempting to woo her. The girlish lightness she felt as he led her toward a door in the wall was tempered by guilt that curled around its edges.

The door, like the key, was wrought iron and covered in a design of intricate roses. Shakespeare unlocked it and pushed it inward, and then offered her his hand. As they crossed the threshold, through the wall, she let out an audible gasp.

"It's like nothing I've ever seen!" she said. This was true. It was like Eden within London: inside the walls was hidden a large and beautiful garden, full of trees and every imaginable flower. Marietta noted many varieties of delicate roses, purple asters, the blossoms of sweet William, phlox, peonies, lilies of the valley, cornflowers, and forget-me-nots. The whole place was as peaceful as paradise. The noises from the London streets could not be heard within the walls surrounding them, and butterflies flitted delicately through the blooming flowers while honeybees lazily gathered nectar from each blossom.

Shakespeare led her to a bench under the shade of a lovely alder tree. He offered her a seat before lowering himself beside her.

"Yes," he said, quietly. "It is magnificent, isn't it? This private garden belongs to a wealthy patron of mine in the city. He allows me to borrow the key whenever I like, but I do so only for special occasions. And meeting my muse... well, I thought that was certainly one such occasion!"

"Surely a handsome playwright of your stature meets one muse per week, at least," Marietta teased, trying not to be so overcome by the beauty of the garden that she lost all her wit.

"No, Marietta." Shakespeare sounded wounded, as though she had deliberately insulted him. His face, she realized, looked actually pained. "You must believe me. You are the only muse for me. You deserve not just entry to this garden, but to a larger and more beautiful garden all your own."

She chose her words carefully. "I only meant to tease," she said. "Please forgive me, William."

He took both of her hands and brought them to his breast. "You are forgiven, always," he said. "But it's true, I never jest when it comes to my inspiration—for I have been in a fever of writing since I was first blessed with your presence last night."

"A fever?" Marietta's mouth felt dry. She was supposed to seduce William Shakespeare, and it seemed to be working quite well.

"Yes. It makes a man insane, but you must be used to driving men mad. Surely they are constantly vying for your attention. I must have many competitors in the form of your suitors."

Marietta laughed, covering her mouth. She had never thought of herself as a beauty worthy of many suitors. She did not have golden hair, fine clothes, or a pedigree. She was nothing like the women who had their rich garments sewn and repaired at the tailor's.

She remembered how serious he was. "I am honored," she said, "to have your affections, Will."

"So you accept me, as your suitor?"

"With pleasure. I have come to meet you here, have I not?"

"I must confess; I was so afraid that you would not meet me here. I paced for a good quarter-hour in the street before I worked up the courage to round the corner to see."

She smiled, and as he gazed into her eyes, she witnessed the hangdog look of a smitten man. He had such deep and passionate eyes. They were unlike any she had ever seen.

He stood, suddenly. "Shall we take a turn in the garden?" he asked.

"Yes," she said gaily, and joined him for a walk through paradise.

The garden, though walled, was extraordinarily large. They strolled and talked for hours, stopping at various flower beds to admire the gardener's handiwork.

"I hope my attentions will not put you off, Marietta," he said, slowly, quietly. "I'm aware that my emotions can appear to be rather…strong. 'Tis only the true strength of my happiness at finding someone who has the power to inspire me so. There's something alluring and mysterious about you that has filled my pen with seemingly endless energy."

"No, Will, I'm flattered, truly. Women such as me simply aren't used to the attention of men such as you."

He laughed. "Women such as yourself? Whatever do you mean, milady?"

Too late, Marietta realized she had almost revealed her secret. Since they met the night before, Will had assumed her to be a lady, and she had never corrected him. She tried to dismiss the subject with a light wave of her hand.

"You're too kind. Are these forget-me-nots or asters? I can never remember."

But Will was not dissuaded by her change of subject. "Marietta DiSonna," he sighed. "It's such an interesting last name. What part of England does your family hail from?"

"London," she said. Her throat was beginning to feel dry.

"Really, London?" he said, seeming intrigued. "Is your father known here then? Is he a member of the court?"

"No, I'm afraid not. My only family member in London is my brother, Nico."

"Ah, Nico DiSonna." Will scratched his chin, as though trying to recall whether he might have met her brother before. "I'm sure I might have seen him at a ball. For that matter, why have I never seen you at a ball? I would have asked you to dance immediately."

Marietta was beginning to realize that there was no way for her to pretend any longer that she was a true lady. Will would find out eventually; it might as well be through her. "The truth, Will, is that you have not seen me at a ball because I've never been invited."

He looked as though he might be about to laugh. "But you're being witty. The lovely Lady DiSonna, not popular enough to be invited to a ball?"

"Yes, you see, it's not Lady DiSonna, though. It's just…Marietta."

He stopped in the garden path and turned to face her. "Just…Marietta?" he asked.

"Yes," she said. "Oh! I'm not a lady, Will. I'm only a seamstress in the tailor's shop. I so loved your play, and so wanted to meet you. When you assumed I was a lady, I didn't want to correct you for fear that you might not care to spend more time with me." Marietta stared at the ground, afraid to look up. What if he grew angry and left her? What then? There was a long silence.

"Marietta, you may not be who I thought you were, but at this point, nothing could stop me from spending time with you. Not after I've looked into your eyes. Not after I've heard the easy laugh on your lips. Not after you've met my friends, my comrades at the theatre. Marietta, you have entranced them, and moreover, you've entranced me. I've never been so happy to have met someone."

She looked up. In Will's eyes was the same smitten look he had worn earlier. She felt a flutter in her stomach and said quietly, "I'm so glad to hear you say that."

They continued walking, and she spoke with him of her work as a seamstress, and of how much she loved London. For the most part, he was quiet, once again reticent, and yet attentive to her. He asked genuine questions about her work and from time to time, he would share a fact about a flower or quote her a line of poetry. He was, she realized, beginning to open up to her.

Marietta lost all track of the time until the light of the sky became rosy with sunset. "Oh my," she said suddenly. "I must return home at once!"

Shakespeare looked puzzled. They had stopped, once again, to admire the English roses. "Of course, my dear," he said graciously. "We shall hire a carriage to escort you home."

"Oh no, that won't be necessary. I prefer to walk," said Marietta hastily, thinking what Nico's reaction would be if she arrived at home in a hired carriage.

Together, Marietta and Will walked toward the entrance

of the garden. The sun was moving too fast toward the western horizon. She wished she could slow it down, just this once.

"Marietta, it has given me so much joy to see you again," Shakespeare said. He held both of her hands in his. She was aware of her hands trembling and her heart beating wildly.

"Thank you for bringing me here."

"The pleasure is all mine." He drew her closer. The air was redolent with the scent of peonies. She wished she could stand like this all night, feeling the protection of his arms around her. What had she thought last night, that he was too intimidating and too quiet? After today, she had met a different man. A man who was open with his heart.

The rich light of the setting sun streamed through the leaves on a nearby tree, backlighting Will as he leaned toward her, and then kissed her. It was brief, but passionate, leaving her light-headed and craving more.

"Good night, sweet Marietta," he said, not letting go of her.

She caught her breath. "Good night, Will," she said, and stepped away, so he could lead her to the gate and squeeze her hand once more.

She exited into the street alone, so no one could see where she had come from or who she had been with. She was so full of pent-up energy and desire she felt she could run all the way back to the East End.

Careful, Marietta, she cautioned herself.

This giddiness was so unlike her; she was usually so cautious and practical. But Will, with his sturdy arms and that kiss! She had to ask herself, who, now, was seducing whom?

Chapter 9

STEALTHILY, MARIETTA CREPT through the front door and into her bed before Nico could wake and realize she had just arrived home. After such a dizzying night, she finally felt tired, and remembering that she would have to be at the tailor's shop early the next morning, she wasted no time during her nightly routine. Once she was in her bed, sleep overtook her almost instantly.

She was in a kind of dreamy state, feeling safe in Will's arms as he spoke to her, repeating the word *muse, muse, muse*…and then suddenly, she was aware of the piercing sunlight streaming in through the window. With the baffled stupor of the newly awakened, she opened her eyes and sat up in bed. Someone was knocking at the front door.

Marietta shook herself awake. What time was it? Nico appeared to have left already. Still in her rumpled clothing, she stumbled toward the front door.

She opened it to reveal a man she didn't recognize. Medium build, dark hair, a pinched nose.

He thrust a scrap of parchment toward her, before she had time to speak.

"Christopher Marlowe sends this," he said.

Marietta blinked. "Marlowe," she said, staring down at the note in his hand. "And who are you?"

"One of his players, miss. Edmund Wells is the name. I'm merely a messenger." He delivered all this information in a flat tone of voice that made Marietta doubt his acting abilities very much indeed.

She took the note and read the tiny scrawl.

Hoping you have succeeded in finding what you were looking for, after your night at the White Hart. Surely enough time has passed?

Marietta clenched her fist around the note. It had only been two days, and already Marlowe was reminding her of their deal. But what she felt was not anger; it was fear. What if she couldn't prevent Marlowe from hurting Nico before she stole Shakespeare's play?

She looked Edmund in the eye. "Tell him to be patient. It's close to done, but I need but a little time."

Edmund went a shade paler and stumbled over his words. "He—he told me to tell you: beginning with the night he spoke to you, a fortnight is your limit."

"Tell him to be patient," Marietta said again, this time with more intensity.

Edmund hesitated, then nodded. "I will tell him."

"Good," Marietta said. "Remind him of our pact."

Edmund stood dumbly.

"Is that all?" Marietta finally asked.

"Um—yes, miss."

She waved him off. "Go then. Tell him," she said impatiently.

As she watched Edmund walk away, she thought frantically about how she would see Shakespeare once more, and gain enough of his trust to get access to his latest work. She needed to move fast.

Chapter 10

THE GLOBE THEATRE in daylight was perhaps even more impressive than it was in the evening, when it was lit with candles. Marietta stood in the emptying auditorium, gazing at the round of seats as crowds pushed past her toward the exits. She had come after the commoners' matinee performance, hoping that he would be in the back room.

She stalled, feeling suddenly nervous. Last night he had said that she was his muse and that he had been in such a fervor from his writing. She hoped he still felt the same way about her, but what if the spell had worn off? He was an artist, and she'd heard tell that artists were fickle.

But she smoothed her dress, taking comfort in the light-blue wool material that was one of her favorites. Then, wishing she could see her reflection one last time before meeting him, she steeled herself and marched toward the back room.

She had thought that the sight of a woman strolling backstage might give the Chamberlain's Men pause, or that they might recognize her. But by and large they ignored her, allowing her to walk behind the curtains and pick her way through the debris of props and costumes. A few of the men, recognizing her, gave little waves.

"Marietta!" someone called out.

She turned around. It was Richard Burbage, the blue-eyed actor who played Bottom.

"Good afternoon, Richard," she said. "I was looking for Will. Is he at the theatre today?"

"Why yes, yes he is," Richard answered. "Am I to assume that you liked the performance so much that you came back for a second time?"

Marietta laughed. "Perhaps you should assume, rather than know the truth," she teased.

Richard smiled. "As I suspected," he declared. "You're only here to pay your compliments to the playwright. Another siren appears for Shakespeare, ready to lure him onto the rocks."

Marietta kept a smile on her face, though she detected a harsh note to Richard's comment. *A siren?* Did he know something of her plan?

"I ought to see him now," she said, wanting to exit as quickly as possible.

Richard nodded, so she made her way to the back room. It was most important that she be able to see Shakespeare again, for Nico's sake. And because she remembered Will's perfect, sensuous kiss from the late evening last night.

Once outside the door, she took a deep breath.

And just as she was about to open it, she stopped short.

Because someone else had left the room first.

A female someone.

Marietta couldn't move. She simply watched the woman as she exited the back room holding a broom. She was young and pretty in a simple way, dressed in plain woolen clothing. She gave a slight nod in Marietta's direction as she walked toward the theatre.

Was Shakespeare so womanizing that he was wooing several women at once? Was Marietta only the fairest of the lot to him?

Did that make her a pawn in his scheme? The notion shook her to the core. She had been foolish enough to think that she was the manipulator, but perhaps it'd been him all the while.

With every muscle in her body, she wanted to leave the Globe. She didn't want to open the door and find Will, who may have recently said good-bye to a different lover. She knew better than to fall for a man like that—an arrogant man, a man of the theatre, and a man with a reputation. And yet, regardless of whether he was playing her, he was also being played.

But this was all for Nico's sake.

Swallowing her pride, Marietta knocked on the door.

Will opened the door. Even though she had just seen that woman, Marietta felt herself soften at the sight of his face. He looked delighted, if surprised, to see her.

"To what do I owe this pleasure?" he said, opening the door wide so that she could enter the green room.

She brushed past him, a little coldly, and sat in one of the chairs in the corner. Part of her wanted to ignore him, to punish him for being a rake, but another part of her remembered that this ruse was not yet over.

"What better place for a playwright's muse to surprise him than the theatre?" she asked.

He laughed. "True, true. Though there is no place where you could ever surprise me, Marietta, that you wouldn't be welcome."

"I'm pleased to hear it."

He shifted his chair closer to hers and lifted a strand of her hair, twirling it on his finger. "Every strand dark as the finest chocolate," he marveled.

She felt herself blushing. "I must meet you tonight," she blurted. "I came here to see you without the knowledge of my brother."

He dropped the strand of her hair. "Your brother?"

She glanced around the room. They were alone. "My brother is very protective of me. He would be angry to know that I was the...muse...of a playwright with such a reputation."

Shakespeare chuckled, and put on an innocent face. "Pray tell, what is my reputation?"

Marietta played shy. "Don't make me say it."

He feigned a grave countenance. "I'm afraid you must."

She sighed, and placed a hand on his knee. "That you court many women and sometimes, all at once."

He froze and stared at her, and she thought for a moment that this must mean she had caught him in a lie. But then she saw blotches of red and white pop out all over his skin. He began laughing, a thin, nervous laugh.

Marietta was appalled. He had been with another woman, and welcomed her in only seconds later, and he was laughing about the gossip that preceded him. He hadn't a care how others were affected by his actions.

But then, he said in all earnestness: "Marietta, you can't believe that, after our walk in the garden last night?"

She was playing a role; she had to remember she was only playing a role. She stilled her angry tongue and took in his features. His eyes were wide and his lips were parted. The longer she looked at him, the more it seemed as though, perhaps, he was being sincere.

"No," she said finally, looking him in the eye. "I don't believe you are courting more women than me."

"Good," he said, satisfied. "Because you are the woman I would like to see tonight. And what of this brother of yours? How strapping is he?"

She did her best girlish giggle. "He is harmless, only he has a temper. He's very protective of me because you see, we lost our parents when we were young. He and I are the only family we have."

She felt pierced by Will's look, by his true sympathy for her. And yet she was grateful that he did not respond with pity as did so many others.

"We all have our sorrows," he said, as if he were one who had experienced his share.

"Yes," she agreed.

What was she doing? She should be seducing him! Not discussing life's sorrows.

"Meet my carriage at the fountain tonight after our performance," he said. "I'll take you somewhere. Your brother, with any luck, will already be asleep."

"Take me to your home," she said, suddenly choosing to be forthright with him. Tonight—she needed to get the play tonight. "I want to see where you live."

"And I where you live! Your desire is my mandate. I will hardly be able to concentrate thinking of you." He ran the edge of his finger along her cheek. Then, he drew her toward him, into a passionate kiss.

She couldn't deny that if this was a ruse, it was at least an enjoyable one.

When they finally pulled away from their embrace, Marietta pushed her hair behind her ears and, feeling dizzy, had to steady herself. Shakespeare walked with her out of the back room and into the Globe, where some of the actors in the company were rehearsing onstage.

"Tonight then," she said.

"I shall count every moment until then," he answered.

Soon, she would have the play for Marlowe and this would all be over. But she wasn't sure if foreseeing the end of the affair made her feel sad or relieved.

Chapter 11

MARIETTA WORE DARK clothes to the fountain that night. She hadn't needed to avoid Nico, since he was out at the public house and would probably stay late. He'd likely come home and go straight to bed without noticing her absence. She loved her younger brother, but she did worry about him. His recklessness reminded her that it was best if she follow through with Marlowe's scheme quickly, before he could get himself into a fight.

There was nobody else around when Shakespeare's hired carriage arrived from across the Thames. Will stepped down to help her up. Once inside the carriage, close together and covered with a blanket, Marietta felt alive with excitement. Although she felt conflicted over the secrecy and the deception of her actions, and she couldn't tell if she loved or hated the man beside her, she had to admit she had never done anything so thrilling. Marietta DiSonna, seducing a famous artist in order to steal from him. She knew it was wrong, but there was a part of her that loved the excitement of the game.

The carriage pulled up in front of a fine Tudor house. Even in the dark, Marietta could see how impressive it was.

She turned toward Will in awe. "This is your home?" she said. She couldn't help herself. So much for trying to be a graceful, secretive seductress.

He laughed. "Do you like it?" he asked, shyly. "I asked to have fresh flowers cut, to please you."

"Oh, yes, I like it very much," she said as he helped her down from the carriage and took his arm before they walked through the front door. Three stories loomed above Marietta. It was a far cry from the small cottage she called home.

Inside, candles in wall sconces cast shadows down the hall. He led her into a sitting room and gestured for her to have a seat in a stuffed armchair while he lit the lamps. She unwrapped her shawl as she looked around at handsome portraits of people she didn't know and paintings of countryside landscapes.

"How was the night's performance?" she asked, finally, feeling at a loss for words.

"We did fairly well. Though Quince tripped and fell on-stage. It was terrible for him and wonderful for the company. Would you care for some wine?"

"Certainly," Marietta said, though she never drank wine. But she thought a seductress would be likely to say *certainly* in answer to that question.

He went to a bar cart in the corner of the room and poured from a bottle into two goblets.

"It's from Italy," he said as he crossed the room to join her.

When he handed it to her, she noticed that the goblet was silver and engraved. She tasted the wine. It was a rich red, oaky and masculine.

"Do you like it?" he asked.

"Mmm," she said, although she found it heady.

He started to chuckle. She was confused; then she realized he was laughing at her expense.

"What could possibly be so amusing to you?" she said, feeling indignant.

"My apologies," he said, trying to stop. "It's only that—there's something about you, something I've never encountered in anyone else. It's so difficult to see through your many facades. Your expressions are as fathomless as the clouds."

"Oh," she said. "It isn't my intention to seem confusing."

"No, no," he said, leaning closer. "It's something I enjoy. Trying to unravel the mysteries of what you're really doing, what you're really saying."

Nervously, she gulped her wine. Perhaps it was better than she initially thought. She was starting to feel warmer and more relaxed.

Shakespeare continued. "I've written many sonnets about you, Marietta. You know you've inspired my new play, but there are even more poems you've sparked that I haven't yet sent to you."

She perked up. He was starting to get that feverish look he got when he talked about her being his muse.

"I inspired your new play?" she said.

"Yes," he answered. "But first, the poems."

He strode across the room to a desk that Marietta hadn't noticed, being distracted by the magnificent room and by her companion's conversation. From a drawer, he pulled a few sheets of parchment, and, still holding his wine in one hand, cleared his throat to read.

"Shall I compare thee to a summer's day?
Thou art more lovely and more temperate.
Rough winds do shake the darling buds of May,
And summer's lease hath all too short a date."

Yesterday, Henry had read her a poem written by Will that had put her in awe. Now, hearing Will's words from his very own lips, with such emotion weighting each word, she was struck dumb.

After a moment of silence in which he stood with the parchment in one hand and the glass of wine in the other, he said, "Please, say something."

"It's…it's beautiful," Marietta said, and she meant it. "I am—I'm overcome."

Standing in the low lamplight, Will didn't seem to her at all like a rake, not a bit like her old beau Jacob. She forgot all about the mysterious woman who had exited the back room that morning. All she could think about was this honest and passionate man before her.

"I'm afraid I'm the one who is overcome. This is what your beauty and vivacity drives me to," Shakespeare said. "There is a character in my new play—I'm calling it *As You Like It*—and my inspiration for her is you."

And all at once, Marietta snapped back to reality. She felt as sober as she had before her first sip of that Italian wine.

His newest play.

"*As You Like It* is the name of your newest play?" she asked.

"Yes, and the character's name—your character's name—is Rosalind."

"Rosalind," Marietta repeated. It was a beautiful name. "Tell me how we're alike."

"She is willful, strong, and independent. She brings light to all the dark corners with her cleverness and her gaiety. She goes where she likes and dresses as she likes."

Marietta smiled. This was exactly how she would like to think of herself, even if others often underestimated her abilities.

Shakespeare continued talking as he refilled her wine.

"It's superstitious of me, but I suppose that's the stage. Sometimes I don't know if I dreamed Rosalind into being, or if by
creating Rosalind, I brought you to me. Such was the process
of writing the play, that I can't be sure which is the reality, if
either of them at all."

He went to his desk and brought back a stack of papers—
the play itself. This was what Marlowe had sent her for, the
whole reason she was here. To take *As You Like It* from its author and bring it to a lesser thief so he could pass it off as his
own.

"This is Rosalind," he said, "after her father's kingdom has
been usurped and he has fled to the woods with a band of
followers."

> *Dear Celia, I show more mirth than I am mistress of; and
> would you yet I were merrier? Unless you could teach me to for-
> get...*

Something in her gave way. The line *I show more mirth than
I am mistress of* seemed to her so perfectly shaped to hold
her hidden feelings about her life and its disappointments.
Or perhaps it was the mention of the name Celia, Marietta's
friend and confidante, though Will could not have known
when he named the characters. But she was suddenly overcome by a fervor and need for him.

At once she was across the room and in his arms. He
kissed her roughly, his hands gripping at her hair and then
moving to untie her bodice. She ripped at the ties with him,
until the bodice was off. She breathed a sigh of relief. He
lifted his tunic and threw it on the floor, and then they were
together on the rug, caught up in a total, absolute passion.

Much later, Marietta blinked awake and sat up before remembering what she had just done. The wine had left her

head foggy. She realized that she was unclothed, then looked over and saw Shakespeare—*Will*, she thought—asleep with his arms beneath his head like a pillow. Quietly, she gathered her clothes. Out the windows, she could see that the light of dawn was just beginning to creep into the deep blue sky. The stars were disappearing. After she was dressed, she was about to tiptoe out of the room when she saw the play. It had landed on the floor beside her chair.

She stole one last glance at the sleeping genius who had written her into his masterpiece. Marlowe did not deserve this play.

But it was a desperate situation; it was for Nico.

William, a renowned playwright, would have other successes. He would know she was the thief. And she would never be able to see him again.

Though Nico, her only brother, her only family—his life would be spared.

She snatched for the play, lifting its heft and turning. Just as she was about to leave the room with it, she heard a mumble.

Behind her, Will was beginning to move and mutter. She froze. His eyes opened and he looked right at her.

She dropped the play and ran out the door. Before she even knew what she was doing, she was halfway back to the fountain in the square.

And she was sobbing. She knew she had ruined it, ruined everything. Now that Shakespeare had seen her, she could never retrieve the play for Marlowe. Her lover knew she was false. And Nico—Nico was in danger once more.

Chapter 12

MARIETTA MANAGED TO wash her face and arrive
for work at the tailor shop, where Celia mercifully chose
not to pry. Marietta was sure she could tell something was
wrong, though. They threw themselves into their sewing,
and because they had a busy day ahead of them, Marietta
found that she did not have time to dwell on her problems until she was walking home alone. She wondered if
Shakespeare would seek her out to confront her about her
dishonesty, or if he would simply go on as if she didn't exist. She and Nico could find another way to pay Marlowe
the money he was owed. She could sew fine ladies' clothing at home after work, and perhaps they could take on a
boarder.

But when she arrived home, she found a single red rose
laid across the doorstep. She picked it up and smelled it, cautiously. It was a perfect flower. Underneath it was a piece of
parchment that read,

Marietta,

I must see you again. Meet me tonight on your side of the river, near the bridge that separates the stage from the rest of the dreary world.

With great fondness,
Will

She stared at it, reading it over and over again, for a full minute before she went inside.

"Nico?" she called. There was no answer.

Marietta went to her bedroom, where she hid the rose and parchment in a drawer.

What could Will want? Surely he didn't write that he must see her again because he felt he was still courting her. He had witnessed her trying to steal his play. What if this was a way of confronting her, asking her to confirm or deny that she was indeed a charlatan? But then, why the rose, and why *with great fondness?*

She knew that she should not go to meet him. She had already exposed herself for what she really was. Yet she couldn't bear to think that she might never see Will's face again. One last time, one last good-bye—what was the harm in that?

Chapter 13

SHE WAITED UNDER a streetlamp near the bridge, shrouded by a cloak and hood lest someone recognize her. She knew she was being dramatic, but she was wary. Horses and carriages clattered by her as she paced along the dark water of the Thames.

"Marietta," said a voice behind her.

She jumped.

When she turned around, she saw Will laughing.

"What in the world has you so frightened? Did you think I was a pickpocket?"

She composed herself. "No, no! I'm glad it's you."

She steeled herself for his rebuke, his account of what a liar and thief she was, but it didn't come.

Instead, he moved toward her and embraced her. And she forgot for a moment about Marlowe and Nico, about everything but Will and his kiss. This was where she belonged—in his arms.

He pulled away from her. "I've been writing again. You inspire me so! This morning I wrote a new sonnet and continued with Rosalind's character—"

He stopped. "Something is upsetting you. Why are you so stiff?"

"No, no, nothing is the matter," she said, attempting a smile. "I'm delighted to see you."

He took her arm and gestured that they should walk to where his carriage was waiting at the bridge.

"I wish I could read the depths of your eyes to find out what you're truly thinking," he said. "I suppose that never knowing what you'll say next is one reason I enjoy your company so much."

"Do you? Enjoy my company?" she asked. He seemed so relaxed. She didn't understand why.

He helped her into the carriage, then followed to sit beside her. "Why, of course! I was disappointed this morning when I awoke and you had already taken leave."

She was stunned. So he *hadn't* been awake when she tried to leave with the play!

"My sewing was calling me," she said.

"Yes. Tell me, did you embroider this?" He touched the hem of her skirt, decorated with tiny white vines and flowers.

"Oh, that. Yes, I do little embroidery projects as well."

"There's no need to be humble," he said. "It's quite intricate, quite detailed. Your work is a kind of poetry in itself."

She laughed. "You are full of silver-tongued words tonight."

"I'm sincere, Marietta. It's beautiful." He turned her chin toward his face with a finger and gave her a kiss.

When the carriage pulled up to his door again, she wondered how she could be doing this. Sneaking off to spend scandalous nights at the house of none other than William Shakespeare! If Celia only knew. This wasn't like Marietta at all. Well, not like the old Marietta, anyway.

Again, she was in his living room, again drinking wine. And he was sharing with her parts of the play, new lines about Rosalind from Orlando.

"From the east to western Ind,
No jewel is like Rosalind.
Her worth, being mounted on the wind,
Through all the world bears Rosalind.
All the pictures fairest lined
Are but black to Rosalind.
Let no face be kept in mind
But the fair of Rosalind."

"The words are lovely," she told him. "It's hard to believe that you write them for me."

"The words come easily when the muse is so lovely," he said, and kissed her. "No other woman has ever inspired me as you have."

She hesitated, remembering something. "No other woman?"

He nodded and leaned in again, but she avoided his kiss.

"Who was the woman who came out of the back room before I went in yesterday?"

He looked puzzled. "What woman?"

She straightened and set her wine on the table. "Do not pretend for my benefit that you don't know what woman. As I've told you before, I am aware of your reputation, William Shakespeare, as anyone is in London!"

It was his turn to straighten. He seemed to be stifling a laugh. "And I have told you, whatever the rumors, there is no truth to them." He took a sip of his wine.

"How can you say that when you aren't aware of the rumors?"

He sighed. "They say that I love beautiful women?"

"Yes."

"That I woo many women and break many hearts?"

"Yes."

"No. I write of love and of women, and it makes the

masses think that I must live exactly as I write. But that's not true—to write well of romantic affairs, of friends and brothers and warring families, a man must live a life of solitude."

Marietta stayed quiet. Perhaps the rumors were only rumors. After all, she remembered, the first person to tell her of Shakespeare's reputation as a rake was his enemy, Marlowe.

"And the woman who left the back room yesterday afternoon?"

"That must have been the maid, Greta. She comes to clean the back room and the stage between performances."

The maid! All at once, Marietta realized how foolish she was being. Here was a man who was confessing his admiration only for her, and she was inventing stories of his misdeeds.

"I'm sorry, Will," she said, moving closer to him. She put her hands in his. "You must forgive me. I am only afraid of being wronged."

"I forgive you," he said. "I'll always forgive you. I forgive you a thousand times."

They kissed passionately. The room smelled of the redolent smoke from the lamps he had lit, and of her lily perfume.

"You are slow to trust. Whoever it was that wronged you before, he was a fool," William told her. "As for me, you are the only woman I have eyes for."

She let him kiss her until she felt dizzy, and then he let him lead her upstairs to the bedroom. The play was downstairs on the desk. But Marietta knew that she would never be able to give it to Marlowe now. Not when it was written by the man she loved.

Chapter 14

MEANWHILE, NICO SAT again at the White Hart Tavern, drinking ale with the men with whom he had worked to build the wall. Construction work always meant pocket money, and this was his second night of carousing. Nico and the other men were watching some women dance in the middle of the room. It was a bawdy scene—the dancers lifted their skirts and posed seductively. He was feeling light, happy, relaxed. Having a pint was the only thing that made him feel this way; the rest of life was work and pain. Well, gambling had a certain appeal, of course. But he was doing his best to avoid it after the incident with Marlowe.

Unsteadily, he stood and reached in his pocket for his coins. He needed only one more drink, and then he would go home. The barmaids were all busy, so he brought his mug to the bartender for another pint of ale.

The tavern was packed tonight, with what seemed like half the men in London enjoying the entertainment. He made his way through the crowd, but once he got close to the bartender, someone else pushed him. Nico whirled around.

The man was bigger than he was, and clearly tipsy.

"Careful," Nico warned.

"Out of the way," the man slurred. "I'm try'na get a pint of ale."

"You'll get your ale," said Nico. "But you'll wait your turn first."

"Hey—aren't you the one with the sister who runs around with the playwright?"

"What did you say?" Now the man had Nico's full attention.

"The harlot. She's the one who visits Shakespeare's house nightly. I've seen her with my own eyes!" The man flashed a mean grin.

Before Nico knew what happened, he was on top of the man, punching him hard in the face. But the man, bigger than Nico, quickly got the upper hand.

All around them, men were chanting "Fight! Fight!" and Nico was angrier than he had ever been. No sister of his would be called a harlot.

Then someone lifted him off the floor and dragged him out of the bar, throwing him out on the street.

"Go home and see about your wicked sister!" the voice shouted. There was laughter floating out the door, followed by a slamming door.

Nico groaned, and picked himself up. He thought about forcing his way back into the tavern, showing them all what he was made of. But Marietta's honor was at stake. He had to stop what she was doing, before the gossip had spread too far. A woman without her honor had nothing at all.

He wiped some blood from his face with his tunic and began the arduous task of walking home. When he arrived, the cottage was dark. Marietta was gone. He began to fear the worst—had she, in fact, followed through on Marlowe's plan? Was she attempting to seduce the playwright? He couldn't believe that his sweet sister would do such a thing.

Angrily, he searched her room—under the bed, in her meager dresser. There was very little to search at all. Then, finally, he opened the drawer that contained one red rose and the note from Shakespeare, asking Marietta to meet him near the Thames.

Nico howled. Not only was his sister secretly meeting a man by night, but she was deceiving that man by stealing his play. And it was all for him, her brother! She was destroying her reputation to spare him his rotten gambling debts. And he had not even been able to defend her by winning the fight at the bar.

Silently, Nico vowed that he would put an end to Marietta's misery. He would step up and be a man. It would be he, not Marietta, who would be the one to steal the play for Marlowe.

Chapter 15

MARIETTA WAS SO happy that she came into the tailor shop humming the next morning without realizing it.

Celia looked up with a smile. "Someone is in a good mood today. You're like a little robin!"

Marietta laughed. "How can you know? You know everything."

Celia turned back to her sewing. "Well, not everything. Pray, tell me, have you been well? I feel as though we've hardly spoken since the night we went to see *A Midsummer Night's Dream*."

Marietta felt the sickness of guilt. She picked up her own sewing, a bodice for which her skilled embroidery had been commissioned. She wanted to tell Celia everything, but she was also afraid that her friend would judge her harshly for her actions. Celia had been honest, hardworking, and loyal her whole life. She would never be able to understand what possessed Marietta to immerse herself in this scheme.

"I've been well," she said, keeping her eyes on her work. "Thank you for asking. I've missed you, too, dear friend. How have your days been lately?"

Celia was about to tell her, when they both heard a commotion in the front of the shop.

"What in the name of the heavens?" Celia exclaimed.

It sounded like someone was shouting. They both put down their sewing and came from the back of the store to the front to witness the scene.

Marietta almost fainted when she saw. The blood rushed away from her face. It was none other than Christopher Marlowe, dressed in his signature oversized collar and raising his voice with the tailor. Poor Mr. Buckley was stammering.

"I-I-I'm sorry, sir, when the seamstresses are working we try to give them peace, and we handle customers' requests at the front of the store. I am at your service."

"I don't have a customer request. I told you, I need to see Miss DiSonna on personal business," Marlowe answered. He carried himself like nobility, drawing himself up to his full height in order to tower over meek Mr. Buckley.

"I'm here," Marietta heard herself saying. "We'll only be a moment, Mr. Buckley. We'll be outside."

Marlowe turned on his heel and marched out of the store, and Marietta followed quickly, lest he make another scene. She glimpsed the glee on the faces of the young shopgirls, and the confusion in Celia's eyes. There was no way she could keep her secret from Celia now.

She beckoned Marlowe a few feet away, at a safe distance from the shop, out of sight. She was sure the two front girls, Elizabeth and Agnes, were making excuses to clean near the windows so they could spy out.

"I'm pleased, Marietta," Marlowe said. She instinctively recoiled from his unctuous manner. She had not seen him since the night she danced at the White Hart with Shakespeare, but now she realized she hated everything about him, down to his perfectly groomed mustache.

"And what has pleased you so?" Marietta asked. She had not yet obtained the play. What other reason could there be?

"I've been hearing some wonderful rumors," Marlowe said, "about you and Shakespeare."

Marietta's heart sank. All of London must know! And she thought she had been so careful.

"Since you have succeeded in seducing Shakespeare—and of course you have, beautiful as you are—there should be no challenge in getting the play for me tonight."

"Tonight?!" Marietta exclaimed. "Two days ago, a player from your company sent a message that you would wait a fortnight."

"Yes," Marlowe said, "But you have done so well, even better than I thought you would."

He looked her over with a gaze that she found impertinent. She crossed her arms over her chest.

"You're quite the master at this. Therefore, tell him you must see him tonight, distract him with your wiles, and find a way to smuggle the play out for me."

"Seduction," she said, "isn't always a one-night affair, Mr. Marlowe. Though perhaps you are not aware?"

He dropped his smile and looked annoyed.

Marietta continued with her bluff. "By the time I'm finished, William Shakespeare will be so in love with me he'll be eating out of the palm of my hand. But I can't accomplish that in one night. He must trust me completely."

Marlowe grimaced. "Love, Miss Marietta, is not the task I set you to. I told you that if you wanted to save your brother's life, you would need to *seduce* Shakespeare. And seduction, Miss Marietta, as I'm sure you know, *is* a one-night affair."

His attitude so offended Marietta that she wanted to slap him right there in the square, in front of all the shoppers and merchants. She and Marlowe were keeping their voices relatively hushed, but she was afraid that passersby might still hear.

"Tomorrow, Marietta," Marlowe said. "The play is mine tomorrow, or your brother will be made responsible for his debts." Then he turned and walked away as if they had never spoken at all.

Marietta stood dumbfounded for a moment. She had no idea what she was going to do. Stealing the play would mean losing Will, and not stealing it would mean losing her brother.

She went back into the shop. The two girls seemed as if they were trying not to look at her. They suppressed giggles. Mr. Buckley was attending to a customer. Marietta walked past them with her head high, as if today were a day like any other.

When she got to the back door, she heard Elizabeth whisper to Agnes, "Romeo, sweet Romeo!" Both girls started laughing.

Marietta darted through the back door and stood against it as if she were guarding from intruders.

Celia looked up. Worry lines creased her forehead. "Marietta," she said. "You must tell me what is happening. Are you in trouble?"

Before Marietta could answer, there was a knock at the door.

She brushed her hair back from her face and opened it. It was Mr. Buckley.

"Marietta," he said, "perhaps you should return home."

"But—" she protested. Taking the day would mean losing her daily wages, and it was a poor time for that, when she was trying to find a way to keep Nico out of trouble.

"I'm sorry," said Mr. Buckley. He blinked rapidly, as he did whenever he was nervous. "I can't have this type of commotion with customers in the shop."

Marietta nodded. She gave Celia a little wave, and walked past Mr. Buckley to the street outside.

A lot of good Nico had done her. She should have stayed far away from this tangle of misdeeds—though he had told her as much. Why did she have to rush to be involved, to defend? He was her little brother. Alas, she thought, perhaps there had never been a way for her to protect him.

Chapter 16

LATER THAT NIGHT, Nico found himself in a pleasant district of London, on a street full of grand houses. A friend of his who held gentlemen's horses at the Globe Theatre had told him that William Shakespeare always attended performances of his own plays, and so Nico knew that he would undoubtedly be in attendance at tonight's performance of *A Midsummer Night's Dream.* Shakespeare's home would be empty.

Nico had stayed sober for the occasion. He guessed he probably had an hour to complete the task. He skulked around the street corners, avoiding carriages because he might look out of place.

When he arrived at Shakespeare's address, he snuck around the back, looking for an entry that might already be provided for him. Before too long, he had it. A window had been left open.

The house was dark. It appeared there were no servants or family present. Nico carefully opened the shutters the rest of the way and hoisted himself into the room, falling onto the carpet with a light thud.

He stood up and dusted himself off. He was in a large sitting room, with chairs situated before a fireplace. He fumbled around until he found a lamp and matches on a table. He lit it, and held it up to look around.

It was a beautiful room, filled with oil paintings and books. And what great luck: Shakespeare's desk was right next to the window!

Nico brought the lamp over to the desk and began sifting through papers. Before too long, he found a sheaf of parchment with a cover page: *As You Like It.* It was hefty enough; perhaps it was the play that Marlowe wanted.

Nico looked through the drawers for anything else that might resemble Marlowe's desired play, but nothing seemed to be quite as long. Only a few poems. He sat down in one of the chairs by the fireplace, realizing that he had never read a play before.

It began with Orlando. Nico read:

> *"As I remember, Adam, it was upon this fashion bequeathed me by will but poor a thousand crowns, and, as thou sayest, charged my brother on his blessing to breed me well: and there begins my sadness."*

Nico stopped. The words were dense and confusing, but there was also something beautiful about them. And something wonderful about this place. He noticed, on the table, a bottle of wine and two goblets.

Glancing at the door behind him, he guessed that Shakespeare would still not be home for three quarters of an hour. What would he notice if a little wine was missing? By the time he realized, Nico would be long gone with the only copy of the play.

And so Nico poured himself a generous goblet and took a big sip, and then another. He settled into a chair with the play—just for long enough to enjoy life in William Shakespeare's very rich shoes.

Chapter 17

NICO WOKE UP with a start, not understanding where he was. There was a noise at the door....

In a flash, he remembered that he was in Shakespeare's house, and realized that he might be hearing the sounds of the playwright coming home. How long had he slept? He bolted for the window, sheaf of parchment in hand.

He almost got out in time, but wasn't fast enough. "You there!" someone behind him shouted.

Nico didn't wait to find out who it was. He jumped from the window and started running down the street as fast as his legs could carry him. But his pursuer was close behind him. One glance told him it was Shakespeare himself. Panting for breath, Nico ran faster.

"Stop! Thief!" Shakespeare shouted.

Nico ducked down a side street, hoping to lose his pursuer, but Shakespeare stayed close on his heels. He ran down another side street, and another, until he didn't even know where in the city he was.

He turned right, into a dark, narrow alley. Perhaps Shakespeare would be afraid to follow him down there. Nico took a sharp left, only to find himself faced with a wall. It was a dead end.

He rotated around to find himself face-to-face with the man he had just stolen from. Instinctively, he hid the play he held in his hands behind his back. But that only left him exposed and defenseless. In a sudden surge of movement, Shakespeare put a knife at his throat.

"Wait," Nico said. "Sir, please. It is not what it seems."

"If it's not what it seems, then I expect it to be quite a tale," the other man said wryly.

Nico assessed his situation. One man wanted an incredible sum of money, a play, or his life, and another man might be willing to kill him to retain his own play. It was not a good situation. Nico had to say something intelligent, something clever, to trick his way out.

Instead, he found himself blurting out, "What are your intentions with Marietta DiSonna?"

Shakespeare looked surprised. "You know Marietta?" Then he seemed to grow suspicious. "Ah, are you another suitor of hers?"

"Nay, I'm her brother!" Nico exclaimed. "And she is a woman with the heart of a saint. Any man who hurts her must do his reckoning with me."

"My intentions with Marietta are honorable. But if you're her brother, what are your intentions with my play?"

"Sir, I did not mean to take it, but I have made a bargain with the Devil. Please forgive me," said Nico.

"And who might this Devil be?"

"Christopher Marlowe."

"Ah," said Shakespeare. Nico felt the coldness of the steel press into his throat. "A devil indeed. Christopher Marlowe sent you to take something of mine?"

Before he could stop himself, Nico felt the story pouring out of him. "I owe him a great debt. He sent Marietta to seduce you to take the play, but I cannot let her destroy her reputation over me. Please, if you must harm anyone, it should be me. Everything that has happened in this sad tale is my fault."

Nico expected vengeance. But Shakespeare only dropped the knife, leaving him holding the parchment with one hand and rubbing his throat with the other.

"Marietta was sent by Marlowe?" he asked. "This whole time?" He looked dumbstruck, like a man who had been told the sky was not blue.

"It's my fault, sir. She didn't think she had a choice. She is honest and good; it's all my fault."

"No matter," Shakespeare spoke very quietly. "No matter. You can take the play."

Nico was stunned. "I can?"

"Take it. It was for her," he said softly. "It was all for Marietta. Now that I know that her love was false, it means nothing to me."

Nico didn't move.

"Take the play," Shakespeare said in defeat. "And get out of my sight."

Nico ran past him into London, racing as fast as he could toward his redemption.

Chapter 18

NICO DID NOT stop until he reached his cottage door. He hesitated. Inside, he heard the soft sounds of someone weeping.

"Marietta?" he called quietly, as he pushed open the door. There was no answer.

He found her in the little kitchen, pacing back and forth. For a moment, she didn't even see him.

"Marietta," he said again. She turned around. He could see streaks down her cheeks from her tears.

"What's wrong?" he asked.

She didn't answer. He realized she was staring at the sheaf of parchment in his hand.

"Marietta?"

She moved toward him. "What's that?" she asked, reaching for it.

"This?" He moved his hands behind his back. "It's our good fortune! I can see how you have been distressed by the predicament I've created. But you needn't worry any longer. I have the play! I will give it to Marlowe tonight, and all my debts will be repaid."

Marietta didn't respond right away. "You have... you have the play?" she asked.

"Yes," he said. He brought it forward again, for her to see.

"The work by the playwright William Shakespeare?"

"Yes," he said, now wondering if there was something wrong with her.

"And it's here, in our home?"

"What's wrong, Marietta? I've ended our troubles. I promise, you'll never have any dealings with that nasty Marlowe again."

Marietta was still standing stock still, looking as though she had received a shock of some kind. "You have Shakespeare's play?"

He didn't say anything this time.

"But how do you have it? What did you do, Nico? What did you do?"

"I—I took it from his house."

She seemed to go weak for a moment. She made her way to a chair in the corner and sat down. He stayed where he was, on the other side of the room.

"But—how?" she asked.

"I came through the window when he was away. This is good, Marietta. This means that you no longer have to risk your reputation to help me! Marlowe will have what he wants and life can resume as usual."

"You don't understand."

"What?"

"You don't understand—I was not risking my reputation."

"Yes, yes, I'm afraid you were. But not to worry; I have defended it! All is well." Nico was beginning to get agitated. Was there something wrong with his sister?

"No! Nico, you must understand, Will and I—"

"Will?"

"Yes—what I have with Will, it's not a lie. It only started

out that way. I wanted to help you, but it grew into—into something more."

"Marietta, are you saying that the rumors are true?"

"I don't know what the rumors are, but I do know that I care for him. And how can he trust me now that his play is missing?"

Nico clenched his fist around the rolled parchment. He knew from his encounter with Shakespeare that Marietta had been seeing him, but her admission still made him angry.

"He does not care for you, sister," he said, feeling a contemptuous smile grow across his face. "I told him the truth, and he said he did not even want the play, for it was tainted by your lies to him."

Marietta stood, rage shaking her limbs. "Nico, tell me that isn't true. Tell me that you did not convince William Shakespeare of my indifference."

She walked toward him.

He backed away. "You were out in secret every night, sullying the name of the DiSonna family!" he yelled.

"A lot left to sully, with all your gambling, drinking, and debts, Nico!" she shouted back.

She made a grab for the play, but he was too quick for her. He pushed her away, roughly, and ran toward the door, holding the play firmly in place behind his back.

"At this point, would you have even taken the play for Marlowe, as you were supposed to do? You would have chosen your affair over your own flesh and blood?"

"Nico…" Now Marietta looked stricken. Tears began to roll down her face once again.

"He never would have treated you honorably, Marietta. You, a poor seamstress, and him, a famous playwright! At least what I'm doing will get us out of trouble now. I'm bringing this play to Marlowe tomorrow night and laying this ordeal to rest for good." Nico was almost crying, too.

Before Marietta could say anything else, he ran out of the house with play in hand.

Chapter 19

AFTER NICO LEFT, letting the door slam shut behind him, Marietta crumpled to the floor. She couldn't keep herself from sobbing. All the secrecy and all her shameful hiding had been revealed, and now she was afraid that Shakespeare would never speak to her again. She should never have tried to get involved. She had tricked him, and she never deserved him in the first place.

And now, even worse, his masterpiece was gone. And that terrible Marlowe was going to have it delivered straight into his hands. There was nothing she could do—Nico was determined to save himself. She would have to learn to live without Will and move forward, loveless and alone.

She sobbed for a good long while, until her eyes were red and her throat scratched from the crying. Then she remembered—she was not completely alone. There was still Celia. Marietta hoped she was not angry for the way she'd been behaving lately. She would have to go to Celia's house and hope that, ever constant as she was, Celia would forgive her and take her in. Marietta would tell her everything.

She looked at the clock. It was too late an hour to call upon Celia. Tonight, Marietta would get some rest. But tomorrow, she would pull herself together, splash some water on her face, and pay a visit to her only true friend.

Chapter 20

THE NEXT DAY, in the empty round space of the Rose Theatre, Christopher Marlowe stood with a well-dressed, wealthy man.

"Philip, you know us artists! Crafting a masterpiece takes time. But the new play is coming soon. I expect to have it on the stage within one month's time."

Philip Henslowe, the theatre's owner, pulled on his fine wool vest and cleared his throat.

"We cannot wait too much longer, Marlowe," he said. "We must have entertainment for the people. We have already been charging for tickets."

Marlowe smiled, his lips curling up to match his waxed mustache. He clapped Henslowe on the back.

"Yes, yes! Entertainment for the people! And what entertainment it will be, I promise you. I'm quite excited about this next project. Just wait until you see it."

Henslowe smoothed his beard nervously. He was about to say something, but they were interrupted by Marlowe's player, Edmund Wells, when he ran into the theatre. He reached Marlowe, then cupped his hands and whispered into the playwright's ear. "I was just at the White Hart. The boy, Nico, will repay his debts tonight," Edmund whispered.

Marlowe nodded and patted Edmund on the shoulder. "Very well, Edmund. Thank you for letting me know."

He turned to Philip Henslowe. "Do not worry, dear sir," he said, putting his hand on Henslowe's back and steering him toward the theatre's exit. "I have absolute confidence that the play will be in rehearsal within the week. Why, I'll finish the thing tonight."

"Very well," said Henslowe, seeming satisfied. "I shall come to view rehearsal at the end of the week then?"

"Yes, that's right. I think you'll be very pleased, very pleased indeed!" said Marlowe.

Henslowe donned his hat and mounted his horse. The men said their farewells, and Marlowe strode back into the theatre, where Edmund was still waiting, still and silent as ever.

Marlowe rubbed his hands together in excitement. "This is fantastic news! I was beginning to think the DiSonna siblings would never come through with the play."

Edmund smiled the pleased grin of one who has been congratulated on a job well done.

"Edmund, you know what terrible writer's block I've had," said Marlowe. "And that hack, Shakespeare, always seems to have a new play on at the Globe. Well now I'll be able to beat him at his own game. The play will arrive in as good a shape as it is, and I'll fix it up as my own. And of course, Edmund, there will be a good part in it for you."

Edmund grinned. "The hero or the villain?"

"Whichever you prefer, loyal Edmund," Marlowe said. "Whichever you prefer."

Chapter 21

MARIETTA PRACTICALLY RAN all the way to the little room Celia rented in a young women's boardinghouse. They sat together on Celia's bed, and Marietta started sobbing all over again. Then the whole story spilled out.

"I was so concerned for you yesterday, when that man…"

"Christopher Marlowe."

"…when Christopher Marlowe came to speak with you. It seemed you were in grave trouble!"

"Oh, Celia, I have been, and I'm sorry that I kept it from you. It was only to protect you, Nico, and myself. I didn't want to get you involved."

Celia leaned forward and wiped Marietta's cheek with her embroidered handkerchief. "Of course you didn't. It's all right, Marietta. You're telling me now."

"Oh, Celia, if you only knew. I thought I could be a secret spy or a dramatic thief, like someone in a play. But he's so handsome! And so romantic."

"Tell me about him," Celia said, leaning back against the wall. "What is he like, the playwright William Shakespeare?"

"Oh, he's a gentleman, always looking after a lady first," Marietta said dreamily. "He's quiet. At first I couldn't tell what he was thinking, and I had no idea how he felt about me. But he would leave me the most beautiful little notes and write me poems. He took me to a breathtaking secret garden…and that's where he opened up to me."

Celia smiled to hear her friend describe such a man, but then Marietta frowned and sighed.

"But it's of no use now. Nico has told him that everything was a lie, and William was apparently so upset that he gave Nico the play. How would I ever explain this to him and win his favor again?"

"But you have to try!" exclaimed Celia.

"How?" Marietta asked, surprised by her friend's insistence.

"With a man like that, and when you are so in love, how can you not?" Celia said. "You must go to him. If he has these strong romantic feelings for you, as you say he does, then none of this will matter."

"But what of the play?" Marietta said. "Celia, how will he ever forgive me—how will I ever forgive myself—for being involved in the theft of that wonderful play? And after he put me in it?"

"Yes," Celia said. "The play…"

"What?"

"Well—when you told me what Marlowe said yesterday, you never said the name of the play."

"It's called *As You Like It*."

"Yes, yes, I know that. But," Celia leaned forward, "did you say it in front of Marlowe?"

"Did I say what?"

"The title of the play! Does he even know what it's called?"

"No…no! He doesn't know what it's called. I've never told him."

"Do you think that Nico might have told him the title already?"

"I don't think he's been in contact with Marlowe. He said he plans to bring the play to him tonight."

"So there is still some time."

"Time for what, Celia? I don't understand."

"Time to give Marlowe a decoy play." Celia sat up, enthused by her idea. "If he doesn't know what William Shakespeare's newest play is about, it could be anything. As long as he doesn't know the difference. The important thing is that you get to Marlowe before Nico does, so he never gets his hands on the real play."

Marietta gasped. "Celia, you're brilliant!" She threw her arms around her friend.

"Oh, shush, it's nothing," Celia said.

"But where will I find a decoy play?"

"Well—there is a man of letters who I believe could help."

"Really, who?"

Celia laughed. "Why, your Shakespeare of course! Go and tell him the truth. See if he can provide some kind of decoy—an old, unknown play, or one by another playwright Marlowe wouldn't recognize."

"Yes," Marietta said, straightening herself and fixing her hair in the mirror. "Yes, you're right. I'll have to tell him the truth. Even if he casts me aside, things can't be any worse than they are now. What have I to lose? And yet Will could still avoid losing his work of art."

"You'll have to work fast," Celia said, dabbing at Marietta's face again with the vanilla-scented handkerchief. "There isn't much time. Where do you think he'll be?"

"Well…he's recently lost a play and a woman. I expect he, like most men, might be indulging in a pint at the pub."

"Good," said Celia, opening the door. "Now go, go!" Marietta flew out as fast as she had come in, blowing her friend a kiss on her way.

Chapter 22

MARIETTA RAN ALL the way into town, hoping that this plan would work. As her feet pounded down on the pavement and she whisked past horses and carts, she flashed back to a memory of the moment when everything started, when she raced to the White Hart to save Nico from Marlowe's wrath. How things had changed in such a short time!

Today she hoped to avoid that particular tavern at all costs. She couldn't risk Marlowe seeing her out. She prayed Shakespeare would instead be at the Boar's Head Inn, another public house he'd told her he frequented. When Marietta reached the tavern doors, she paused to catch her breath. What if Will didn't even want to look at her? No, she couldn't even think about that. She would just have to go and find out.

She marched into the center of the tavern. All the men turned their heads, surprised to see a woman in their midst in the middle of the afternoon. She walked straight to the one man who didn't look up from his pint, his unkempt hair falling into his eyes as he leaned over it, as if he could see his future in the liquid.

She paused next to him. He didn't move.

"Will," she said.

She saw him tense when he recognized the sound of her

voice. She was not even aware that she had been wringing her hands together, until he turned toward her. Her heart melted when she saw his face.

"Marietta," he said. Her name came out as a rasp, a dry choking in his throat.

"May I sit down?" she asked.

He seemed to hesitate, but his gentle manners got the better of him. He pulled out the seat next to him to make it easier for her.

She sat, feeling the fluttering in her stomach that once came about because she had been thrilled to see him, but was now accompanied by the sickening feeling of nerves.

"What is it you're looking for?" Shakespeare said. He wasn't looking at her. He was still staring into his drink, expressionless.

"Please, Will, don't behave this way," she said.

"In what way am I behaving?" he asked.

"As though you cannot bear to be near me!" she said. "Please, look at me."

He turned his sweet, baleful brown eyes toward her. He was obviously trying not to seem too emotional.

"I know what Nico said to you," she told him.

"Then you know that I am aware of your lies," he said.

"I was not lying," she said. She looked him in the eye. Every nerve in her body pleaded with him to believe her.

He let out a little laugh and brought his attention back to his pint.

"Please, I beg of you, believe me!" Her voice rose in pitch, as she was starting to feel desperate. "It did begin that way, with Marlowe telling me that if I wanted to save my brother I must seduce you, but then—"

"And the tune of truth begins to play…"

"—but then I began to know you, and I—I developed

feelings for you. I realized that I could never steal your play, the play you wrote for me. I knew that there must be some other way to clear my brother's debts."

"Yet when you introduced yourself to me, when you professed a love for that performance of *A Midsummer Night's Dream,* when you spent time with me—all that was a trick."

"No! No, my love for the performance was real, and though my initial intentions were misguided, I quickly realized that I hadn't the heart to wrong you."

Shakespeare, who had been drinking his pint with an affect of indifference, now turned his body toward hers and raised his voice. "How am I to believe someone who came into my life intending to seduce me and steal from me? You have already built your story on a foundation of lies."

"I know. I understand—I would never be able to believe one who had so planned to deceive me, either! But look at me. I—"

He turned his eyes, icy cold on her, and the words *I love you* got lost in her throat. How could she be the one to first say that to a man of his ilk? She'd be laughed out of the pub. A lady never showed all of herself like that.

"What I mean to say is...

Shall I compare thee to a summer's day?
Thou art more lovely and more temperate."

She found herself standing up. Some other men had turned to watch her speak the words of poetry. She hadn't even realized how much the words of Shakespeare's sonnet had meant to her until they poured out of her. She was astonished to find that she could recall them. And at just the moment when she needed to prove to him how much she cared.

Then, Shakespeare was standing with her. He took her hands.

"Rough winds do shake the darling buds of May,
And summer's lease hath all too short a date."

There was a silence. In his eyes, there was forgiveness.

"I believe you," he said.

Then he kissed her, a soft and sweet apology that made her lips tingle. She almost swooned with relief that he still cared and had not scorned her forever.

Men in the tavern began whooping their approval. Marietta pulled away and blushed.

"Shall we talk somewhere, er, more private?" Shakespeare asked her, grabbing his hat off the table and taking the last swig of his pint.

"Yes, let's. Because there is still one problem…"

"We must get the play back from your brother! Of course. Now that I know you aren't the spy and seductress you intended to be"—he winked—"I must put the finishing touches on my lady Rosalind, so that she may shine brighter than any other star of literature."

Shakespeare put his hand on the small of her back to lead her out of the tavern.

"Where is that rascal brother of yours? I daresay he's a better runner than he is a gambler."

"Well—I believe my friend Celia and I have actually hatched a plan that will satisfy on all fronts."

"What do you mean?"

He held the door for her. She squinted in the bright sunlight outside. He motioned to a boy who was holding his horse for him.

"I mean that there is a way for you to have your play, for

Marlowe to believe that he is in possession of your play, and for my brother consequently to be free of his debts."

He stopped and stared at her, a bemused smile on his face. "It seems I'm not the only talent in London these days! How do you propose we accomplish your undertaking?"

"I'll tell you when we get to your library. But we ought to hurry—we haven't much time before my brother meets with Marlowe."

He helped her to mount the horse and then lifted himself to sit behind her. With his arms around her, hugging her sides, she couldn't help feeling giddy. She put her hands on the horse's warm neck. Then he gave the command and they galloped through town, on their way to return the play to its rightful owner.

Chapter 23

NICO HAD FINISHED with his shift at the stable. He had kept the precious play tucked carefully in a satchel in the hayloft, where he checked on it obsessively throughout the day. But before he went to see Marlowe, he decided it wouldn't hurt to nip into the pub for a quick pint. There, he had run into a friend who bought him another.

By the time Nico came out of the pub, he was feeling a little tipsy. He felt for the pages in his satchel, and, seeing that they were there, began his long, victorious walk to Christopher Marlowe's house. Earlier that day, he had sent a message to the effect that he would be coming. He didn't want Marlowe to harass Marietta. The messenger sent word back that Marlowe would be quite pleased to receive the play at his home that night.

As Nico trod down the street, warm from the alcohol in his blood, he felt elated to know he would soon be free. The knowledge of his debts had weighed as heavy on him as a woolen cloak. Without them, he might be able to turn over a new leaf, become a little more responsible. He could make Marietta proud. Then perhaps she would forgive him for ruining her chances with Shakespeare.

He did feel bad about the hurt look on his sister's face that

afternoon. He never liked to see Marietta upset, and he especially didn't like to be the cause of her pain. His sister was his
only family in the world. Sighing, he told himself he would
have to make it up to her. She would move on. Heartbreak
was only temporary.

When he reached Marlowe's door, he couldn't help but
be intimidated by its great height. The stone lions guarding
the entrance didn't help, either. He waited, alone in the dusk,
suddenly concerned that he had taken the right play. What if
there was another? What, exactly, did Marlowe want?

The door opened. Nico squinted through the flood of
light at the silhouette of a person who had opened it. The
man seemed to be a butler. He beckoned Nico in and,
silently, led him down a carpeted hall to a drawing room.
Nico stood in the doorway with his satchel at his side.

Marlowe stood with his back to the doorway, next to
a roaring fireplace. He was wearing a burgundy smoking
jacket, and he was completely still. He appeared to be con-
templating something. Nico looked around, but the butler
had disappeared from the hallway into some unknown room.
Nico didn't know whether he should come in the drawing
room and sit down, or stay standing at the door.

Marlowe turned, smiling as he did so.

"Nico," he said, smoothly. "I've been looking forward to
this visit." He was sipping what appeared to be brandy from
a glass.

"Can I offer you a drink?"

Nico, who almost never drank anything stronger than ale,
couldn't resist.

"Don't mind if I do," he said, making his way to Marlowe's
expensive-looking bar cart. He couldn't help but feel a pang,
looking around at the luxurious surroundings. It seemed that
Marlowe obviously didn't need the money that Nico owed.

Though it was true that Nico had lost at gambling, a kinder man might have forgiven at least part of the sum.

Marlowe handed him his own brandy. Nico took a sip, looking around at the rich-looking paintings. The brandy burned and then warmed his throat. Marlowe motioned him to a plush upholstered chair.

"My courtly patrons have been good to me," he said, motioning around him.

"Yes, sir," Nico said, finding his vocabulary significantly reduced in such intimidating surroundings.

"They'll be quite pleased, I'm sure, with the new play I'm about to present as well," Marlowe continued. "I trust you understand that this transaction that is about to take place is of the utmost confidence?"

Nico almost choked on a sip of brandy. "Oh, yes. Of course, sir," he said.

Marlowe twisted his mustache. "Good," he said. Then his tone became chilly. "Because if I find that word gets out about the origins of this play, I'll have no qualms about slitting the throat of a poor stable boy."

Nico stared. He reached for the satchel, his hands trembling.

"You understand that, right, Nico?"

"Yes, sir," Nico whispered.

"All right, then," Marlowe said. He waved his hands to motion Nico away from the satchel, which Nico had been about to open.

"There's no need for that yet," Marlowe said. "A gentleman always entertains his guest before he handles matters of business."

"Oh," Nico said. "Of course." He took another gulp of brandy, hoping that the faster he could finish it, the faster he could leave.

Chapter 24

"HURRY, HURRY!" URGED Marietta, who was sitting beside Will at the desk in his study. He was writing like a madman, dipping his quill in ink every few seconds, and she was blotting and blowing on each paper as he finished.

"Are you sure we couldn't simply take a play from your shelf?"

"And pass a published play off to another playwright? Marlowe's a bad writer, but even he isn't enough of a hack not to recognize an existing play."

"How much more do you have?"

Shakespeare completed the page with a final flourish. "It's done!"

"Thank the good Lord!" Marietta said as she blew on the ink frantically. "What if Nico has already arrived?" she said, gathering the parchment together.

"Have faith, Marietta. I feel nothing can go wrong with my muse by my side." He planted a kiss on her lips even as she was trying to rush out the door.

"We must hurry," she said, noting that they hadn't a moment to waste on amusements.

"Yes, yes, we'll take the carriage," he said.

And they rushed out into the night.

Chapter 25

MARLOWE HAD SPENT the better part of the last hour telling Nico about the various artists whose paintings graced his drawing room. Most of them, he claimed, were friends of his. Nico kept taking long pulls from his drink, wondering if he would ever be able to leave. Marlowe, to his surprise, seemed like a lonely man, eager for some companionship, even if it was from a gambling, indebted, thieving stable boy.

Finally, Marlowe stood. Nico copied him, reaching for the play.

He had just untied the leather strings on the satchel to pull out the parchment inside when the front door opened and slammed shut. He and Marlowe both turned toward the noise. Someone was running down the hall.

It was Marietta. Her hair was flying loose from its pins, and the sleeves of her dress were almost falling off of her shoulders as she raced into the room holding a sheaf of papers.

"I have the play!" she shouted. Then, realizing that it was only Marlowe and Nico, and that she had their attention, she said more softly, "I have the play."

She turned to Nico, flashing him a warning with her eyes. Then, she approached Marlowe tearfully, thrusting the papers forward. "Nico was doing his best to protect me by submitting a counterfeit on my behalf, so that I might not have to betray the playwright William Shakespeare," she said. "He is a good brother. But I cannot let him lie for me any longer. I have stolen the real play, and this is it."

Marlowe didn't move. He appeared to Nico to be shocked, and more than a little suspicious.

"Here, take it, before I change my mind," Marietta insisted, letting out another sob. Marlowe suddenly came to life. He reached out and snatched the pages from her.

With tears still in her eyes, Marietta turned toward Nico and grabbed his hand. He was still holding the satchel in the other. She took it from him, complete with the original play inside, and led him from the room, as Marlowe greedily perused the new play she had given him. Nico, drunk from the night's activities, said nothing as he followed Marietta down the hall and out the door. If anything, he felt grateful that she had come to lead him out of Marlowe's home.

"Please, don't say a word," Marietta said. "Just…thank you, bless you, dear brother. I'll explain everything in a moment."

Chapter 26

NICO, DUMBFOUNDED BY what had just happened, followed Marietta down the street. They stopped when they were a good distance from Marlowe's house.

"Did it work?" said a voice from the darkness.

Nico jumped. "Who goes there?" he shouted, reflexively.

Out of the shadows emerged none other than William Shakespeare. Nico put his hands up in front of them as though he was ready to fight. What was happening?

"Nico, Nico, all is well," Marietta said, laughing.

Shakespeare moved closer to his sister, and Nico was surprised to see them embrace.

Marietta handed Shakespeare the satchel with the real play. He opened it and eyed the pages as if they were precious gold.

Seeming elated, Shakespeare leaned forward to shake Nico's hand. Nico accepted the handshake dumbly.

"Well done, Nico. Thank you for your help in this matter."

"W-what?"

Marietta interjected. "We found a way to give Marlowe the play he thinks he wants and keep *As You Like It* safe."

Nico was about to ask for more of an explanation, but a

carriage came from around the corner, as if from nowhere. Marietta and Shakespeare got in and bid Nico join them. Then they were off at a trot.

Shakespeare continued, "Marlowe had no knowledge of the play I had been writing. He only knew he wanted one of my plays for himself."

"So we decided to give him an original Shakespeare," Marietta said, laughing.

"What did you give him?" Nico asked. He was nervous. What if Marlowe found out and came after him?

"We wrote him a play all his own," Shakespeare said, his voice trembling with laughter. "In just a few hours, I penned a light farce about a famous playwright who secretly steals his plays from greater men. Once he finds out what it actually is, it will be too late, you see. If he admits that he knows it was a counterfeit, he'll be revealing his plot to steal from me. If he puts it on at the playhouse, as he'll probably have to, he'll always be aware that the joke is on him."

Nico was speechless.

Finally, he said, "But have you thought that perhaps Marlowe will grow angry and strike back at us out of spite?"

Shakespeare now put a hand on Nico's shoulder. "If ever that scoundrel so much as threatens to harm you or Marietta," he said, "he will certainly have to contend with me and my Chamberlain Men."

Nico saw how well his sister looked with Shakespeare, and how she glowed with happiness now that the play was safe.

"Marietta," Nico said gravely. "I owe you an apology. I'm sorry I tried to take matters into my own hands and stole the play. Any man who makes you this happy has my blessing as your brother."

Marietta was so overcome with joy that she hugged Nico,

who squirmed out of her grasp. He was uncomfortable with displays of emotion.

The carriage stopped abruptly, and Nico saw that they were in front of the cottage. He was flooded with relief at the realization that he was home. He stepped down and bid his good nights, knowing well enough to let Marietta say a private good-bye.

Chapter 27

ONCE NICO HAD gone inside, Shakespeare turned to Marietta and kissed her passionately. It had felt like she'd wanted to kiss him forever. When he finally pulled away from her, she was breathless.

"Will," she said.

"Yes?"

"It's a tremendous gift you've given me, to immortalize me as Rosalind in your play."

"Nonsense," he said, cupping her chin in his hand. "I am the one who has received a gift. When I met you, Marietta, and when you became my muse, you changed my life. I was suddenly more prolific than ever; but also, I felt complete. Marietta, the way you protected your brother—it makes me want to be a better man, one as good as you. Truly, you make the world a better place."

He kissed her again, and then looked at her silently, his eyes roaming her face.

Marietta grew uncomfortable and giggled. "What are you thinking?" she asked.

"Only," he said slowly, "of how madly in love I've fallen with you."

She was completely lost to him now, and so unbelievably happy. For Will—who had been so shy and slow to open up—to say he was madly in love with her! She felt as light as air.

"Will," she said. "I love you, too."

And in the blue-black dark, outside of a small thatched cottage on the edge of London, a carriage sat still for a very long time while two soul mates embraced: a playwright and his muse.

ABOUT THE AUTHORS

JEN MCLAUGHLIN is a *New York Times* and *USA Today* bestselling romance author. She was mentioned in *Forbes* alongside E. L. James as one of the breakout independent authors to dominate the bestseller lists. She is represented by Louise Fury at the Bent Agency. She loves hearing from her fans, and you can visit her on the web at JenMcLaughlin.com.

SAMANTHA TOWLE began her first novel in 2008 while on maternity leave. She completed the manuscript five months later and hasn't stopped writing since. She is the author of *The Mighty Storm*, *The Bringer*, and the Alexandra Jones series. She lives with her husband, Craig, and their son and daughter in East Yorkshire, England.

TABITHA ROSS has an MFA in creative writing. She lives in Brooklyn with her husband.

LOOKING TO FALL IN LOVE IN JUST ONE NIGHT?

James Patterson has more BookShots Flames for you!

Read on for a sneak peek at the next story in the McCullagh Inn series by Jen McLaughlin, *A Wedding in Maine.*

Original romances that fit into your busy life.

JEREMY WATCHED CHELSEA PALE. She looked like she was about to turn and run, and he'd expected nothing less. Chelsea and change weren't exactly the best of friends, which was why he was trying to keep this moment as low-key as possible. Still, after all the shit they'd dealt with to get where they were now, there was no doubt in his mind that this was the right move for them to make.

It was time to make this thing between them official.

Chelsea subtly turned her head from side to side, and he knew she was mapping out her most efficient exit strategy. When she got scared, her fight-or-flight instinct kicked in.

His Chelsea? Yeah. She was a runner.

But he wasn't going to let her disappear. It was time to move on to the next chapter of their lives. The happily-ever-after part.

"Don't go. Give me a chance to talk before you react."

She was holding the doorknob so tightly her knuckles were white, but she wasn't making a break for it. He called that a win, thank you very damn much. "What are you doing?" she asked.

"I'm on one knee with a tiny little box in my hand, and it just happens to have a diamond ring in it. Don't read too much into it." He ran his hand through his hair, giving her his most charming and reassuring smile. "I'm just a guy, kneeling on the floor, who wants the woman he loves to spend the rest of her life with him. No big deal."

She choked on a laugh. "Not at all."

That laugh was a good starting point. "Originally, I had a big, romantic proposal in mind. Like, something in a fancy restaurant in Bangor. Maybe with a string quartet, or an opera singer, or something else ridiculously romantic. You're the best damn thing that ever happened to me, and you deserve the biggest and best of everything in the world, Chels."

She instinctively shuddered at the idea of an elaborate proposal, and he smiled, because he loved the unapologetic realist beneath those sweetest blue eyes of hers. She looked like an angel, but was tougher than steel. "Jeremy—"

"But I know you hate big, romantic gestures because you tell me they're too clichéd and a waste of time and money. So I settled on the most unromantic thing I could think of— proposing to you over cheap take-out Chinese food, in our home, after a long day at work, while wearing an old T-shirt and a ripped pair of jeans."

She tilted her head, still not letting go of the doorknob, still looking unconvinced of this whole thing. "I like cheap Chinese food. And your ripped jeans."

"I know." Jeremy wiggled the ring box, drawing her gaze to it again. She looked so damn beautiful standing there, almost in a full panic. "Also, I like you. A lot."

A smile played at her lips, and she tugged on a piece of her long hair and rolled her eyes in that sarcastically adorable way she always did. "Yeah, I guess you're all right, too." Her eyes widened slightly after they focused on the black box in his hand. "Is that…I saw a picture once…is it…?"

"Your mother's ring?" He glanced down. It was a princess-cut diamond, and the band had tiny little diamonds all around it. It sparkled in the light from their bedroom chandelier in a way that was stunning and majestic. Most importantly, it meant something special to Chelsea, and he'd do anything to make her eyes sparkle, too. "Yes. I went to ten different pawn shops in Maine trying to find it. Paul told me your dad hocked it a while back, but wasn't sure when or where." Well. At least that was what Paul had said after Jeremy badgered him for information. They weren't exactly the best of friends. "I knew I only had a shot in hell of finding it, but luckily it never sold, and I found it in Bangor at a pawn shop of questionable legality."

"Sounds like Dad's type of place." Chelsea finally released the knob, her body relaxing with the movement. This was the moment of truth. Jeremy held his breath, waiting to see if she'd retreat or come closer. "You did all of that for me?"

"I'd do anything for you." He resisted the urge to groan when she took a step toward him, then stopped. "There's no doubt in my mind that we're destined to spend the rest of our lives together. I've lived a life without you for too damn long, and I have no intention of ever going back. You've made me the happiest man alive, and I believe everything we've been through led us to this moment. Let me spend the rest of my life making you as happy as you've made me. Marry me, Chels."

"That wasn't a question," she said, taking another step toward him.

Damn right it wasn't a question. He had spent way too many years as her friend, utterly blind to the fact that they loved each other. It wasn't until she left town, disappearing without a trace, that he'd realized the truth. Once they reconnected, once he had her back in his arms, he knew he was never going to let her go. That was never going to change.

"I'm not asking," Jeremy said. It may not have been a

question, but he felt like his entire life hung on her answer. Even the inn itself seemed to hold its breath with him, waiting. "I love you. Marry me, Chels."

She crossed the room, stopping in front of him. He was eye level with her stomach, so he tipped his head back to meet her gaze. She looked so damn gorgeous, standing there, with that quizzical look, as her fear seemed to fade into bemusement. She pushed her hair back off her face and the chipped nail polish on her fingernails danced in cheerful spurts of lilac against her pale skin. Then she smiled. "If it's not a question, am I still supposed to answer?"

In the DEA, Jeremy had learned to read the slightest nuance in body language and could decipher the meaning behind the smallest facial tic. With Chelsea, though, he didn't need any of those tricks. There was no one in the world he knew better. Looking at her now, seeing the look in her eyes, the way she held her lips together, he knew.

"Yeah." His heart pounded so hard and fast it echoed in his head. His pulse surged into the danger zone. "Go ahead."

AVAILABLE NOW!

THE McCULLAGH INN IN MAINE

Chelsea O'Kane escapes to Maine to build a new life—until she runs into Jeremy Holland, an old flame....

LEARNING TO RIDE

City girl Madeline Harper never wanted to love a cowboy. But rodeo king Tanner Callen might change her mind...and win her heart.

SACKING THE QUARTERBACK

Attorney Melissa St. James wins every case. Now, when she's up against football superstar Grayson Knight, her heart is on the line, too.

THE MATING SEASON

Documentary ornithologist Sophie Castle is convinced that her heart belongs only to the birds—until she meets her gorgeous cameraman, Rigg Greensman.

THE RETURN

Ashley Montoya was in love with Mack McLeroy in high school—until he broke her heart. But when an accident brings him back home to Sunnybell to recover, Ashley can't help but fall into his embrace....

BODYGUARD
Special Agent Abbie Whitmore has only one task: protect Congressman Jonathan Lassiter from a violent cartel's threats. Yet she's never had to do it while falling in love....

DAZZLING: THE DIAMOND TRILOGY, BOOK I
To support her artistic career, Siobhan Dempsey works at the elite Stone Room in New York City...never expecting to be swept away by Derick Miller.

RADIANT: THE DIAMOND TRILOGY, BOOK II
After an explosive breakup with her billionaire boyfriend, Siobhan moves to Detroit to pursue her art. But Derick isn't ready to give her up.

EXQUISITE: THE DIAMOND TRILOGY, BOOK III
Siobhan's artistic career is finally successful, and she's ready to start a life with her billionaire boyfriend Derick. But their relationship has been a roller-coaster ride, and Derick may not want her after all....

HOT WINTER NIGHTS
Allie Thatcher moved to Montana to start fresh as the head of the Bear Mountain trauma center. And even though the days are cold, the nights are steamy...especially when she meets search-and-rescue leader Dex Belmont.

A WEDDING IN MAINE
Chelsea O'Kane is ready to marry Jeremy Holland in the inn they've built together—until the secrets of her past refuse to stay buried. And they could ruin *everything*.

BOOK**SHOTS**

CROSS KILL
Along Came a Spider killer Gary Soneji died years ago. But Alex Cross swears he sees Soneji gun down his partner. Is his greatest enemy back from the grave?

ZOO 2
Humans are evolving into a savage new species that could save civilization—or end it. James Patterson's *Zoo* was just the beginning.

THE TRIAL
An accused killer will do anything to disrupt his own trial, including a courtroom shocker that Lindsay Boxer and the Women's Murder Club will never see coming.

LITTLE BLACK DRESS
Can a little black dress change everything? What begins as one woman's fantasy is about to go too far.

THE WITNESSES
The Sanderson family has been forced into hiding after one of them stumbled upon a criminal plot. Or so they think. No one will answer their questions. And the terrifying truth may come too late....

CHASE
A man falls to his death in an apparent accident....But why does he have the fingerprints of another man who is already dead? Detective Michael Bennett is on the case.

LET'S PLAY MAKE-BELIEVE
Christy and Marty just met, and it's love at first sight. Or is it? One of them is playing a dangerous game—and only one will survive.

HUNTED
Someone is luring men from the streets to play a mysterious, high-stakes game. Former Special Forces officer David Shelley goes undercover to shut it down—but will he win?

113 MINUTES
Molly Rourke's son has been murdered. Now she'll do whatever it takes to get justice. No one should underestimate a mother's love....

FRENCH KISS
It's hard enough to move to a new city, but now everyone French detective Luc Moncrief cares about is being killed off. Welcome to New York.

$10,000,000 MARRIAGE PROPOSAL
A mysterious billboard offering $10 million to get married intrigues three single women in LA. But who is Mr. Right...and is he the perfect match for the lucky winner?

TAKING THE TITANIC
Posing as newlyweds, two ruthless thieves board the *Titanic* to rob its well-heeled passengers. But an even more shocking plan is afoot....

KILLER CHEF
Caleb Rooney knows how to do two things: run a food truck

and solve a murder. When people suddenly start dying of food-borne illnesses, the stakes are higher than ever....

THE CHRISTMAS MYSTERY
Two counterfeit paintings disappear from a Park Avenue murder scene—French detective Luc Moncrief is in for a merry Christmas.

COME AND GET US
When an SUV deliberately runs Miranda Cooper and her husband off a desolate Arizona road, she must run for help alone as his cryptic parting words echo in her head: "Be careful who you trust."

BLACK & BLUE
Detective Harry Blue is determined to take down the serial killer who's abducted several women, but her mission leads to a shocking revelation.

PRIVATE: THE ROYALS
After kidnappers threaten to execute a royal family member in front of the Queen, Jack Morgan and his elite team of PIs have just twenty-four hours to stop them. Or heads will roll...literally.

HIDDEN
Rejected by the Navy SEALs, Mitchum is content being his small town's unofficial private eye—until his beloved fourteen-year-old cousin is abducted.

THE HOUSE HUSBAND
In the suburbs of Philadelphia, someone is committing a series of heinous crimes: familicides. Can Detective Teaghan Beaumont catch him before it's too late?

THE BEAR MOUNTAIN DAYS ARE COLD, BUT THE NIGHTS ARE STEAMY....

Allie Fairchild made a mistake when she moved to Montana. Her rental is a mess, her coworkers at the trauma center are hostile, and her handsome landlord, Dex Belmont, is far from charming. But just when she's about to throw in the towel, life in Bear Mountain takes a surprisingly sexy turn....

Read the fun and flirty love story, *Hot Winter Nights*, available now from

THE MOST ELIGIBLE BACHELOR ON CAPITOL HILL HAS MET HIS MATCH.

Abbie Whitmore is good at her security job—until Congressman Jonathan Lassiter comes along. The presidential hopeful refuses to believe that he's in danger, even though Abbie's determined to keep him safe. But how can she protect him while she's guarding her own heart?

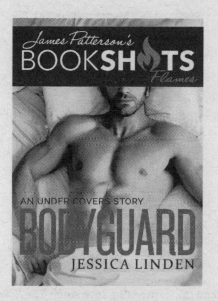

Read the suspenseful romance, *Bodyguard*, available now from

WITH BEATING HEARTS AND BATED BREATH...

Ashley Montoya was in love with Mack McLeroy in high school—until he broke her heart. When an accident brings him back home to Sunnybell to recover, Ashley's determined to avoid him, but Mack can't stay away. And the more she's with him, the more she can't help but fall into his embrace....

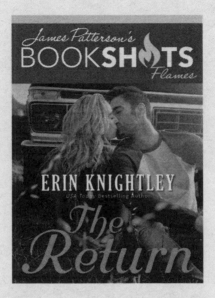

Read the captivating love story, *The Return*, available now from

SPREAD YOUR WINGS AND SOAR.

Rigg Greensman is on the worst assignment of his life: filming a documentary about birds with "hot mess" scientist and host Sophie Castle. Rigg is used to the celebrity lifestyle, so he'd never be interested in down-to-earth Sophie. But he soon realizes she's got that sexy something that drives him wild…if only he can convince her to join him for the ride.

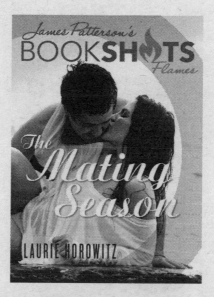

Read the heart-pounding love story, *The Mating Season,*
available now from

SHE NEVER EXPECTED TO FALL IN LOVE WITH A COWBOY....

Rodeo king Tanner Callen isn't looking to be tied down anytime soon. When he sees Madeline Harper at a local honky-tonk—even though everything about her screams New York City—he brings out every trick in his playbook to take her home.

But soon he learns that he doesn't just want her for a night.

Instead, he hopes for forever.

Read the heartwarming new romance, *Learning to Ride,* **available now from**

HE'S WORTH MILLIONS, BUT HE'S WORTHLESS WITHOUT HER.

Siobhan Dempsey came to New York with a purpose: she wants to become a successful artist. But then she meets tech billionaire Derick Miller, who takes her breath away. And though Siobhan's body comes alive at his touch, she doesn't know if she can trust him....

Read the steamy Diamond Trilogy, available only from

"I'M NOT ON TRIAL. SAN FRANCISCO IS."

Drug cartel boss the Kingfisher has a reputation for being violent and merciless. And after he's finally caught, he's set to stand trial for his vicious crimes—until he begins unleashing chaos and terror upon the lawyers, jurors, and police associated with the case. The city is paralyzed, and Detective Lindsay Boxer is caught in the eye of the storm.

Will the Women's Murder Club make it out alive—or will a sudden courtroom snare ensure their last breaths?

Read the shocking new Women's Murder Club story, available now only from

BOOK**SHOTS**

CAN A LITTLE BLACK DRESS CHANGE EVERYTHING?

Divorced magazine editor Jane Avery is content with spending her nights alone—until she finds *The Dress*. Suddenly she's surrendering to dark desires, and New York City has become her erotic playground. But what begins as a sultry fantasy has gone too far....

And her next conquest could be her last.

Check out the steamy cliffhanger *Little Black Dress,* available now from

BOOK**SHOTS**

SOME GAMES AREN'T FOR CHILDREN....

After a nasty divorce, Christy Moore finds her escape in Marty Hawking, who introduces her to all sorts of experiences, including an explosive new game called "Make-Believe."

But what begins as innocent fun soon turns dark, and as Marty pushes the boundaries farther and farther, the game just may end up deadly.

Read the new jaw-dropping thriller, *Let's Play Make-Believe*, available now from

BOOK**SHOTS**

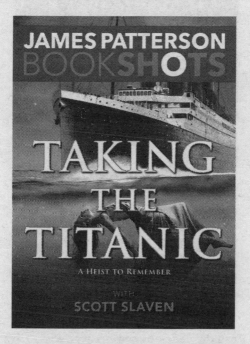